Lovestruck

LIANE MAE

Lovestruck

LIANE MAE

Copyright © 2025 by Liane Mae

All rights reserved.

No part of this book may be reproduced in any form or by any electronic or mechanical means, including information storage and retrieval systems, without written permission from the author, except for the use of brief quotations in a book review.

This book is a work of fiction. All names, characters, locations, and incidents are products of the author's imagination. Any resemblance to actual persons, things, living or dead, locales, or events is entirely coincidental.

All teams, leagues, rules, and calendar of events within the league are fictional and should not be compared with any real professional football leagues.

Editor: James Gallagher, Castle Walls Editing

Proofreader: Rosa Sharon, Fairy Proofmother Proofreading

Cover Design: Kari March, Kari March Designs

Formatted by LC Formatting

Dedication

This book was inspired by the queen herself, Taylor Swift. As a huge Swiftie (understatement), her real life love story that has taken over the world is a romance writer's dream. However, this is not her story, as she is still writing it. It's just this writer's own version, inspired by the woman herself and the fairytale romance we have all swooned over for the last year.

To Taylor, you will probably never ever see this, but I want you to know just how much I love and adore you and think you're not just a talented singer, songwriter, and businesswoman, but an amazing person and role model to everyone as well. Thank you for sharing who you are with the world and inspiring people to never stop reaching for their dreams. This one is mine.

To the readers, enjoy my version of what I deem to be the best love story ever.

Lovestruck (Liane's Version)

CHAPTER 1
Allie

JULY

"Please don't do this," I sobbed, bending over at the waist to try to stop the pain that took the breath from my lungs. My knees hit the hard stage beneath me and the phone clattered to the ground, but I still heard his voice as it echoed through the empty stadium. His words were distorted enough for me to pretend I couldn't clearly hear what was coming from the speaker.

Workers milled around, checking the stage and seating, but none of them paid attention to my world crumbling. The backing music still played throughout the stadium, sheltering the sounds of me on the stage, listening to my world fall apart. It wasn't often in my life I felt completely alone, but at this moment I was nothing more than a single ant in an anthill. When my phone rang just minutes ago, I'd sent the dancers backstage to rest until the show.

"Allie. Baby." His soft voice just made me sob harder. I had heard that tone so many times in our relationship. It calmed me and set my head back on my shoulders. But not this time. This time, he used it to crush my soul. I attempted to take a deep breath, knowing at any moment someone would hear the racket I made and come out here, and I couldn't be seen like this. But all that came out of my mouth was a strangled, animalistic moan.

"P-please," I managed to say again, rocking back and forth on my knees. "Not like this." I picked up the phone and sat back, my backside hitting the stage. I wiped the tears from my eyes and gulped in oxygen. I felt like I might be sick.

"You won't be back for weeks, and you'll be on this tour for over a year. I haven't spent more than a few hours with you in months. It's over, Allie. I'm sorry. I just can't do this with you anymore. I want more out of life than waiting for you to decide I'm a priority." His soft voice delivered the dagger I would've never thought he'd send through my gut.

I'm on tour, I wanted to scream. *How can you do this to me? We've been together for five years! You said we were forever! We are supposed to be getting engaged! Starting our life!* I opened and closed my mouth, but no words would come. He was really doing this to me. The love of my life. The one I thought was going to be the father to my children. He was abandoning me over the phone while I was hours away from the first show of my most successful international tour to date. Because I didn't make him a *priority*? Since when?

"Josiah," I sobbed. "I love you. You said you loved me, that I was the love of your life. Five years and you're just going to throw it away? After everything? Whatever it is, we can work it out. You know you are always a priority to me."

"Allie," he said again. "I will always love you. It's just not enough. I met someone. She has a normal life. I'm so sorry."

I shook my head, wishing my phone hadn't been in my pocket during rehearsal and I could continue living the delusion that my life wasn't imploding. He met someone else—with a *normal* life. Those words reverberated through me and settled like a boulder in my gut. What he meant was *I* wasn't enough. This life I led. Who I was, *I* wasn't worth it. I've heard this lyric a time or two. *Normal.* What did that make me?

"I'll have my stuff moved out before you get back," he continued, like my heart and soul weren't fractured into pieces beneath me. I stood, my legs moving without me realizing I was headed off the stage. I needed to get to the dressing room so I could continue this meltdown away from anyone who could record it and put it all over social media. All it would take was one of these workers with a cell phone and it would be the next viral story. *I met someone. She has a normal life.* The words roared in my ears. Did I know her? Who was she? How long had this been going on? How stupid was I to not see this coming?

I gripped the phone in my hand. I wanted to ask all the questions, but I couldn't make my mouth work. Josiah was speaking, but I couldn't hear it anymore. Tears blurred my vision and I gulped, bile threatening again. No one could see me like this. I couldn't admit to anyone that Josiah dumped me. Had we been fighting more than usual? Sure. But didn't all couples? I didn't think it was that egregious. Had I practically begged for a ring for the last three years? Also yes, but Josiah always had a good reason to wait. Mainly my career. He was a successful entertainment lawyer and his life didn't resemble mine one little bit, but that was what worked for us. Had worked. No longer worked, apparently.

I stumbled down the cavernous hall toward my dressing room, which was the visitor locker room for the football games played here. My sobs echoed off the walls, which only made me cry harder. Thankfully, it was blissfully empty, so I didn't have to explain myself to anyone mulling around. I was rarely alone this long—it was a miracle. Guess my team was busy enough and figured I was safe inside the empty stadium, surrounded by security.

"Allie?" a voice finally broke through my panic. I looked down at my phone, realizing Josiah was still there. I turned the corner to enter the final hallway before I'd reach the locker room area, and that was when I hit a brick wall and my phone went flying out of my hand, clattering to the floor somewhere out of reach.

Before I could recognize what was happening, strong hands gripped my arms and kept me from falling. I gasped, my tear-filled eyes unable to see who held me.

"Hey there," the deep male voice said, and I knew instantly it was no one from my team. Fear gripped my stomach, overtaking the grief from moments before. In my world, an unfamiliar voice equaled danger. I blinked, attempting to step back away from the stranger. My tears cleared as fear took over my sadness, and my eyes widened.

In my tennis shoes I wore for rehearsal, this man loomed over me by at least six inches, and I was not a short girl. My eyes scanned his short dark hair, his neatly trimmed facial hair, concerned blue eyes looking down at me, and . . . holy shit. This man was the finest guy I'd ever seen.

Dressed in a pair of loose-fitting gym shorts and a T-shirt, he smelled like he just got out of the shower. Muscles bulged in places I'd never seen up close. This guy could throw me over his shoulder and take me away. With that thought, I stepped back out of his reach, forcing myself to remember that I didn't know this guy and I may not be safe. My mind reeled with ways to escape.

"You okay?" His eyes crinkled with concern, and I once again found myself staring into them. They reminded me of the water at my favorite beach. I shook my head, ridding myself of noticing anyone's ocean-blue eyes.

"F-fine," I said, finding my voice. I looked around for my lost phone, hoping I could get to safety if this guy had ill intentions. *Why are you so stupid? You know you shouldn't be alone.* Those damn eyes scanned me again, scrutinizing my face like he could look right through me.

He stepped back and spotted my phone. I watched, rooted

to the floor, as he picked it up and returned it to me. He looked down at the photo on my lock screen and then back to me. He gave me a smirk I could only describe as panty melting before putting the phone in my hand. The impact of my phone falling must've disconnected Josiah. What a shame.

"That the guy you're crying over?"

I sniffled on cue, and tears filled my eyes again. *Shit.* I needed to get away from this guy. I turned to walk away, but he reached his hand out to stop me. When his giant hand made contact with my forearm, simultaneously gentle and scorching, I gasped. Our eyes met and a smile played on his lips, like he knew exactly what I felt when he touched me. He was probably used to women falling at his feet. But this woman wasn't going to. I was done with men. All they did was lie to me and cause me heartbreak. I pulled my arm back, refusing to register anything having to do with my reaction to this guy.

"Seriously, are you okay?" His voice felt like velvet caressing my skin. "Allie, right?"

I shoved the phone into the pocket of my yoga pants and tried to stop the tears from dripping from my eyes. *Dressing room. Now.* I had less than an hour to get my shit together before hair and makeup would be here to transform me into pop princess Allie Witt, Global Superstar. I needed Bailey. She could talk me down. And this guy knew who I was, and I still had no idea who he was.

"I-I have to go," I said, stepping around him. "Thank you."

"Let me walk you to your dressing room," he said, holding out his arm. "You're using the visitor locker room, right?"

I looked around, alarm bells still ringing in my head.

"Hey," he said.

My gaze snapped back to his handsome face.

"I'm not going to hurt you."

A sharp laugh escaped my lips. "That's what someone says when they—they . . ." I couldn't continue because a fresh wave of grief gripped me and I began sobbing again. His promise to not hurt me reminded me of Josiah when we first met. The Josiah who just ended our five-year relationship with a phone call while he was in our home that I paid for with our shared dog that I picked out. The nameless handsome stranger took my hand in his, and I pointed in the direction of my dressing room. I let him lead me there, sobs racking my body so violently I thought I may actually throw up this time. His large, warm hand surrounding mine kept me upright as we approached the dressing room.

He opened the door and I stepped in. He guided me with his hand lightly on my back to the couch against the wall. I sat and dropped my head into my hands. Seconds later, a water bottle appeared in front of me.

"Drink," he said, that voice sending a shiver down my spine. I took it without looking at him and gulped the water. He handed me some tissues from the table next to the couch and I wiped my eyes and nose, but it didn't stop the steady stream. I couldn't make it stop. When I finally took deep breaths and the tears subsided enough for me to breathe normally, I realized this huge hulk of a man was rubbing my back, his fingers filtering through my ponytail.

"Can I call someone for you?" I closed my eyes at the concern in his voice. I shouldn't be sitting next to him, allowing him in my space, but I couldn't find it in me to make him leave.

I turned my swollen eyes up to him. "No. Thank you for helping me, but you can go. I'm sorry. I'm sure all you wanted was a crying female to deal with today."

He smiled, and I almost groaned. Dimples. Of course he freaking had dimples.

"There are worse things I could be doing." He dropped his hand from my back and tucked a stray piece of hair behind my ear. I fought not to shiver. Why did a touch from a stranger feel so . . . good?

"Do you want to talk about it? I've been told I'm a good listener."

I opened my mouth to tell him no because I was trained to not tell your personal business to anyone if you don't want it all over the internet. I sure learned that one the hard way. More than one time. But he had no phone or recording device that I could see, and I found myself turning my body to face him. What was the worst that could happen? He sold the story to a pap without any pictures or any evidence we'd talked at all? Those stories were a dime a dozen.

His arm rested on the back of the couch, a fraction of an inch away from touching me. "You know who I am," I stated.

"Hard not to," he responded. "Mainly because you're kind of plastered everywhere right now—including around the stadium. But also—is there anyone in the world that doesn't know who you are? But I don't care one bit to talk to the press, if that's what you're worried about."

"Why?"

He smirked, and I tried once again to not notice those adorable freaking dimples that peeked out from behind his short facial hair.. Or the way his muscles rippled under his T-shirt when he moved. Or how he ran his hand through his short hair, making his arm flex. "You do not follow football."

I laughed, even though it sounded hollow and forced to me. "You could say that." At this point, I wished I did.

He held his arms out. "This is my stadium. I play for the Blaze."

I blinked. That made so much sense for why he was in this stadium when I had a show here tonight. And also for his massive size and freshly showered self. I heard the team was in the practice area today, but they were supposed to be long gone by now.

He held out his hand. "Theo. Theo Nolan. Otherwise

known to my teammates as T-Bear number twenty-three, short for Teddy Bear, if you couldn't figure that out."

I stared at the size of him, remembering those hands holding me steady as I almost catapulted to the floor. I reached my hand out, and the moment we touched, I bit my lip to stop myself from gasping again.

"Allie Witt. Mallorie. I've been Allie most of my life, though." I wasn't sure what made me say my real name other than it was the opposite of what Josiah called me, and it was the real me. I didn't want to psychoanalyze that right now.

"Mallorie." The three syllables of my given name rolled so nicely off his tongue. "That's a beautiful name for an even more beautiful woman."

My phone vibrated and I took it from my pocket, seeing a message from Josiah on the screen. I whimpered and Theo took the phone from my hand and put it on the other side of him on the table.

"Josiah?" he said. "That's his name?"

I nodded, squeezing my hands together so tightly my nails dug into my skin. I was not going to cry again. Apparently he was not worth my effort. No matter what I did, he still didn't want me.

"We've been together for five years. He just ended it. He said there was someone else and he wanted someone who was around more, who had a 'normal' life." My voice broke, and I looked down at my hands as my eyes welled again. "Whatever the hell that means. I guess it means someone who isn't me."

Theo lifted my chin with one finger, his eyes staring into mine for several beats. He really did have the prettiest eyes. I bet he heard that all the time. "He just ended your five-year relationship over the phone on the opening night of your tour?"

I nodded, and damn if those tears didn't spill over again. This time, Theo took a tissue and dabbed my eyes and cheeks, and I refused to allow myself to register his gentle touch. "I've been busy preparing for the tour. I-I guess I didn't pay enough attention to him." What the fuck was I doing letting this guy in my dressing room and spilling all my secrets to him? I had seriously lost my mind.

"Mallorie." He paused, seeming to think through his next words before speaking. "I am sorry, but if any man is such a piece of shit that he breaks up with his girl after five years with a phone call on one of the biggest days of her life, that man is a complete and utter douchebag and does not deserve her. And do not put this on yourself. Did the man not know who you were and what you did for a living when he met you?"

"He did," I said. "He loved who I was at first. I thought we were going to get married. Have kids. N-now I'm alone. Again." I laughed. "Oh boy, the media is going to have fun with this one. 'She can't keep a guy,' or 'Another one bites the dust for pop princess Allie Witt.' Even better are the ones that are like, 'Oh wait until she annihilates another guy on her next album.'"

Theo blew out a breath. "I am so sorry you're having to deal with this today. I know how hard it is to compartmentalize and be able to pull off a big performance. Do you want to know what helps me?"

I stared at this man, this stranger who rescued me and helped me, and I realized that I did want to know. He got it. Maybe not exactly in the same realm, but close. He was in the spotlight and had a lot of pressure to perform, no matter what was going on in his life.

Just then, the door opened and in came my publicist, Zoey, followed by my hair, makeup, and wardrobe team. They were early. Figured. Zoey saw my tear-stained, puffy face, and then Theo sitting next to me and stopped in her tracks, her eyes widening in surprise.

"Allie." My name had many meanings in that tone of

voice. Zoey and I had been together since my first album, and she was like a big sister to me.

"Hey, Zoey," I said. "This is Theo. Theo helped me in the hall when I almost fell."

Zoey stepped closer to us so the rest of the team wasn't part of the discussion. She crossed her arms in front of her chest and sized him up. Zoey didn't play around, and it was one of the things I appreciated the most about her. She always had my best interests at heart.

"Theo Nolan, right?" So apparently she did follow football. Then again, it was her job to know things.

"Yes, ma'am," he responded, holding out his hand. Zoey shook it, but her eyes were on me. I knew what was about to come out of her mouth.

"Do we need an NDA?" she asked me pointedly. My face flamed at her implication.

Theo held up his hands. "I was never here."

Zoey looked him up and down. "You weren't recording anything?"

He turned his pockets inside out. "I don't have my phone with me. It's in the locker room."

I rested my hand on Zoey's arm to stop her. She was my little bulldog and I loved it, but she was directing her scrutiny to the wrong person. "It's okay, Zo. He helped me."

She nodded and her body language relaxed. "Thank you," she said to him, then turned her gaze to me. "Why were you alone?"

"The guys are making sure the stadium is ready for tonight, and the dancers were finished practicing," I said. "It's okay. Really." I knew that no matter what I said right now, Zoey was going to tear up my security team for not being near enough to me. On one hand, she was right. Theo could've been someone with nefarious intentions and I could've been long gone by now. But on the other hand, he wasn't and I was fine. Her argument would be that wasn't always the case, evidenced by the many stalkers I'd had in my career.

"You do not look okay." She turned back to Theo. "Thank you for your help. If you will excuse us, Allie has to get ready for tonight."

Theo met my gaze over Zoey's head. He didn't get to tell me how he compartmentalizes, and I actually really wanted to know the answer. Though I have had to fake it until I made it enough. I could do it and I would do it. My fans deserved the Allie that was 100 percent with them, and honestly, when I performed for them, nothing else mattered.

"Thank you," I echoed to him. He nodded and walked toward the door. I felt Zoey looking at me, no doubt scrutinizing my puffy eyes and blotchy face, but my gaze was on the man walking away.

Before he opened the door, he turned back to me. "Mallorie. How I deal with it? You channel those emotions into putting on the best show of your life. For me, I challenge myself to have the best game to spite whatever is going on. You do the same. Get out there and show those people just who the hell you are, and don't let him take this experience from you. All of those people that will be out there tonight? They traveled from near and far to see you because of the amazing performer you are. Don't give him another thought," he said. "There's someone out there that will appreciate and love you for exactly who you are. Don't settle until you find that person. Don't ever make yourself smaller for another person. Ever again."

I sucked in a breath and held it, unable to respond other than a small nod. How had I known this person for mere minutes and he hit the nail right on the head? He winked at me and turned away. The door shut behind him, and I turned to meet Zoey's intent gaze.

"Start talking," she said.

CHAPTER 2
Theo

"YOU WANT TO DO WHAT NOW?" my best friend, quarterback Spencer Green, said to me. He stood in front of his locker in nothing but a towel, having just finished his workout and shower.

I had just come back from leaving Allie's dressing room, and I couldn't quite channel my emotions about the whole thing into a box. Never in my life did I think I'd ever see that woman face to face, much less have an entire conversation with her.

"Stay and watch Allie Witt in concert tonight from my box." I had the idea and now I couldn't talk myself out of it. I had to see her perform.

He furrowed his brow. "I mean, I get that she's hot, but why? Her music isn't really our vibe, T."

I definitely wasn't telling him the real reason, that I had caught her in the hallway today and then listened to her cry over some douchebag guy that didn't deserve her. Or that I'd been crushing on her forever. Or even that I thought her music was amazing and she knew how to write lyrics.

"It'll be fun! She's talented. It's her opening night and it's in our stadium! You got something better to do?"

Spencer pulled a shirt over his head and crossed his arms in front of his chest. My friend since college days, Spencer knew me as well as anyone did. Being an only child, he was the brother I never got.

"Why do I feel like there's more to this story?"

I shrugged. "Maybe there is, maybe there isn't."

Spencer studied me. There was no getting away with shit with him. "Are you crushing on her?"

Flashes of her body shuddering with tears as I rubbed her back made me look away from him. The pain on her face, the anguish in her voice, the way she thought it was *her* who was the problem made my gut clench.

"Definitely not."

Spencer punched me in the arm. "Shut up. You're lying. You are crushing on Allie Witt, the pop superstar, one of the most recognizable people on the planet? Isn't she in a serious relationship?"

I almost laughed because he claimed not to be a fan of hers but sure knew info about her.

I wouldn't give him the details I knew—I promised her that. Plus, it wasn't his business. When I didn't answer, Spencer held up his hands.

"Okay, shit. Let's do this. Let's go eat first because I'm fucking starving. Then you can tell me how I missed that you have a crush on the biggest pop star in the world."

The lights pulsed around her and she danced like she was born to do it. I couldn't stop the grin on my face as her fans echoed back a part of the song they obviously knew was their part.

I put my phone back in my pocket after recording another snippet of her performance. Allie was amazing. The crowd—all eighty-five thousand of them—screamed every lyric with her and danced along like they were in their own living room. Her guitar hung from her neck, and she strummed it while belting the lyrics out and dancing. Her band and backup dancers moved around her like a well-orchestrated machine. Happiness radiated from her, and I smiled. She did it. She put that idiot in the box where he belonged and gave the audience a show of a lifetime.

We'd been watching her about an hour now, and she'd already changed outfits three times. She went from a glittery pop princess to a sexy vixen to now a beautiful queen. I knew some of her most popular songs, but not all of them. Despite that, it was still an experience to watch her. No one but me and her publicist Zoey would even know that her heart was broken under all that beautiful exterior. Thinking of it made my chest twinge. I hated that she felt the way she did about herself, but I also didn't blame her. The insecurities this guy just gave her were unacceptable.

Spencer walked in and handed me a second beer. "You still drooling over her?"

Over dinner, I told Spencer I ran into Allie after practice. I did not give him any information about our encounter, just that I saw her face to face and we had a brief conversation. He still reminded me that she was a taken woman, and I still denied anything more than just wanting to see her perform. I also attempted to dissuade him from the years-long crush I had on her, which I never told him about because it was just an innocent schoolboy crush. I never thought I'd meet her in a million years. But when I came out of the locker room on my way out and saw her stand up and run off the stage, obviously upset, there wasn't a single part of myself that could stop me from helping her.

As evidenced by his comment, he still didn't believe me one little bit. The truth of the matter was, Allie became popular when I was in college, and I thought she was hot as hell, like most guys did. I wasn't the type who had posters of women on my dorm wall, but if I had, she would've been front and center. Now that I was in my early thirties, I noticed when I saw a story about her and I followed how successful she'd been over the last several years, but it wasn't like our social circles intermingled. Unfortunately for her, most of her news stories revolved around which guy she was dating, breaking up with, or whom her next album was about.

A quick Google search earlier told me that she had more awards than any other artist in history, yet that wasn't the top news story. It angered me for her, thinking about her saying that the media was going to go wild with this story once they found out about her breakup. Josiah. What a putz. I looked up information about him, too. It wasn't hard to find since he was connected to her. Josiah Abbott. Apparently he was an entertainment lawyer and that was how they met. You'd think someone in that line of work would be even more understanding, but instead, he crushed her.

The media wouldn't highlight any of the amazing things she did for those in need, the way she loved her fans, the gatherings she did for the Allie-Cats (her fans' name for themselves), or the families she sponsored every holiday season. No. It was all about her being unmarried and a man-eater at the age of twenty-nine. Shit, it was a damn good thing no one had cataloged the number of girls I'd been with since high school. The double standard was unreal. It was expected from us, the professional athletes, but she was judged for it.

"Spence," I said in warning. I turned my attention back to the show as the colors changed and Allie reappeared on the stage to earsplitting screams.

"She's good," he said, stepping up to the window with his phone. "Lacey loves her and hates me a little bit right now for being here without her." Lacey was Spencer's fiancée and a sportscast journalist who was out of town, or she'd be here with all her Allie garb on. When Spencer had called her at dinner to tell her we were going to see her, the squeal from the phone caused everyone in the restaurant to turn and look at us. "She wants me to FaceTime her during a song where she wears a black-sequined bodysuit. Apparently that's her favorite."

"She *is* good," I agreed, my brain whirling. How could I talk to her again? I needed to make sure she was okay and that she didn't believe that idiot who said she wasn't enough. This girl was the entire package—drop-dead gorgeous, talented, full of charisma, and with a genuine love for her career. I should've put my number in her phone, given it to Zoey, something.

I'd lost my chance. I'd never get to her now.

Spencer waved his hand in front of my face. "Earth to Theo. Are you going to be for real and tell me what's going on with you?"

A thought came to me. "Do you think George is still around?"

"George? Security George?"

George was our buddy and often came over to shoot the shit and have a drink or two.

"Yes."

"I'm not sure. Maybe he's working the event. You have his number. Why don't you text him? What is going on? You look like you've seen a ghost."

"Do you think our George would have access to Allie's security?"

"Theo Nolan. Tell me what the fuck is going on."

"I just—" How did I explain this without sounding like I'd lost my mind? "I need to get something to Allie."

"You. Need to get something. To Allie Witt." Spencer laughed. "You and everyone else here, man."

"But everyone else here is not Theo Nolan."

Spencer laughed again. "That is true. You are one of the most recognizable faces in the entire league. Something about you being hot and the number-one eligible bachelor in the league or something." He crinkled his nose, and we both laughed. "Did she know who you were when you 'ran into her' earlier?"

"No. She doesn't follow football."

Spencer laughed at my expense once again. "This shit is gold. A female that doesn't know who Theo Nolan is, and Theo Nolan himself is losing his shit over her."

"I am not losing my shit." I tapped a text to George to see if he was here and stared at the screen, waiting to see the bubbles appear.

"Am I watching you become an Allie-Cat? Should I record this for history?"

Spencer directed his phone at me, and I flipped him off without looking at him. I heard the camera click as he took a photo of me giving him the vulgar gesture.

"And tell me, Spence, how do you know what an Allie-Cat is?" I looked up from waiting for George's response to see the incredulous look on Spencer's face.

"Lacey."

"Uh-huh," I said.

"But you also knew what they were," Spencer argued.

I shook my head, not dignifying that with a response.

Pyrotechnics went off, and our good old-fashioned ribbing stopped. Allie appeared from under the stage in the famed black-sequined bodysuit, and Spencer's attention was immediately on his phone as he attempted to quickly call Lacey.

George responded moments later, and I smiled at the screen. A plan formulated in my head—I just had to make it happen. I texted him back and waited for the response.

When the song ended, Spencer turned back to me. "Uh-oh. I know that look."

"What look?"

"What are you planning? It's your scheming look."

"George is here. I'll be right back." I didn't give Spencer a chance to comment before I hightailed it out of the suite.

I stopped as the music pulsed and I heard Allie sing some ridiculously high and powerful notes, the crowd screaming at the top of their lungs. This was why this girl was so popular. Her voice was killer. I made my way back to the locker room and pulled out a pad of paper and a Sharpie. The door opened and George stepped into the room.

"You got it?"

George, a mid-sixties man who had worked for the Blaze his entire career and was one of the best guys I'd ever known, grinned at me. "Sure did." He held out the oversized women's jersey he got from the team store with my name and number on the back.

"Perfect." I took it from him, and he watched in silence as I wrote the note. I carefully opened the plastic the jersey was wrapped in and pulled it out. I signed the number with my scrawled signature and nickname on the back and then slid the note inside the fold. I put it in the plastic and handed it to George. "You can take care of this?"

"Have I ever let you down before?" George looked at the note just peeking out. All you could see was *Mallorie*.

"Never. Just don't let this be the time." I slapped him on the back, and we walked out of the locker room together.

"I made friends with her head bodyguard this afternoon. Juan's a good guy. We bonded over his love of the Blaze. Should be no problem to get it to him. I have heard she doesn't do any meets after the show, though, so don't ask me to get that for you."

I stopped. "Wait. Why didn't you say that? Let's go get him a signed jersey, too. I want him to have a reason to give this to her."

George smiled. "I like seeing this side of you, Theo."

"What side is that?" We walked side by side back to the locked team store. The music was so loud it was hard to hear, so he didn't answer until we were inside the store and the music was muffled.

"You're the best guy I've ever known, and I've known a lot of guys. You have such love for everyone around you, and you use your influence for good. Plus, you're hilarious and a kick-ass dancer. It's just nice to see the side that still acts like a boy with a crush. I know Beth did a number on you, so I'm glad to see you putting yourself out there again."

I groaned at the mention of Beth's name. She was a cheerleader for our team, and we'd been together for three years when I found out she was cheating on me. We hadn't been together in over a year now, but it had wrecked me at the time. I'd thought she was the one for me. We met when I was in my first year at Blaze, and we were casual for about a year before we got serious. I thought she was going to be my wife and even had a ring bought. But fate saved me from making a terrible decision. I guessed that was one of the reasons I understood Allie's situation—she was blindsided in the worst of ways. I found out Beth was cheating on me right before one of our biggest games of the season, seeing if we would qualify for the playoffs. Much like Allie, I used that anger and heartbreak to go play the best game of my career. It was obvious that Allie was great at using her feelings to lay it all out on the stage because this woman was incredible.

"You could say I understand some things about Allie," I said.

George indicated the note. "Mallorie?"

"Her real name," I explained. He nodded and took both jerseys as we headed out of the room. He didn't ask how I knew that or why I cared so much about getting this jersey to her. What he couldn't see, and I hoped no one else looked at other than her, was what I wrote on the note. Nothing that could be misunderstood, but enough for her to get my meaning.

"Let me know," I said as we parted ways. He waved and I headed back to my box to watch the rest of the show.

"Hey, T," Spence said. I turned and he was stopped in front of Allie's life-size cutout, a shit-eating grin on his face.

She wore her colorful sequined outfit from her opening set, her long hair curled around her face, beaming with a brilliant smile. I looked into those big blue eyes and immediately remembered the tears filling them. I forced myself to focus back on the stunning picture in front of me.

Across the top, *ALLIE WITT—LOVESTRUCK TOUR* announced who she was like she wasn't one of the most recognizable people in the world. The identical posters were everywhere around the stadium and around our entire city as they dedicated this as her "hometown opener" and named the city hers for the weekend. I'd never seen anything like it. "Want a pic with it? You can point at the *lovestruck* word in it since you've got it bad."

I laughed, despite him trying to continuously give me shit. This is what we did. When he met Lacey, I was just as bad. However, I just met the girl and she had her heart broken. I had a little crush flaring up at the worst possible time, which was just typical of my luck. No one was marrying us off. I just wanted to make sure she was okay. That really was it. Mostly. Well, I could try to convince myself of that.

People moved all around us as they filed out of the concert. Some fans sang together, some of them wiped tears from their eyes, and many smiled like it was the best night of their life. This was the Allie effect. It was so neat to see in person, and I wondered whether she ever got to see this part anymore. I snapped a couple pictures of them as they moved around us, thinking maybe someday I'd get to show her. All of a sudden, cheers erupted from whoever was left inside the stadium. People around us stopped, and I watched them. What was happening?

I heard people talking about Allie coming out from behind

the stage to leave, and I found myself wishing I was still in the stadium so I could spot her again. Maybe she would've seen me.

"Go ahead," I said, posing in front of her cutout. I wrapped my arm around the life-size Allie and pretended to kiss her cheek. Spencer took several pictures, ribbing me the entire time. I had no shame. "You get in here with me, you idiot. Make Lacey happy and send it to her." We took a selfie, both of us making a foolish face.

"What's this?" Spencer asked, picking up a heart from behind the cutout.

"No idea," I said, taking it from his hand. It was a hot-pink felt heart with the Lovestruck logo on it. "Maybe someone dropped it."

"You should keep it," Spencer said. "To remind yourself of the night you told your best friend you had a massive crush on the biggest pop star in the world."

"Shut up," I said, but I slid the heart in my pocket anyway. It was cute and would remind me of meeting her today.

After a few moments, people around us started to notice us, and while the majority kept walking, a few lingered as they put together who we were. I heard our names as I saw a few snapping pictures, so I turned to Spence.

"Let's go." I was probably too late to keep those off social media. But hey, I was just a fan taking a picture like every other person here. It wasn't like they got the real pictures of me sitting next to Allie as she sobbed. Those images were just burned into *my* brain.

CHAPTER 3
Allie

SEPTEMBER

"Have you heard from him?" Bailey's voice echoed throughout my house. The beachfront house that used to be *ours*.

It was my first time home after our breakup. I had a two-week break between tour stops, so I decided I had to deal with this once and for all. Our dog Charlie lay at my feet. He was *my* dog now. No way I was giving him to Josiah.

I looked out the back sliders to the long stretch of beach, the waves lapping the shore. My Florida home was one of several I owned across the country, but it was my favorite and what I considered home base. For me, there was nothing like the sound, sight, and smell of the beach to inspire me.

"No. I don't plan to hear from him, though. As long as he is lying low as we discussed and not going to the press, I am fine." Not to mention the NDA he signed years ago. I knew he had as much desire to go to the press about me as he did to step in dog poop. He hated the press.

"When are you putting it out there?" Bailey Lee was a successful, popular country singer, and we'd been best friends for over ten years after meeting at our first-ever awards show as teen stars. She was one of the few who really understood everything about this life I led. Her home base was Nashville, while mine was in Florida, so we didn't get to meet up as often as we wanted. In typical fashion, people had tried to pit us against each other our entire careers, but we didn't give it a second thought, and we always made sure to show the world how much we loved and appreciated each other. We even had crossover fans who called us Ballie or Wittlee and begged for a collaboration. The internet was funny. Sometimes. If only they knew how much we sang and brainstormed together. Our labels were the ones hesitant for us to "cross over" together.

"Zoey is working on 'the leak' that we broke up. She will handle when to do it. Sometime this week, since I'm on a break from the tour and that news can settle before I go back out. Right now, I'm just enjoying the calm before the storm." There had been speculation about why Josiah hadn't been seen with me or at any of my shows, but the good thing was he didn't do much of that when we were together, so there wasn't much off about it.

Bailey sighed, echoing my feelings exactly. She knew what was going to happen once the media got the news story. Not that people weren't camped out outside the gates of my house every day anyway. But right now, that was for a good reason—my fifth headlining tour, an all-stadium sold-out international tour. It literally broke the internet when I announced it after my newest album, *Lovestruck,* went number one globally for a record number of weeks.

We even added two more rounds of dates to help with demand. My team said I could tour for years from the demand of this one tour. Once this story broke, the shouts outside my house would be questions about why I couldn't make another one stay rather than the success of my album and tour. It got old. Really, really old. Some would say I signed up for this, but in reality, I signed up to live out my dream, not be judged for the men—or lack thereof—in my life.

Tears threatened, but I refused to cry over him one more second. For me, it had been two months. For the public, it would be a fresh story, and I'd have to relive it again. And again. And again. Until they got tired of it and moved on to another female to harass. Or they'd just talk instead about the size of my ass, from teenage me to late-twenties me, and whether me being too thin or too fat was why a man wouldn't commit to me. And let's not forget the pregnant rumors anytime someone got the wrong angle of my profile in a picture. Was there any wonder women had eating disorders, and I'd spent most of my early twenties trying to meet their unrealistic expectations?

"Just one more man-eater story I'll have to deal with," I said. "What else is new? The narrative never changes."

"Why they can't focus on our accomplishments instead, I will never understand."

Bailey had had her share of news stories about her dating life as well. Two years younger than me, she entered the country music scene at sixteen also, and her dating life had been just as scrutinized as mine. Sometimes I'd like to ask people just what they thought teenagers and twentysomethings were supposed to do, but I didn't. It wasn't worth it. When I did interviews—which was rare now—I got my digs in, but even that wasn't worth it anymore. I just focused on the lyrics to my songs and left it at that.

I tried to focus on continuing to live my dream and ignore them, but as I neared thirty years old, the opinions got louder and more frequent. My "biological clock" was ticking, I wasn't getting any younger, etc. etc. etc. Reporters asking me about my work no longer focused on just me, but what I wanted for my future—a.k.a. *who* I wanted, and when I was going to start popping out babies. It wasn't that I didn't want all that—I just didn't want it on someone else's time frame or according to some mythical biological clock. I had goals to meet before all that. And, you know, finding the right man, apparently.

At least while I was with Josiah, the only news story was when we were getting married or if we were already secretly married. That story surfaced a few times a year. Since Josiah was not a fan of the press, he didn't often accompany me to awards shows or other public events, and if he did, he went in through another entrance and met me inside. He did not enjoy the whole pap-walk thing, and there were only a handful of pictures of us publicly in five years.

I had come to realize this was more of an issue for me than I originally thought. I could understand that he didn't choose public life, but he did choose me. He knew when we met, ironically when I was at a meeting in his office with another attorney after someone accused me of stealing their lyrics (even though I write every word of all my songs). He knew who I was and what my life was like. And before we became official, we'd had a lot of conversations about what he was comfortable with. I initially liked the privacy our relationship gave us. But it became annoying when he refused to have anything to do with that part of my life and used it as a reason to not commit to me forever.

I guessed the final realization was that I just wasn't what he wanted after all. I couldn't see it—or refused to see it—at the time, but, as they say, hindsight is twenty-twenty. I really was past him at this point. I've cried my tears, written my lyrics, recorded my songs, written in my journal, and dumped the whole thing on my poor mother, my assistant Conor, Bailey, and Zoey.

"Hey." Bailey's voice snapped me back to reality. "You okay?"

"I am. I'm as over him as I'm going to get. I don't want him by any means, but it just hurts, you know? I know what's about to happen, and it'll take the attention off where I want it—on my tour and my successes and right back onto my personal life. When is my life not going to be too much for someone? When is it my turn?"

She laughed, even though neither of us thought it was funny. "I hear you."

"I know you do, but I'm also sad that you have to understand this, too. We are beautiful, successful women at the top of our games. Why does this have to be so hard?"

"The same reason why they talk about our bodies on social media but never about men's. It's not the same standard they hold us to. Men can date as many girls as they want and it isn't a news story. But we are. And heaven forbid we don't look the same as we did when we were sixteen, or if we show some skin at our performances now or our lyrics say a bad word. It's like we are stuck as teenagers."

Silence enveloped us for a moment. We didn't have the answers to these things, but at least we knew we weren't alone in it. Together, we'd made a lot of progress with the public over the years, but you couldn't change them all. Old ideologies died hard.

"Hey." Bailey's tone indicated a change of subject. "Did you contact Theo to tell him thank you?" He hadn't left me his contact information, but I knew I could get it easily. I just didn't think it was a good idea.

I looked immediately over at my desk, where the signed jersey sat inside the plastic I'd received it in. I thought about the note inside it, written to my real name with the words of encouragement written in neat block letters. The kindness he showed me that day. On top of that, the fact that in two months, I hadn't heard him utter a single word about running into me that day or what I told him.

Integrity in a man. Imagine that. The only other things I saw other than the jersey he sent me were the viral pics of him kissing my cheek on my life-size cutout at the tour and some pictures of my fans leaving the stadium, but even then, he didn't post them. Fans who saw him posted them. That was cute and broke the internet temporarily with comments about "shipping" us, but without knowing Josiah and I broke up, the story died and it was chalked up to him being a closet Allie-Cat. I did find that quite funny, but he seemed to run with it, and it didn't bother him.

"Nope."

Bailey laughed. "You have to admit, that was pretty ballsy. And sweet. He's hot as fuck. I'd climb that man like the tree he is."

I laughed, imagining her doing just that. Bailey was pocket size, and Theo was not. Yes, my Google search showed me quite a few drool-worthy pictures and videos of Theo Nolan. I learned way more about football than I ever thought I would. I learned he was a running back and played offense, neither of which I knew a thing about before looking them up. Thank goodness for a lot of downtime on my plane traveling to different cities. It wasn't like I had a lot of time for watching football growing up, but I may actually give it a try. "He is hot, I'll give him that." I thought back to seeing him up close. Definitely hot.

"And successful on his own," she continued. "Did you see he's part of a documentary? They're filming the life and career of five of the top American Football League players."

"I did not," I said. As a general rule I stayed off the internet because it was a toxic place that made me spiral. I posted on my own social media sometimes and lurked on fan videos, but that was about the extent of it. My team took care of what I needed to know and shielded me from the rest.

"The first episode came out last night. You should watch it. I did. It's good. I think I need to get me a football player. I think Theo Nolan has his eyes on someone else I know."

"His eye on me? No. He was just a nice guy."

Bailey laughed. "If you say so. Watch the show. You may

like it, and it may finally make you want to contact him and thank him for the jersey."

Dread dropped like lead into my stomach. "Does he mention me?"

"Not in the way your mind went to, but he does mention you. Want to watch it on FaceTime together?"

"Bailey."

She giggled. "It's good, Al. You know I am not a fan of men dropping our names, but it isn't like that."

"He doesn't mention the worst day of my life?"

Bailey sighed. "I'm going to queue it up and put you on video chat. He's hilarious. His best friend, Spencer, is in it with him. They've been best friends since college and are like brothers. Spencer is engaged, or I'd say for you to tell Theo I'd like a setup when you finally contact him."

I chewed my lip as she switched us to FaceTime and then turned her phone so the show appeared on my screen. An intro with five sexy football players in the gym, on the field, and then lined up together for a photo in their respective team gear immediately caught my attention. Well, to be honest, the one who'd sat next to me and rubbed my back while I fell apart was the only one I watched. I couldn't tell you a single feature on the rest of them, but Bailey's commentary told me they were all hot.

I knew the day I saw him for the first time that he was hot. I wasn't dead—I was upset. But seeing him on the screen made me hold my breath. Theo Nolan was drop-dead gorgeous, much like I remembered. His dimpled smile and the ease with whom he was standing out the most, despite him having chiseled cheekbones and a scruffy beard that made me weak in the knees—despite never being a beard girl before. His perfectly styled short brown hair and bright-blue eyes seemed to sparkle behind the camera. He was a natural.

They cut to footage of each of them during a game and

then showcased each one on their own field. Spencer and Theo were together in their spotlight, running plays.

"Theo, you've had a great year so far professionally. You've been a top performer for the Blaze for eight years now."

Theo laughed and clapped Spencer on the back. "We are a great duo. I couldn't do it without the support of this guy right here and my amazing family."

"Family is important," the interviewer commented. "You're an only child, right?"

Theo nodded. "They stopped at perfection." Everyone laughed, and I couldn't stop myself from joining in.

"It gets better," Bailey interjected off the screen.

"My parents did everything they could for me as a young boy once they realized my passion. My dad played all the way through college but got hurt and didn't go on. He's been my biggest supporter my entire life. And my mom—she's my best friend. I wouldn't be the man I am without them."

"Swooooon," Bailey said, and I laughed. "You hearing this? Oh, just wait. It gets even better, my friend."

"What do you do for fun when you're not on the field?"

Spencer prattled off first about his fiancée, Lacey, his charity work with a local school, and his love of golf and the beach. The camera panned to Theo and he sat back, completely comfortable. I envied him. I didn't think I'd ever been that comfortable with a reporter in my face. Then again, inevitably, whatever question they started with, it turned into who I was dating or who I was rumored to date.

"I actually love to cook. I have a degree in culinary arts. I run a culinary program for teenagers as part of a local high school program. I don't get to do as much as I'd like during the season, but I still make sure I stop by and do at least one meal a week with them. I love music, even though I can't sing or play any instruments, so I try to go see live music whenever I can. It's a good stress reliever for me."

Spencer smirked, and I heard a noise from Bailey. My hands started sweating. "You saw a really good concert recently, didn't you?" I thought back to the pictures of him from social media during my concert—in his box, the lights of the stage reflecting a broad smile on his face.

Theo turned his gaze to his friend, and a silent conversation happened between them. My breathing accelerated and I sat forward.

"Relax," Bailey's voice came through the line. "There's nothing bad. I promise."

Theo grinned, his dimples on full display and his perfect teeth all showing. "Why yes, I did, Spence. And you were lucky enough to join me."

"Who did you see?" the reporter asked.

"Just so happened that the extremely talented Allie Witt was here at our stadium for her opening night for her new tour. So Spence and I caught the show. It was phenomenal. I know why everyone loves her and she's at the top of her game. That girl could probably run circles around me. Singing and dancing for over two hours? On top of that, I think her stage was like a mile across, and she changed outfits more in those two hours than I do in a month."

I knew Bailey said something, but I couldn't rip my attention from his face. He said *I* could run circles around him?

"And you sent her a special gift," Spencer added. "The boy was dead set on getting it to her. He pulled every string he could."

I covered my mouth with my hand. My gaze darted to the jersey and back to the small screen of my phone.

Theo laughed. "She played in my stadium. I wanted to show her how appreciative I was of her talent. So I sent her a signed jersey."

"And did she get it?" the reporter asked.

Theo shrugged. "I think so, but I'm not sure. I wanted to deliver it myself, but Allie doesn't do meet and greets after shows, even for football players who play in that stadium. I'm not gonna lie, my feelings were kinda hurt." With that, Spencer put his hand on his shoulder like he was consoling him, and I couldn't help but grin. Theo winked, and something strange happened in my lower belly.

"Allieeeee," Bailey moaned off-screen. "I want to jump that guy for you." I shook my head at her once again, referencing her small self climbing this man.

"You put something else with that jersey, didn't you?" the reporter prodded.

This time, Theo shot a warning glance at his friend before smiling back at the camera. "I just wrote her a note and said I thought she was talented and I enjoyed the show."

That wasn't what the note said at all. I blew out my breath and sat back, my legs jumping in nervous anticipation.

The video paused and Bailey's face appeared. "That's not what it says, right?"

I shook my head no. "Not one word of what he just said."

Bailey nodded. "I thought so. He's protecting you. I love it." She flipped the screen and pressed play again.

The reporter whistled. "You shot your shot to Allie Witt? Rather sure she's taken, even if you are Theo Nolan. Maybe you can change her mind."

I saw a look cross Theo's face so fast most people would probably miss it, but I caught it. He shrugged and held up his hands in surrender. "I meant no harm. It was just a thank-you. I would never try to get any woman to change her mind about anything, much less something as serious as already being in a relationship." There went my stomach again.

Bailey turned the screen around so I could see her face. "Al. Seriously. That man is the hottest man I've ever seen in my life."

I sighed. "I know, Bai."

"Did this convince you to get his number yet?"

My stupid heart, which always failed me, said one thing, but rational me spoke. "No. I am not ready."

"You could get it. You know a lot of people. Your people could contact his people. You're Allie freaking Witt." Bailey prattled on as if I didn't even speak. "You could just tell him thank you. You don't have to get married tomorrow."

I sighed. I knew she was right, and I did owe him that thanks after the way he protected me just now in that episode. And for the jersey and the sweet words on the note. Plus, Juan was over the moon that Theo included him in the gift, too. He wore it every Sunday and made sure to tell me what the score was of each of the Blaze's games. Rico, my other main security, was jealous and Juan took every opportunity to rub it in to him that he got one and Rico didn't.

"I'll think about it. Let me get through this disaster first." I didn't admit, even to myself, that I was afraid to get his phone number because I wasn't sure I could guard my heart against him, and my heart was already weak from being stitched back together.

Conor, my assistant and cousin, sat next to me on the plane, Zoey across from him, my mom on the other side of me. We were headed to my next tour destination, six shows in Texas. Security sat in the front, as they did, going over the security plan for the stadium.

"How's it going?" I asked, not sure whether I wanted the answer. The "news" of my breakup with Josiah got "leaked" five days ago while I was on my small hiatus at home. I stayed off my phone and the internet even more than usual. The only people who came through my "do not disturb" were the people on this plane and Bailey.

Zoey looked up from her laptop. I was glad she sat across from me so I couldn't see what was on her screen. She typed on her phone and looked at her laptop at the same time. Zoey had been with me since I was a young girl fresh into this life. She had been part of every decision, every up and down, and every bit of drama I've had to deal with, whether true or fictional.

"It's typical. People coming out of the woodwork stating they know you or him. People commenting on their own opinions of it all. Adding to the rumor mill of whose fault it was or what you or he supposedly told them about your relationship. The biggest rumor was that he wouldn't marry you, so you ended it. Of course they're using 'It's the End' as the proof that you were giving him an ultimatum."

Of course. One of the songs on *Lovestruck*. They were not that far off, but it wasn't me who ended it. Was that song me working through that he still hadn't married me? Yes. It also hit a chord with people because it was one of the most successful songs from the album so far, and it wasn't a single.

I sat back and looked out the window. My mom took my hand and I smiled thinly at her. For as hard as this was for me, it was just as hard on her. It had been me and my mom for my entire life. I never knew my dad and she was my sole supporter. Every once in a while, someone came out for media attention and claimed to be my father. That has yet to be true, and I had no desire to go any further with it. I knew what my mom told me about that time in her life, and that was good enough for me. It wasn't something she wanted to get into details about, and I accepted that.

Once my career took off, my mom started working for me full time. She was my bookkeeper and scheduler. My aunt Tiffany, my mom's sister, and her husband, my uncle Daniel, Conor's parents, lived next door to us growing up, and we'd spent most of our time together as one family. Conor was two years younger than me, and when I got famous, he purposely went to college to work for me. Before he was my assistant, my mom and my aunt and uncle did it all. Allie Witt was a family affair. Of course now we had many more people that made up our organization, but they were still and always would be the heart of it.

"Is it the top news story? Over my tour?"

Zoey and Conor exchanged glances. "Yes. But your show tomorrow will put the focus back where it belongs, and before you know it, it'll be old news."

"What are the Allie-Cats saying?" Zoey and Conor ran my official fan social media page, Allie-Cat Post, which they worked hard to keep all fans and no trolls. It was a full-time job, so they did have some trusted moderators, but they tried to keep their hands on it at all times.

Conor ran his hand through his curly blond hair. "They're sad for you. They know how hard this is going to be for you to get up there and sing. They've got some sweet tributes for you for tomorrow. I'm not going to tell you, though. I want you to be pleasantly surprised."

"Ha," I said. "If only they knew I already got through the worst part two months ago." Back then, when I had tears in my eyes during a song I'd written for Josiah, they chalked it up to my emotions about seeing my fans screaming for me. When I sang with extra venom in my voice about people who let you down, it was at the injustice of being a woman in a male-dominated world or the haters who constantly posted negativity about me.

"You are loved," my mom said in a quiet voice, and Conor nodded. "Focus on those that know and love you, and not on the ones that say your name on social media just to get attention."

"I know," I said. I laid my head back against the headrest, closed my eyes, and thought about the stadium tomorrow night, full of people who wanted to be there. Who paid a significant amount to be there, with family and friends, in their outfits, singing my lyrics back to me. The ones who stayed with me no matter what the news said, what guy I was linked to, or what drama someone concocted. Even ones who had been fans first as teenagers and were now bringing their own kids to the concert. Those were my favorite ones. We grew up together. Seeing the little Kitty-Cats, as they named themselves, in the audience made all the rest of it worth it.

I stuck my headphones in my ears. I needed to focus on what was important, and that was being ready for my show tomorrow. The rest was just noise.

I opened the door to my dressing room, wiping the sweat from my forehead. I was as ready as I could be for tonight, so now it was time to eat, shower, and relax.

Being from Florida, I was used to the heat, but even in my yoga pants and crop top, I was still dripping. Changing outfits tonight would be fun. They may need some extra fans backstage tonight. Forget my long blond hair. It would be a frizzy mess. Maybe I'd just go natural tonight and not straighten it. September was still summertime in the South. Fall who?

Conor and Zoey both turned when I walked in, and that was when I saw the most massive flower arrangement I'd ever seen in my entire life. It took up much of the table it sat on. My mouth dropped as I noticed the color—the colors of my *Lovestruck* album, pink and purple pastels. There had to be hundreds of small flowers inside it. Next to it was a pink glitter gift bag. Glitter was by far my favorite color, and that was definitely not a secret.

"What's this?" I asked.

Conor and Zoey shared a look. "It was delivered a few minutes ago by security. I guess it was cleared."

Cleared meant that whoever sent it wasn't a deranged fan or unhinged stalker, and yes, I had both of those. It was someone I knew. I stepped toward it, my hands shaking for some reason I didn't want to read into. Bailey. It had to be from her.

The flowers didn't have a card. I touched the soft petals, looking at the intricate colors on each one. They were gorgeous. I could hear Conor and Zoey whispering behind me, and the door opened and closed, but I stared at the gift bag like it was a snake that would bite me if I touched it. What was my problem? The list of people that it could be from was so small I had no reason to have the nervous shakes.

"Are you going to open it?" my mom's voice came from next to me. She put her arm around my shoulders. "Ew, you're sweaty."

I laughed. "Yeah, it's rather hot out there if you didn't notice. I've been rehearsing for two hours."

"Who is it from?" She gestured to the massive gift in front of us.

I shrugged, reaching out for the card sticking out of the bag. "I don't know yet. I'm guessing Bailey."

"Love that girl," she said. "You hungry? I'm going to have food service get lunch ready."

"Starving," I said. "Thanks, Mom." She walked away and I turned back to the bag. An envelope was tucked on the side, but it didn't say anything on the front. I looked over my shoulder to see both Conor and Zoey busy, so I opened the envelope and slid out the handwritten card.

And knew immediately it wasn't from Bailey. The very obvious male block handwriting I'd seen once before stuck out to me first.

Focus on what's in your control and not what some people who don't even know you say. Know you're better off, and you don't need anyone who doesn't know your worth. But if you need something to hug or to get out some stress relief, enjoy your gift. Much like this lioness, you are fierce and unstoppable. The flowers remind me of you and your music—beautiful, colorful, and inspiring. Kick ass tonight, Mallorie.

~T-Bear #23

Tears blurred my vision as I removed a stuffed lioness out of the bag. I smoothed its soft fur and looked into its dark eyes. Something shiny caught my attention, and I laughed out loud when I saw the necklace dangling from its neck. The Allie-Cat symbol of a black cat with a heart on its chest with my initials, AW, inside it. He really thought of everything.

"Girl," Conor appeared next to me. "You've got to be kidding me right now. Theo Nolan sent you this?" Apparently Conor knew who T-Bear #23 was. Two months ago, I'd have had no idea, but it seemed I was definitely in the minority.

That got both Zoey's and my mom's attention, and they made their way back to the table. The three of them read over my shoulder, and my mom slapped her hand over her heart.

"Mallorie." My mom was the biggest romantic ever—which was ironic since she never married and spent her life with me. She didn't need to say anything else—I knew what she thought. She was always good about letting me have my own opinions about the guys in my life, even if she always told me afterward what she really thought. I smiled when I thought about her rant after I told her about Josiah's phone call.

"I know," I said. I had the incredible urge to call Bailey, but she was unreachable right now, shooting a music video. Instead, I snapped pics of the flowers, the lioness, and the note and texted them to her, smiling at what I knew would be her reaction once she saw them.

"Zoey?"

"Yeah?" She still stood next to me, and I could see her wheels turning from this new gift.

"If I wanted you to get someone's number for me, could you do that?"

She furrowed her brow. "Of course."

Conor grinned, and I felt my mom watching me with a dreamy look. If Bailey were here, she'd jump up and down. Zoey looked at them, then at me. "Is this about Theo Nolan?"

I bit my lip. What was I doing? I had no business finding him. I was in the middle of a shitstorm of bad press once again, thanks to Josiah, the media spewing all sorts of shit that wasn't true. I didn't need another man—a famous one at that—connected to me. But he was already kind of connected to me. He'd mentioned me in his documentary, and he'd been all over social media at my concert and with my cutout.

Now he'd sent me a second gift without any presumption. He didn't add his phone number to anything. He didn't give away details about me to anyone. He was just—there. Supportive. Showing me that I wasn't alone. I thought about why this felt different to me, but I couldn't put my finger on it. He just felt—safe. And I wasn't the type of person who felt that often with someone after just meeting them.

It could blow up in my face. That had happened to me before. I trusted too easily sometimes, and people took advantage of it. But all I wanted was to say thank you. I didn't have to go any further than that. I just wanted him to know I appreciated all he did—and didn't—do for me since that day I ran straight into him.

"Yes. Get me Theo Nolan's number, please."

CHAPTER 4
Theo

I TURNED the ignition off on my SUV and pressed the close button on the garage door. Exiting the vehicle, I grabbed my bag from the back seat and made my way into the house. I was exhausted. We were leaving tomorrow afternoon to travel across the country for our game this weekend, and practice had been grueling. I was grateful we were getting out of the heat of the South to play in a cooler climate. There was no such thing as fall in Florida that was for damn sure.

My phone vibrated and I took it out of my shorts pocket. A delivery confirmation showed that Allie had received my gifts. A smile crept across my face. I hoped they gave her just a minute of peace. I had followed the story of her douchebag ex once it hit, and of course I knew this was months old, but I knew that no matter how well she was doing now, the attention this would get in the media would put her right back there.

I was a fraction of the celebrity she was, and even I had more media attention than I ever wanted after I broke up with Beth for cheating on me. She, of course, took that attention and ran. It was all my fault and not hers. I didn't even care to defend myself. In Allie's situation, she couldn't—and didn't

—say anything. All people would do would be to twist it, no matter what the truth was. She'd stopped discussing anything about her personal life years ago, which only fueled speculation. I definitely understood why she stopped, though. It wasn't their business.

After my mention of her in the documentary, things kind of blew up. I felt bad about that, but I figured maybe I was helping detract from the media shitstorm over Josiah. I would've asked her if I had a way to talk to her, but I knew she wasn't in the right place right now, so I decided to support her from afar and just let her know I was thinking of her. All she needed was another guy trying to get her attention publicly.

I knew I could find some live streams of her show tonight on social media—I'd taken to watching some of them when I could. I met a lot of famous people, and in my line of work, I met very successful people. But the more I learned about her, the more I realized Allie was something else altogether. Studying her had become my second full-time job. *Way to sound like a stalker,* I chuckled to myself. But that wasn't it at all. I just genuinely wanted to know her. I'd prefer to know if what I read about her was true by knowing *her*, but for now, I'd take what I could get and hope I could get the real story about many of the things I sometimes read from the source herself.

My phone dinged with a text, and it was my publicist, Jamie. *Hey T, I have a request you may be interested in. I was contacted a few minutes ago by Zoey Levine, publicist to the one and only Allie Witt. She is asking for your contact information. Are you okay with it? I know this answer, and I kind of wish I had Face-Timed you to ask instead so I could see your face. Let me know. Also, yes, I did completely freak the hell out once I realized it was actually Zoey Levine. I may or may not have asked for proof it was her.*

I stared at my phone, my heart pounding so hard I heard

it in my ears. Allie. Mallorie. Asked for my phone number. I would laugh at Jamie's obvious fangirling over Zoey, but I couldn't seem to move. Was this really happening? Allie really wanted to talk to me? She reached out to get my information? I had dreamed of this moment for the last two months, but no way did I let myself actually think it would happen. I intentionally didn't put my number on anything, so the ball was in her court, so to speak. I knew she wasn't in the right headspace for me to start crowding her.

I forced myself to suck in a deep breath. Hands shaking, I FaceTimed Jamie instead of responding. When her face popped up immediately, she was already laughing.

"This is for real? You aren't fucking with me?" Jamie was amazing, but we had a silly, fun relationship with each other when she wasn't busting my ass. She knew all about my crush on Allie and my kind of putting it out there in the documentary.

Jamie nodded, her bright eyes wide on the screen of my phone. "Trust me, I couldn't believe it was Zoey, either. She actually video called so I could be sure it was her and not someone else calling. You'd be proud of me. I acted like the professional I am and didn't scream, but I wanted to."

I finally laughed. "She wants to contact me?" I wanted to pinch myself that this was really happening and I wasn't dreaming.

Jamie nodded. "She does. Zoey mentioned her receiving your gift today and asking to talk to you. She has a show tonight but wanted your info for after. You're okay with this, right?"

There were few times in life that I was speechless, but I couldn't make my mouth form words, so I nodded. I was going to talk to Mallorie. Tonight.

"I'm going to be honest; I never thought she'd contact you. Not because you aren't awesome, but because . . ."

"She's Allie Witt," I finished the sentence. Jamie nodded,

and we both kinda stared at each other for a moment in disbelief.

"One more thing," she said, her face turning more serious. "Zoey emailed me an NDA. I know it's awkward, but . . ."

"Sign it."

Jamie laughed. "You didn't let me finish."

"I don't need you to. Sign it. And give Zoey my number for Allie."

"Do you want me to read it first, or are you just in the habit of having me sign your name to things you haven't read?"

"I know you. You'll read it. But I trust her. And I would never, ever say anything that could hurt her. To anyone. So sign it."

Jamie nodded. "You seem pretty rattled for you, T. You good?"

I looked around like I was afraid someone was going to hear me in my empty house. "Jamie, I'm not going to lie to you. I never have. I'm so fucking excited I could go run through ten guys right now. When I hang up, I may scream like a little girl. In fact, I know I will. It's a good thing I don't have a neighbor for at least a mile."

Jamie threw her head back and laughed. "I get that feeling. When I hung up with Zoey, I absolutely screamed at the top of my lungs and jumped up and down. Definitely a 'will remember where I was forever' moment, so thanks for that. I cannot even imagine seeing Allie in person or talking to her on the phone. I may pass away. I think—no, I *know*—I'm jealous of you right now, but also so happy for you. You deserve this so much after that bitch."

Jamie was protective of me after Beth. They had become friends, and Jamie felt a lot of guilt over what Beth did to me. I would never, not ever, tell her not to be friends with her, but she refused to be part of her life after she dragged me through the mud and made a media spectacle of me in an extremely personal way.

I laughed at her fangirling because I got it. I took a deep breath and let it out slowly, forcing myself to calm down. "Thanks, Jamie. For everything."

"You do not need to thank me for anything. It is my honor to be part of your life. And, Theo? I know I said this already, but I'm happy for you."

"It's just a phone number. Don't be too happy for me yet. Remember, she *is* Allie Witt. But also, thank you because I'm fucking happy as a pig in shit right now. I'm going to go so I can scream into my pillow like a fifteen-year-old and start writing her name in my notebook."

We disconnected and I put the phone down on my counter. My hands shook, and I felt like an idiot because of it. I had never, not ever, been shaky over a woman before. Butterflies, sure. Lust? Absolutely. But this feeling was completely foreign– and I kind of liked it.

"Stop it, Theo," I said out loud to myself. "Just because she asked for your number doesn't mean shit. She's a nice person, and you sent her two gifts. She's just saying thank you." I tried to talk reasoning into my head, but my brain was running rampant. I looked at the time. She would take the stage in about fifteen minutes.

Time for me to go take a shower, heat up some food, talk myself out of acting like a fool, and find a live stream to watch. Thank goodness for these die hard fans on social media.

I paced my room, my phone in my hand. It was well after midnight. Allie's show ended over an hour ago, and I started pacing almost immediately after.

Social media was wild, but I appreciated it in this case,

that was for sure. She was definitely back at the hotel or home or wherever she stayed when she played. I realized I didn't know these details because they weren't something you could google and that if I got to get to know her, I might find out some of those things. That was more exciting than I'd admit to anyone but myself.

There was no damn way I could go to bed. If she didn't call, I'd have to take a sleeping pill. I'd already done another workout and had another shower to work out the anxiety, yet I still felt like I was about to play for the championship. *Be cool, T. Geez. You sat next to her and rubbed her back while she cried. This is not a big deal.* No matter what I told myself, I couldn't stop my racing thoughts.

This was different. She wasn't a girl in crisis who literally ran into me full force, and I wasn't a guy she didn't know. She chose to talk to me. The biggest global pop superstar in our generation, if not ever. I blew out a breath. This was not a big deal. She was a person. I thought about the day we met and how upset she was. A regular person with regular feelings. Just because she was famous and successful didn't change that. In fact, it made everything more pronounced. She was just a girl. I laughed at the ridiculousness of my thought. She was absolutely *not* just a girl. She was *the* girl.

I flipped my TV to a sports channel for noise. I went into the bathroom to brush my teeth, making sure the phone was on full volume and had as many bars as possible. I could *not* miss her call.

I hung the towel back on the rack and picked up my phone, and it dinged in my hand. I almost dropped it trying to turn it on to see who it was.

Theo?

My stomach dropped to my feet as I saw the phone number. Of course, it wasn't one of my contacts, so unless it was a coincidence that someone I didn't know got my number to text me after midnight, it was her. *Be cool, man. Be cool.*

Fingers shaking—and they were too big for these damn keys anyway—I wrote back. It took me too damn long to get the words right and send them.

The one and only. I wanted to say so much more. But I needed to make sure it was really her first.

Send me a picture of you holding up two fingers. The girl wanted to make sure I was who I said I was. Smart. This was not her first rodeo.

I glanced in the mirror to make sure I looked okay. I wore a Blaze shirt and sweatpants. I ran my hands through my hair. It was short, so not much to be messed up. I turned my head side to side to make sure there were no rogue beard hairs. I held up two fingers and smiled, snapping the picture in the mirror. I sent it off, every second I waited feeling like a year.

Hey there. Just had to make sure it was you.

I wanted to ask the same thing. I wanted to see her face. But for some reason, I was terrified to ask her. It was like the me who'd rubbed her back and wiped the tears from her face was long gone, and in his place was a bumbling teenager trying to score his first date. *With Allie fucking Witt.* If twenty-year-old me could see me now.

I understand. It's great to hear from you.

Without me asking, a picture of Allie filled my screen. She still wore her stage makeup, but she was in a T-shirt and what I assumed were shorts, but I couldn't see them over the large T-shirt. Her hair was pulled up in a bun on top of her head, with curls framing her face. I lost my breath at the sight of her.

Just in case you needed proof, too. It's really me and not an impostor. Just got back from my show.

Hey, beautiful. Your show was amazing. How are you holding up?

You saw my show? Again? How? I know we aren't in the same state tonight.

Your fans live stream it every night. I just have to find the right one. It's blurry and jumpy, but I get to see most of it.

Wow. That's dedication. I wanted to thank you. For everything. But—is it okay if I call you?

My eyes widened. She wanted to—call me. My stomach clenched in anticipation of hearing her voice again.

Of course.

Seconds later, the number I for sure would save as hers appeared on my screen again.

"Hey," I said, trying but probably failing to sound chill. I knew my voice shook because I could hear it. I forced the urge aside to stand up and pace again and instead made myself sit on the bed and lean against the headboard.

"Theo," she said in response, and I felt each letter of my name throughout my body. That voice. Sweet, melodic, and just a bit gravelly from singing all night. I loved when I heard that part of her in her music because it was hot as hell. I knew nothing about music other than I liked to listen to it, but in my research I figured out it was called lower register. "I trust you, but sometimes texting is hard..."

"I get it," I answered. "I am glad to hear your voice, anyway." I cringed when I said it, wondering if it sounded ridiculous, but she didn't seem to mind. Since when did I second-guess every word that came out of my mouth? I wasn't this guy. *Since you got a phone call from Allie Witt.* Right. That.

"My voice is tired from singing, so excuse the state of it." She laughed, and my stomach dropped to my feet. God, that sound. "Thank you for everything you did for me that day, but also since then. Thank you for the jersey and the gifts today. I love the lioness. She's now going to go with me to every tour stop. But also, thank you for what you said—and what you didn't—in your documentary and in the notes to me. Somehow, with you not knowing me at all, you hit on so many things I needed to hear. That's why I had to get in touch with you."

She'd seen my show. Or someone told her. Pride filled my chest. "You don't have to thank me, Mallie. I didn't do them for the thank-you. I did them to show you I care and to hopefully make you smile a bit. And as far as the documentary stuff? Not their business. I'm not new to the prying of the press, though I definitely don't have it on your level. I've also had quite a bit of training on how to keep my mouth shut."

"Mallie?"

I realized that the nickname just came out, and I wasn't sure if she liked it. "Sorry. Mallorie. Allie. Which do you prefer?" I realized the answer was very important to me. I wanted to respect every part of her, even something as silly as a nickname from someone who barely knew her.

"No," she said. "I like it. No one has ever called me that. I was either Mallorie or, once I got a record deal, Allie, because it was 'easier for name recognition.' I actually suggested Mallie as my stage name because it was different, but that got shot down. I'm named after my grandmother, so my mom never calls me by any nickname. To her, I am only Mallorie Rose."

"That's really neat," I said. "That's a beautiful name."

"Yeah, we were really close and she passed away right before I got my record deal, so I'm grateful I get a part of her with me all the time. My song "Generations" is about her."

I loved learning these things about her. "I am really close with my grandparents, too. Thankfully they are still a part of my life."

"You're definitely lucky," she said. "I only grew up with my mom, so we've always been really close as well. She's my best friend. I'm close to my aunt and uncle as well."

"I am close with my parents, too. Sure makes things much easier when you have a good support system, doesn't it?"

"I cannot imagine being where I am without them."

"So, how are you holding up? It sure looks like you're killing it out there, but I know that in professions like ours, we also put on a front. Not that we are the same—" Ugh. I needed to stop talking.

"No, you're right," she interrupted.

I blew out a breath, glad she didn't make me feel stupid like my life couldn't possibly compare to hers.

She sighed. "I'm okay. My fans are sweet and trying to protect me. Tonight, they all had signs that said 'Team Allie' on them to show support. It's apparently a trending hashtag on socials, too. Josiah and I haven't had any contact in months. He was gone from our house way before I got back there. I just have to wait out the craziness and let them focus on something else—or, in my case, some*one* else. They will literally try to connect me to anyone. I could sneeze in someone's direction and they'd say I was sleeping with him." She laughed dryly. "Or her. Did you know there was a several-year period there when people were convinced Bailey and I were together? There are still some of them out there that just won't let it go. I mean, I love Bailey like the sister I never had, but not like that."

I knew Bailey Lee was her best friend and a well-known country singer, and the speculation about her was ridiculous, but I wasn't surprised after what I knew of the media with Allie and other successful women.

I thought about the social media posts after my pictures went viral. "I'm sorry if I contributed to them speculating about you," I admitted.

"Theo." My stomach fluttered again, and I bit my lip to not groan at the way she said my name in her tired voice. "Do not apologize. You made me laugh with your pic pretending to kiss my cheek on the cardboard cutout. As a general rule, I do not do much on social media. It's just better that way for my own mental health. There were a lot of years that I was active, but the negative gets to me more than I want to admit. So much garbage out there I don't need to see. Conor, my cousin and my assistant, screens things and shows me things he thinks I will like. He showed me that right away, as well as your and Spencer's videos in the box singing and dancing to my songs. I'm glad to know that my demographic now includes professional football players."

"It was fun. You put on an amazing show. I've been a fan of yours for many years." I cringed again at my lack of filter. *I'm really not a stalker.*

Allie laughed. "Really? Thanks, Theo. I love what I do so much. It makes the rest of it worth it. Wait. Is your name actually Theodore?"

I laughed, too. "No. Just Theo. I was named after my grandfather, Theodore, though. But my mom had mercy on me to not saddle me with that name. But my nickname is T-Bear, like Teddy Bear, because of my size and fuzzy facial hair. Years ago, when I first started playing professionally and grew out my beard, a kid said I looked like a teddy bear, and that was the end of that. My teammates took that and ran with it, and once the fan base got ahold of it, it was mine forever." I smoothed my trimmed beard, even though she couldn't see it. "I may have at one time had a good amount of chest hair, but I shave it."

I felt my face flame. Why was I still talking? She didn't need to know that.

Allie giggled. "Okay, well, if I am Mallie to you, then you are Teddy to me. That's how I'm going to save your number in my phone."

Teddy. I closed my eyes at the thought of being her personal teddy bear, comforting her small frame with my large one. I remembered my giant hand on her small back while she cried. I had to force the images that came after that from my mind and open my eyes again, guilt making my cheeks flame. Thank goodness she couldn't see me because my thoughts just diverted quickly to the R-rated-heading-toward-X category.

"Is that okay?" she asked.

I realized I hadn't answered her, lost in my own daydream, and her voice sounded unsure. "Absolutely. Put the little teddy bear emoji next to my name in your contacts."

She giggled, and I decided that it was my favorite sound in the world. "Yes!"

"I'm putting Mallie with a microphone and a music note in mine."

"Perfect!"

A natural silence enveloped us for a moment, and I wished for this conversation to never end. I couldn't believe how lucky I was right now. I would never, not ever, forget this night.

CHAPTER 5
Allie

I KICKED my feet on the mattress like a little girl. Texting with Theo—Teddy—was thrilling, but hearing his voice? Gave me chills from head to toe.

That first day, in my emotional state, I hadn't paid much attention to the timbre of his voice. Many, many song lyrics could be written about just the sounds of him saying normal words, and I could guarantee I'd write some of those as soon as we hung up. The ideas already swirled in my head.

And *Mallie*? Gah. I couldn't believe I felt like a teenager right now. Bailey would have a field day with this, and I would tell her every single detail the second I could get hold of her.

"Mallie?" There it was again. I shivered, goose bumps on my arms.

"Teddy?" I pictured it now—me, cocooned in his arms, safe and protected. *Mallorie Witt. Stop it right now. What in the hell are you doing? You aren't going to be safe and protected in anyone's arms.*

"I really enjoy talking to you."

I sighed, ignoring the butterflies taking flight in my stomach. "Same."

"Is this just a onetime thank-you conversation?"

Damn if he didn't just put it right out there like that, and damn if I didn't like it. I wasn't one for playing coy or mincing words, either. There was just no room in my life for playing games, not ever, but especially not now. I was done not getting exactly what I wanted and making no apologies for it.

"Because I'm going to be honest with you. I will never, ever sugarcoat or lie to you. I don't want it to be a onetime conversation."

I sucked in a breath and worried my lip between my teeth. He was direct, and I liked it. "I don't want it to be a onetime conversation, either, but I have to be honest with you, too."

"Please do."

"I'm in a crazy part of my life right now. With all this nonsense with Josiah, and I'll be on tour for months . . ."

"Mallie," he interrupted. I had never liked a nickname more. "I have a hectic life, too. I get it. But please, let's just be real with each other. First, you don't have to be superstar Allie with me. You're just Mallorie. Mallie. A girl whose job is to sing and do a damn good job at it."

"And your job is to play football. Very well."

Theo laughed. "Right. We don't need to put conditions or excuses on things. And something you do not have to do? Try to make yourself smaller to talk to me. Like I told you the day we met, don't ever do that for anyone again. Be who you are, unapologetically, and the right people will find you. It does not matter to me one bit that you have an absurd schedule and life. I love that about you. I may not understand it on your level, but I understand it."

I stared at the phone, unable to speak. How did this man do that? He always said exactly what I needed to hear at the time.

"Wow."

"What?"

"You're good with words. I thought I was the lyricist."

Theo laughed. "I'm not feeding you lines. This is just me. I want to keep talking to you. I don't care when that is or how often. I don't care if it's a text that says hi. You don't ever have to wonder who I will talk to about you or what I will do because that's not who I am. No pressure at all."

"Thank you." I believed every word he said because he hadn't shown me any different. That little pessimist in my brain that had been burned tried to interject her objection that Josiah had said similar things when we first met, but I silenced her.

"Mallie?"

"Teddy?"

We both laughed. "I like you," he said.

"You barely know me." It was an automatic response, but I didn't really believe that. Theo just seemed to get quite a bit about me as a person, and there were very few people in the world who knew the real Mallorie. Many people thought they knew Allie Witt, and maybe they did in a way. But Allie, pop superstar, was not the same as Mallorie. And who I was with my fans was not who I was with the people I loved.

"I want to change that," he said, his voice low. The effect went straight to my gut and below. I bit my lip, imagining that big hand touching me. This was not the time, nor was I going to go there. Baby steps. Less than baby steps. Baby crawls.

"Okay," I said.

"Okay?" I couldn't help but hear the hope in his voice, and I shivered again. That voice made me weak in the knees.

"I'll call you tomorrow," I said. "I have another show, but I'll call you after like I did tonight. Maybe we can—" I paused, my bravery wavering. Give me a sold-out stadium and I'll rock the confidence all the way. Give me a handsome man breaking through my exterior? Instant insecurity. But I needed to change that, and now was as good a time as any.

"Can what?" Theo prodded, his voice making me bite my lip in response.

"Maybe we can FaceTime?" I closed my eyes, my stomach flipping while I waited for his response.

"I would love to see you again," he said, and my stomach clenched. "We fly out tomorrow afternoon, so I'll be free after your show for sure. I look forward to it."

"Get some rest," I said, not wanting to hang up but also needing to process all this, preferably by screaming and running around.

"You too, beautiful," he said. "Good night, Mallie. Thank you for calling me."

When the line went dead, I held my phone with the stupidest grin on my face. When was the last time I felt that way about just having a first conversation with someone? I texted Bailey to call me ASAP and then lay back on the bed. I pulled the pillow over my face and screamed into it, kicking my legs. I didn't even care that I needed to rest my voice or not strain my vocal cords. *I just had a whole conversation with Teddy and he wants to keep talking to me.*

Theo freaking Nolan. *Teddy.* The hot-as-hell professional football player who saved me from certain embarrassment on the worst day of my life just told me he liked me and wanted to keep talking to me. The guy who could literally get anyone he wanted. Yes, I was spiraling.

When my phone dinged, I assumed it was Bailey responding. But a grin the size of Texas spread on my face when I saw that it was actually Theo.

I want you to know that you made my whole day. Thank you for reaching out. Sweet dreams, Mallie. Talk to you tomorrow. Xoxo.

I put the phone to my chest, my heart pounding like I just ran across the stage. I squealed again, wishing Bailey was here. Had any guy ever put things out there quite as directly as Teddy did? I didn't think so. He said he didn't play games, and I liked it.

I started and stopped five texts in response and settled on *Thank you, Teddy. You're so sweet. It was great to talk to you. Talk to you tomorrow. Sweet dreams.* I wanted to say much more and talk to him for hours, but I was still hesitant. Experience had taught me that.

"Allie. I am so damn jealous right now." Bailey lay back on her bed, her face filling the screen. "I need you to hook me up with a friend of his. Right now."

I laughed, my phone propped up in front of me as my team worked on my hair and makeup. "You are getting *way* ahead of yourself."

"No she's not!" My mom called from across the room, not looking up from the romance novel in her hand. "I'm with you, Bailey! This man is something else!"

I shook my head. "You two are killing me."

"Tell me that you aren't swooning so hard, Al. There's no damn way."

I grinned and wiggled in my chair. "Okay, I may or may not have had a really hard time falling asleep last night. I wished for you to talk me off the ledge. I wrote two pages of possible lyrics and a melody."

Bailey laughed. "Of course you did. You wouldn't be Allie Witt if one interaction didn't inspire an entire album."

"Not an entire album," I said. "Yet. You know I've always got a book of lyrics."

Bailey shook her head. "Also, no way am I going to be the one to talk you off any ledge when it comes to Theo Nolan. Had I been able to talk to you last night, I definitely would not have calmed you down. This is huge. So you made plans to talk tonight?"

"Yeah. We're actually going to FaceTime tonight after my show. We've texted a little bit today, too. He's traveling to a game."

"Who initiated?"

"The texts? He texted me first this morning and said 'good morning, beautiful' and to kick ass like the superstar I am."

"ALLLLLIEEEEE. I'm dying." She covered her face with her hand and groaned. "Please tell me you're going to see him."

I laughed. "See him? Other than on FaceTime? I'd like to know when." It wasn't that I hadn't thought of it, but our schedules were impossible. And also, I was scared to voice that to him just yet. It felt . . . soon. I needed us to talk a bit more first.

"Girl. You have a private jet. Two of them, to be exact. You could be anywhere he is in a matter of hours."

"Facts!" my mom called again from across the room. I turned and caught her gaze, and she lifted her hand like, *What?* I apologized to my poor team just trying to get me ready for the show and told myself to sit still.

"Let's slow down a bit," I said. "I don't even have a break for another month to even think about seeing him, and I have no idea what his schedule is like."

Bailey sighed like I pained her. "I expect an update later. I have to run. Love you, Al."

"Love you," I echoed as her face left the screen. I caught my reflection in the mirror, the fog of product keeping my hair looking good clouding the mirror. As it cleared, I looked at myself and thought about the girl who once dreamed of being right here, right now. Sometimes I still couldn't believe this was the life I led—that I got the chance to not just do what I loved but be successful beyond my wildest dreams.

The toddler who used anything as a microphone to sing to

anyone who would listen. The young girl who spent so many hours practicing the guitar and piano. The preteen who filled notebooks full of song lyrics. The young teenager who went to every possible open-mic night to get noticed. And then, the sixteen-year-old who released her first record all looked back at me. I never got tired of it—not really.

Some days, it was hard. Doing this for the last thirteen years professionally was the highlight of my life. But sometimes, the day-to-day things that kept this Allie Witt show running exhausted me. However, at the end of each day, at the end of each performance, recording session, or album release, I never took it for granted. As the press liked to remind me, I wasn't "young" as a pop star anymore, so every year I got was a gift I did not take for granted. My favorite part was touring, despite how exhausting it was. Seeing the faces of my fans, whom I dreamed of having my entire life, screaming lyrics back at me invigorated me and kept me going.

"All done!" I grinned and said my thanks as I stood from the chair to get dressed and go rock the stadium. I picked up the lioness that we named Adira after a brief text conversation earlier—since it meant fierce—safe next to my travel bag and held it close to me. I thought of Theo's sweet texts, his sexy voice, and the words he used to soothe my anxiety so well.

"What am I doing?" I asked the stuffed Adira. The butterflies in my stomach had nothing to do with the sold-out crowd filtering into the stadium and everything to do with a certain man who sent me this stuffed animal and told me he wanted to talk to me again.

My phone dinged inside my bag and I picked it up just as Zoey opened the door to get me.

I know you're about to go on. Have so much fun with the people who love you, Mallie. I cannot wait to talk to you later. Thinking of you. Good luck. Not that you need it since you're the most talented person I've ever seen.

I grinned and clutched the phone to my chest. *Good luck to you, too, not that you need it either, Mr. Star Running Back first draft pick (look, I can google too!). I'm getting ready to go out and was just talking to Adira. I like the name.* I sent it before I could second-guess myself and then put my phone and the stuffed animal inside my bag.

"Let's do this," I said to Zoey. I slipped on my boots, took one last glance in the mirror, and forced Theo's handsome face into the back of my mind. I had a job to do.

I looked out at the crowd, my chest heaving after dancing and singing through my first set. The sold-out crowd screamed as my face filled the screens around the stadium.

I smoothed the curls out of my face from my last song and grinned at them. I looked from side to side, from top to bottom, memorizing the feeling of all these people here to sing with me. I knew this wouldn't be forever, and there was nothing like this feeling. No matter how many times I did it, I still soaked it all in. If ever I forgot the dream I had to be here, that would be my last day. One of the dancers handed me my guitar, my favorite one, and then stepped back into the shadows. I put the guitar strap over my head and strummed a few chords.

"Why hello!" I yelled into the microphone, sending the crowd into another frenzy. "It is so great to see you all again! How many of you have seen me in concert before?"

The deafening shrieks told me what I knew—most of them were my lifelong fans. I loved that I grew up with many of these people here, but some of them were my mom's age or older. "And for how many of you is this your first Allie Witt concert?"

I grinned at the shouts and started strumming the guitar again. "Well, welcome to the Lovestruck tour!" I drew a heart in the air, my signature for this tour, and the crowd did it back. "I thought we'd spend a little time just us, is that okay?" This was my favorite part of the show, the part where I just played my guitar or the piano and sang. While the huge production of my shows was incredible, my heart was this right here, where I'd started back in my bedroom as a child.

I began the first chords and closed my eyes as the melody overtook me. I sang, my voice reverberating around the huge stadium. I remembered the many nights singing by myself, hoping one day for what I have right now. When I was up here, nothing else mattered. Not what happened years ago or even minutes before the show. This was my happy place. When I finished, I made eye contact with someone a few rows back and threw my guitar pick at them. I smiled and waved when they caught it and jumped up and down, screaming my name.

The night passed in a blur as I played through my set list, as they seemed to do. I spent so much time prior to my tour rehearsing that doing it was second nature now. I didn't believe in being too prepared—I had been that way my entire career. There was no one in the room who was going to work harder than me.

"Please give it up for my amazing dancers, backup singers, and band! I could not do it without them and the many, many, many people that work behind the scenes!" I screamed into the microphone. The crowd erupted. I caught the eye of several fans in the front rows and blew them kisses. "Thank you so much for coming out tonight. Remember to always stay lovestruck!" I drew a heart in the air again, and the floor I stood on began lowering under the stage. I waved until I was out of sight.

I stepped off the lift, and Conor stood there with a bottle of water. I took it gratefully. "Thank you."

"You killed it as usual," Conor said, pulling me to him in a hug. He didn't even care that I was covered in sweat and probably didn't smell good—this was our routine. We had been mistaken for siblings most of our lives, and dare I say, we were even closer than siblings.

Conor was two years younger than me, and we had the same blond curly hair and blue eyes. We'd been best friends since the day two-year-old me held newborn Conor in my arms. When I started playing music at the young age of seven, Conor was the first person I played for. He still was. When I got a record deal and put out my debut album, Conor was part of all of it. After he graduated from college at twenty years old—add genius to Conor's résumé—he worked for me full-time ever since.

"Thanks!" I pulled back from him, and we walked arm in arm toward my dressing room. I waved to everyone as I passed. "Where's Mom?" To this point in my life, my mom had never—not ever—missed a show of mine. No matter what country I was in, she was the anchor in my life.

"Already in your dressing room," he said. "She got a phone call. I think it's my mom." Aunt Tiffany did not travel as much with us, but she ran our operations from our home base in Florida. Two years younger than my mom, they were extremely close and always had been.

When we stepped into the dressing room, I waved at my mom, who was still on the phone. She blew me a kiss and mouthed. *Great job, sweetie*, like she always did. And instead of going directly to take my costume off and shower and change, I went right for my bag and retrieved my phone.

I couldn't help the grin that broke across my face when I saw Teddy's name. A multitude of texts from the last three hours showed on the screen. I unlocked the phone and opened the text conversation between us.

I found a live stream of someone in the front row and they are losing their shit at being that close to you. I get it, I think I would, too. He is so funny, he's screaming "yasssss bitch" anytime you do something amazing, which is basically the entire show. Girl, you look smokin' hot. I wish I was there. You just waved at him and I think he may die. He just said, RIP me.

I giggled at the message. I loved fans like that, and I wished I knew which fan it was. I tried to see their faces when I could, so the ones right up front were the easiest to watch.

Just you and the guitar is a sight to see. You are SO talented.

Oh and now the piano? You deserve every single award you have received and all the ones you haven't. They should just name an award after you at this point.

I hope I'm not annoying you with all of these messages. I just can't seem to stop. The way you have this HUGE audience just eating out of your palm? Unbelievable. These people on the live stream are losing their minds. I've never seen anything like this. There are a hundred thousand people watching this livestream! That is ridiculously cool. Did you know that many people tune in to these shows?

I'm still in awe that you can do this for this many hours and make it look so easy. I think we need to talk about your workout routine because I may need to do it.

I know I saw this in person, but this was before I knew you. I just want you to know how impressed I am by you. I can't wait to see this from a closer vantage point.

Amazing show. You're a beautiful person, inside and out. The way you make sure to thank everyone who works behind the scenes? One of a kind. I can't wait to talk to you tonight.

I read and reread the messages for long enough that Conor walked up to see what caught my attention. He read over my shoulder, and I could hear the noises in his throat increasing as he read.

"Mallorie." Our gazes met and I nodded.

"I know."

"This man has it bad," Conor said.

"We're just talking," I said, but I wasn't even sure I

believed that at this point. It was ridiculously early, but something just felt—different about him. I shut up the cynic that immediately put negative thoughts in my head.

"*You* may just be talking," he said, packing up the things in the dressing room. "But he isn't. As a man, trust me. I don't think I've ever liked a woman enough to put myself out there like that, much less to someone of your status."

I scoffed. "I'm just a woman like anyone else," I said.

Conor turned his body to me. "Mallorie. You may be a woman looking for the same things as every other woman, but you are *not* a woman like anyone else. You are Allie Witt, the global superstar who has broken more records and gotten more awards than anyone else in history. You are on a short list of the richest—and most powerful—women in the world. You use your platform to influence others in the best ways. That is intimidating to most guys. I think it was intimidating to Josiah, too. You know that who you are is part of the issue you've had with relationships. It's sure as shit not your heart. You're the best person I know."

"You say that because you love me," I said, but my heart swelled at his words.

"No," he said. "Theo isn't intimidated by you because he's the best at his very public job, too. I mean, he's nowhere near the level of you, but he gets it more than anyone else you've ever been with."

"I'm not with him," I argued. My heart squeezed at the thought of dating someone again. I couldn't do it. Not yet, and maybe not ever. I wanted it—God knew I did. I wrote enough songs about the pursuit of love and the aftereffects of its demise—but it seemed impossible at this point to find my endgame.

My mom hung up the phone and walked toward us. "What's this about?"

"Theo Nolan," Conor said. Her eyes widened.

"What about him now?"

"They're talking," Conor answered before I could say anything.

The look on my mom's face was reminiscent of her look after my first Grammy nomination. "*Talking* talking?"

"No," I said at the same time Conor said, "Yes."

She nodded like she completely understood. "It's about time."

CHAPTER 6
Theo

"I SENT her like two hundred messages during her show," I said, pacing back and forth across the room while holding my phone. "What was I thinking? I'm going to push her away. She's going to think I'm some sort of creeper."

Spencer laughed. "Dude. Relax." He turned to Lacey and they laughed at my misery.

"I can't relax," I said.

"Theo," Lacey said. These two had been sworn to secrecy that I was talking to Allie—Mallorie—my Mallie. I trusted them with my life. "Breathe, buddy. She isn't going to think you're a creeper. Did she respond to you yet?"

"Not yet, but her show ended not too long ago."

I could hear the laughter in Lacey's voice. "Has she given you any indication that she's been afraid of your honesty before now? Because it seems that you've been pretty open with her about the way you feel."

I thought back to our numerous texts, the phone call, and the promise for FaceTime tonight. "No."

"Right. So what's the worst that could happen?"

"She realizes I'm a freak and stops talking to me." The thought of this made me want to bang my head on the wall.

Spencer shook his head. "Wow, Theo. I've never heard you like this before. I like it."

The phone beeped and I looked at the screen. I gasped and almost dropped the phone. "I have to go! It's Allie!" I clicked to answer her call so fast I wasn't even sure I did it correctly. That dang accept or deny a phone call screwed me up every time. If I hung up on her, I'd never forgive myself.

"Mallie," I said as she filled the screen. She was makeup-free, and I almost lost my breath at the sight of her natural face. Her hair curled around her features, and I wished to be there to tuck it behind her ear.

A huge grin crossed her face, and it was so much nicer to see her this way than sobbing her eyes out over a guy who didn't deserve her.

"Hey, Teddy."

That low, gravelly voice hit me in the gut again. She settled back against what looked like a hotel headboard, and I saw that she wore a Blaze oversized T-shirt. My heart skipped at the sight. It wasn't the jersey I'd sent her that night. Where did she get it from? "Sorry it took so long. Someone distracted me after the show with a lot of messages, and I needed a shower when we got back. So you get after-show me now. This is what I look like after being on stage for many hours."

Someone. Me. She didn't hate it. She wasn't running away. She was—teasing me? "I love after-show you. It's just as stunning as during-the-show you. Are you wearing a Blaze shirt?"

She nodded and bit her lip, and it took everything in me to not groan at what that did to me. She stood, phone in hand. If she wore anything under the shirt, I once again could not see it. Her bare, toned legs peeked out from under the long shirt, and I almost lost my mind. "Conor got it for me. He's a big fan of yours." I knew Conor was her cousin and assistant, and I thanked Conor in my head for this vision in front of me. I made a mental note to send him a signed jersey as well.

She walked in front of the mirror and turned so I could see

the back. It absolutely had my last name and number on it. She. Was. Wearing. My. Fucking. Name. On. Her. Back.

"You like it?"

I blew out a breath, trying to keep myself under control. It was too early for me to panic—in the best way—about this, but damn if it didn't make me want to stand up and beat my chest. "I love it, Mallie. You look so good with my name on your back."

Her face filled the screen again, and I noticed how wide her eyes were. "Teddy," she whispered.

"What's that, angel?"

She bit that damn lip again, and this time I groaned. "Why are you calling me angel now?"

"Because you look like a fucking angel, and I would give literally anything in the world to be in that room with you right now."

"What would you do if you were?" The look on her face told me she surprised herself with the question.

"Honestly?"

She nodded. "Always."

I took a deep breath. Here went nothing. It may be too soon. I may be out of line. But I couldn't stop the words from coming out of my mouth. "I would grab a fistful of that shirt that is way too big on you and pull you to me. I'd smooth back the curls that frame your gorgeous face, and I would kiss the hell out of those amazing fucking lips. I'd kiss you until you forgot that anyone before me existed."

Mallie opened and closed her mouth a few times, the flush on her cheeks evident even on the camera. "And then?"

Oh, my girl wanted *more*? I wasn't sure she was ready for what was really in my head. "I'd see if you had on anything under that shirt of mine."

Her eyes widened again, and before I could even hope for it, she lifted the shirt to show off a tiny pair of black shorts that definitely didn't cover her ass. The curve of her hips, her flat stomach, her killer legs, and the anticipation of what else was—or wasn't—under that shirt had me hard instantly.

This was probably going too fast. I should probably be the smart one and slow it down. Talk. Ask her how the show was. What her travel plans were next. Anything. But I also wanted nothing more than to continue this.

"I know you get told this a lot in your life, but you are so fucking beautiful."

She blushed, the shirt back over her shorts, and she settled back on the bed. "I do, but hearing it from you is different."

"Different how?"

She shrugged, seeming shy all of a sudden. "I don't know. It just feels—different. Like you mean it more? I don't know. A lot of times people that say that just see my exterior. I feel like you see more than that, and that makes the compliment matter more to me."

"I agree," I said, and both of us knew we weren't talking about what I just said.

"Do you know what I like the most about us getting to know each other?"

"What's that?" There were so many things I wanted her to say here, and I couldn't wait to hear what it was she picked.

"That it feels so . . . organic. I don't know how to explain this or if you have felt this way in your profession, too. Everything with me is so scheduled. Where I am, who I meet, nothing happens accidentally. The people I'm connected to, the parties I go to, the pictures that are taken. I'm not saying it's fake because it isn't, but it is also not something I choose, you know?"

"And you're choosing this?" I wanted this answer more than I'd admit to anyone.

"I am," she said, her voice catching. "And I'm not going to lie, it feels fucking fantastic for me to have something that I chose just for me and I'm the only one that knows about it."

"I'm choosing it, too," I said back. "In case you needed to

hear me say it." I didn't have to think about that answer at all. We looked at each other in the camera for a few seconds, nothing exchanged but the simple yet powerful words we left off with.

"I'm scared," she said finally. "I keep telling myself not to be, but I am."

"Tell me," I said.

"Tell you why I'm scared?"

I nodded. "Let it all out. I'm listening. You have absolutely nothing to be afraid of with me."

"I think that scares me the most," she said. "That you seem like the most genuine, honest person I've ever known, but that's also hard for me to believe. I have had to sift through so much bullshit in my life. People who said they cared about me but didn't. Friends who turned into enemies. Lovers who said they loved me, but at the end of the day, it was too much. Being associated with me is something on another level. No one has been able to handle it. I wish I could be a normal girl dating a normal boy, but that's not the life I lead."

"Angel, let me try to settle your fears. First, I get it. I truly do. I mean, my life will never be on your level, but I'm not immune to the press and people with opinions, either. I was with my ex, Beth, for several years. She was a cheerleader for the Blaze. We had a very public relationship. Our team exploited us for their ratings. They fucking called us Barbie and Ken. There were even shirts made by our team with that on them. Social media was very invested in us, even putting bets on who our kids would look like. I thought I was going to marry her. I even had a ring. Until I found out she cheated on me."

Allie's mouth dropped open and she put her hand over it, a gasp escaping. "You have got to be kidding me. Who would cheat on you?"

I laughed. "Well, I have the same opinion about the moron

that broke up with you on the stage before your first show. It was *truly* his loss."

"Well, it was truly *her* loss too," she echoed.

"I am a big believer in what is meant to be will be," I said, "even if that sometimes means things don't work out the way we want them to. Something better is always out there, even if we can't see it at the time."

"That's a great way to think of things," she said. "So, kind of like you were meant to be there when I ran into you full speed while sobbing my eyes out?"

My heart clenched. I still hated thinking of her that upset. "Kind of like that, yes," I said. "I'm sorry that was such a hard day for you, but I am glad that I got to be there to pick you up."

"Literally," she joked, and we both laughed.

"Literally," I agreed, "but it gave me a chance to see you, the real you."

"Ugh." She covered her face with her hand. "That was so embarrassing. Thank you for being a nice person and not telling everyone you know how pathetic I am."

"Mallie," I said, and she peeked at me through her fingers. "Do not be embarrassed about that at all. And don't ever call yourself pathetic again. Josiah was pathetic, not you. You're not a robot; you're a human being with feelings. Do you want me to tell you something I deem as the most embarrassing moment of my life to make you feel better?"

She grinned, uncovering her gorgeous face. "Yes."

I laughed. "That was a quick answer."

"Well, my every move is usually cataloged by cameras, so there are a lot of moments I wish I could take back in my life, but instead, they are on video for all to see anytime they search it. It's nice to know someone else has had their share of moments, too."

"Oh, this one was caught on camera," I said, and she leaned forward, intently listening. I fought not to be distracted by her large blue eyes and dark eyelashes. "I'm surprised you have never heard this or seen it before. I guess I'm thankful for your busy life and not going on social media. A few years ago, not long after Beth and I broke up, she was still cheering for the Blaze before she was basically run out of there, and she transferred to a team in California. She walked up to me before the game while I was on the field warming up. It was a playoff game, so there was a huge media presence and tons of fans at the game. All eyes were on us because our breakup made a great news story in our football circle. She was apparently tired of my friends—what used to be *our* friends—making her feel like shit for cheating on me, so she decided to walk right up to me in front of God and everyone and tell me that I was the worst fuck of her life, I had a small dick, and that was why she cheated on me. Loudly. With multiple cameras facing us."

Mallie's eyes widened. "No fucking way," she said. "She did not."

"She did," I said. "I'm sure if you look it up now, the video still exists somewhere, but also, please don't. It was the top trending story for weeks. *Weeks*. I had to not only pretend that what she said didn't make me feel two inches tall but also attempt to crush our opponents in the game. Of course the other team started calling me 'Little Cock' on the field, so that was great. The good news was I used that anger to fuel my performance, so it was my best game and we won and advanced. That's one of the many reasons I was able to tell you about compartmentalizing the day we met. I have had to do it many times, but never like that day."

Mallie blinked. "Teddy, Jesus. That is horrible! Did you ever do anything?"

"What was I going to do? There was nothing I could say that would make it better. How do you defend someone that says that? Tell people that wasn't true? I just let people drag me through the mud on social media and in the news, painting me as the bad guy until they were done and moved on to someone else. But was I angry and mortified? Yes. Absolutely yes. They even got 'past lovers' to agree that I was terrible in bed. Of course I knew none of these supposed lovers."

Mallie whistled. "Damn. I can't believe you can trust anyone after that," she said, her voice low. "Someone you loved. For her to do that to you like that. Why? Just why would she do that?"

"She was mad that all of our friends dropped her, and she felt pressured to leave the team. I acted like she didn't exist, but she of course blamed me. So she figured the best way to get back at me was to hit me where it hurt and make sure no one wanted to be with me ever again. The whole 'I don't want you, but I don't want anyone else to have you' thing."

She shook her head. "Okay, you win. That is so wrong. That makes my blood boil, and I don't even know that woman."

"There's no competition here and definitely no winning. I just want you to see that I get both why you are guarded and why you're tired of always being speculated about."

"How can you put yourself out there again?" She looked so sad, so beaten down with that question, that I wished I could reach through the screen and pull her into my lap. I felt like this answer was important and mattered a lot to her.

"It took me a really long time to get over that whole thing," I said. "I haven't dated seriously since her. But I know that at the end of the day, when I look back on my life, more than any of my accomplishments, I want to be able to say that I had a great love story. And I can't get a great love story if I don't put myself out there to find her. And guarding myself against it will not get me there. I'm successful at my job, and I've loved football my entire life. I have an amazing family and friends that I love dearly. I have more money than I'll ever know what to do with. But even as happy as I am with all of that, I want my own family. I want someone to come home to every day, that knows I love her with every cell in my body. I want children that run to me when I get home and wrap themselves around my legs. I want to lie in bed with my wife and feel our child growing in her stomach. I cannot let Beth take that dream from me because she wasn't the right person for me."

Mallie looked away and closed her eyes briefly. I stared at her face, wondering if I just fucked up somehow. I said too much. She didn't want those things. I was going to push her away. When she looked back into the camera, tears shimmered in her eyes. Before I could come up with what to say to backtrack, she began to speak.

"Teddy," she said, and her voice caught. "It's like you fell straight out of my dreams and into my life. That was the most beautiful thing I've ever heard. Don't be surprised if you hear those words in a song soon. Do you really feel that way?"

She wiped a tear off her face, and I once again wished I could be next to her.

"Why are you crying, Mal? I didn't mean to make you upset." I was starting to think there was nothing I hated more than seeing tears on this beautiful woman's face.

She shook her head. "I'm not upset. I'm moved. I don't know how, since the day I met you, you put into words exactly what I feel. I feel the exact same way, but for some reason, it still scares me so much. I've dated quite a bit, but until Josiah, I never saw myself with them long term. I'm sure you know what the press has said about me. But with Josiah, I thought for sure that he was it. But I was so wrong, and now I question myself on whether I even know what I want or how to know if it is real. I spent so many years thinking he was the one. But you're right. Everything you said is true. It's what I want, too. I'm living my dream right now, and singing as my career has been my dream for my entire life. But I'm not a young girl anymore wishing for a date to a high school dance like my first songs. I want someone to come home to, someone that I know has my back at all times. Someone who I don't have to be careful what I say around because I know he'd rather die than ever do something to hurt me. I want someone that helps me live out the song lyrics I've spent my life writing and inspires all the songs I've yet to write."

That line hit me like a punch in the gut. I wanted her to have that, too.

"That got deep fast," she said with a nervous giggle. "Sorry about that."

"Don't," I said, shaking my head. "Don't downplay it. I'm not running away from serious topics with you, and I don't want you to, either."

"Okay," she said. "So. Are we scared together?"

"No. We are brave together."

CHAPTER 7
Allie

NO. *We are brave together*. My heart skipped a beat, and so many butterflies took flight in my stomach that I thought for sure I could float away with them. Our conversation was so ... perfect.

Everything about this man seemed too good to be true. So was he? My cynicism and past hurt said yes, but my romantic nature told me to shut up. He got it. He really did. I thought of the horrible story with his ex, Beth, and thanked all the stars above that at least no one posted a video of me all over the internet while Josiah broke my heart. I'd had enough videos shared of me over the years. Teddy really seemed nothing like anyone else I had ever met before. Maybe it was the professional athlete part. Most of the guys I had been around were either from my industry or Josiah's.

"Brave," I echoed, and he nodded. I looked at the nuances of his face, so handsome on the small screen of my phone. His bright-blue eyes had laugh lines in the corners from all the jokes he told and the laughter he enjoyed. His full lips made me squirm thinking about them pressed against mine, and his neatly trimmed beard made me think about the sinful things he could do to me. And let's not get into the voice that made me shiver every single time he spoke. I wished I remembered more of the day he helped me, but my mind wasn't in the right place then.

I wanted to see him again. The realization hit me like a ton of bricks. I bit my lip, wondering if I had the nerve to say it.

"What is it?" He smirked, and I had to force myself not to groan at the dimple that popped out. It was unfair how delicious he was. And nice. Had I ever seen both in one person?

"How do you do that?"

"How do I read you?"

I nodded, and I felt his gaze from the top of my head to my lips. "I pay attention. You bit your lip. You're trying to decide whether you have the guts to say what you want to say. Now say it. You don't have to be afraid of whatever it is. If you promise to be brave, I will be brave, too."

"Okay. I promise." He smiled, and desire bloomed in my chest. Okay, here goes nothing. I knew my schedule like the back of my hand, so I didn't have to look to know what was coming up. "I have a break in shows in one month. I'll be at my place in New York so I can do some recording while I'm off. Would you—do you want to . . ." I lost my nerve.

"Mallorie." The three syllables of my name had me looking up at him. I had never loved my name more. "Go ahead. Say what you want. Think about all of those talk shows and interviews where you've stood up for what you knew needed to be said." He knew my shows and interviews. The man did homework, it seemed. I love that he cared enough to know about me.

"Would you meet me for a date?" Once the words were out, I couldn't stop the blush from crawling up my neck. "In New York there are places we can be low-key. That way, it isn't a spectacle in the press yet. I have a place with a private entrance, and there are several restaurants where no phones are allowed and you have to be a member to enter." What I didn't say, but I figured he got, was no one had to know if we didn't hit it off in person. I wasn't sure if that was possible, but I had to be sure before blowing up our lives in the press.

A grin the size of Texas split Teddy's face. "Wait one second." He propped the phone up and took his hand and pinched his other arm. When he grimaced, he picked the phone back up and grinned at the screen. "Sorry. I had to pinch myself to make sure this was really happening. It seems I am not dreaming and Mallorie Witt just asked me on a date. *Me*, lowly football player and resident teddy bear."

I laughed, and he joined in. "Stop."

Teddy's face changed and I immediately stopped laughing as well. "I thought the night you asked to contact me was the best night of my life. I jumped around and screamed, and, yes, I'm admitting that to you right now so you will know just how much I would absolutely love to go on a date with you. I need to see our schedule for that time, but let's make it happen for sure."

His schedule. I looked at the time and realized it was the middle of the night and he had a game to play today. "Oh my gosh, I just realized what time it is. I'm so sorry. I'll let you go." I had an unusual schedule and being up this late was typical for me, especially after a show.

"Do not be sorry. Talking to you is more important than any sleep I could get."

"So it's a tentative date," I said, my heart pounding so hard I wondered whether he could hear it.

"It's a 'hell yes' date," he answered. "We're making this happen."

"If it helps, I have a plane."

He laughed. "I know you do, and thank you for offering. We will figure it out when I see when I can come."

He reached a finger out to the screen, and I held my breath. "I wish I could take that curl right there and tuck it behind your ear. I didn't appreciate it enough the first time I got to touch it."

I squirmed, remembering him tucking my hair behind my ear while I cried.

"Then I'd run my finger along your beautiful skin to your lips. I'd pull it out of your teeth and tell you not to abuse those gorgeous lips, that you have nothing to be nervous about with me. I'm ecstatic as hell to be allowed in your world. Then I'd kiss you to show you just how fucking giddy with excitement I am to be given the chance to know you."

My face flamed, and I put my hand on my cheek. It felt like he did what he just described. I had no idea what universe I was in anymore because I was rather sure I floated above the earth. "I-I'd like that," was all I could manage to answer.

"You would," he said, those damn dimples making me weak in the knees when he smirked at me. "But I wouldn't just like it. I'd love nothing more than to taste those fucking lips and to hold that face as I looked into your beautiful eyes."

I blew out a breath, and I knew my face was red. "Too much?" he asked.

"No," I said. "I'm just not used to it."

"Used to what? Honesty?"

I laughed. "I guess so, yeah."

"Expect more of that. And when we see each other? Expect it to happen. Unless you tell me no."

"I don't think I'll be telling you no." Who could? It sure as hell wasn't me.

He groaned now and scrubbed his hand over his face. "You expect me to go to sleep after this conversation?"

Speaking of, I looked at the clock again.

"Good night, Teddy." I not only needed to let him go to sleep but also needed to process what had happened tonight.

"Good night, my Mallie. I'll talk to you tomorrow?"

"Today?"

"Yes. Today. Every day from now until we can see each other in person."

"I cannot remember ever being this nervous in my entire life." I watched as the cars and buildings whizzed past as my blacked-out SUV crossed the city. My leg bounced up and down with nerves as I held the phone to my ear, Bailey on the other end. I've performed in front of hundreds of thousands of people. Done performances and speeches at awards shows. Done intrusive interviews on television and radio. And nothing compared to the amount of nerves in my stomach at this moment.

I hadn't eaten all day. After a month of spending every moment possible talking, texting, and video chatting, I honestly could say I already knew Teddy and I were extremely compatible. We never had a lull in conversation, and the chemistry between us crackled over the screen. It was the pressure of the rest that had me panicking.

He said my life didn't freak him out, but he had no idea what would happen. He was football famous and wasn't immune to the press, but no matter how much he reassured me, I knew he didn't have a clue what he would get into because of me. And behind the nerves was sadness. Sometimes I just wanted to be a normal girl getting to know a normal boy, and that was just not possible. It could be that we both liked each other a lot and it still failed. Hello, track record. Nice to see you again.

Bailey laughed. "Girl, you guys have talked every single day for the last month straight. Don't you think you would know at this point if you don't like him?"

"I think that's part of the problem. I like him too much, and I'm terrified."

"Terrified of what exactly? Him rocking your world with

multiple orgasms tonight? God, that man is fine as hell. I can't believe you've waited a month. I would've climbed him like a tree a long time ago, especially given the things he has said and done for you since you met."

I may or may not have used Bailey as my human diary to process the quickly developing feelings I had for this man. That was nothing to the actual diary I wrote it all in, but she knew most about our conversations, the gifts he sent me, and the anticipation of seeing each other in person.

"Bai." I laughed. "First of all, I've been on tour. Kinda hard to do that while traveling the country. And he's been busy traveling the country for work, too. It's a miracle that he had a week off and was able to travel to me this weekend. We are meeting for dinner at Prism and spending some time together, not over a phone screen."

"You are meeting for dinner to start your night. Are you really not inviting him back to your place? After all this? It's going to be dinner and then 'nice to see you, we will meet up again in a few months'? You are not that stupid."

"I didn't say that I wouldn't invite him back to my place. There are very few places I can go and not have everyone find out I'm with him, and we just aren't ready for that. I'm definitely not. You know what it is like. I can't be seen with a man. And one with his status? Instant trending all over socials and news outlets. Paparazzi camped out outside his house and field. Speculation about us. Digging up all the info on him. Until I know this is going somewhere, I just can't deal with it. It's the best way to make someone I care about run for the hills. So I don't think there will be any orgasms happening tonight."

"If you don't let that man give you the D, you're dumb as hell."

"ETA two minutes," Juan called from the front.

I sighed. "Bai, you know how I feel about all this, and adding sex to the mix just complicates things."

"I do," she said, all joking gone. "You have to give him a chance to handle it, though. Out of anyone, he at least has some idea of what he's getting into. And even if he doesn't get it completely, you have to have some faith that what he says is true. And sex with him will definitely complicate some things, like ruining you for any man ever again. Have you *seen* the size of his hands and feet?"

I laughed and shook my head at her. "Stop it. You're killing me. You and I both know that he won't really know what it'll be like until he's thrown straight into the lion's den." The SUV came to a stop, and Juan and Rico, my security detail, stepped out. "I have to go," I said. "Wish me luck."

"You don't need luck," she said. "That man is head over heels for you, and so are you. What you need is to be properly fucked. I expect a report in the morning." With that, the phone went dead.

I mean, she wasn't wrong. It had been a long time, and I was no prude. I loved sex just as much—if not more—than the average woman. But I couldn't add that pressure to this date. I would let whatever happened happen. The door to the restaurant immediately opened, the establishment having been alerted of my arrival. My bodyguard Juan opened my door and I slid out, walking with purpose to the entrance to avoid being photographed.

Thankfully no one was out here. The door shut behind me and Juan led me through the dark hallway into the main part of the restaurant. I knew Rico walked behind me—the two of them were always with me. Oftentimes I had upward of ten; it just depended on where I was. With the security level of this restaurant and the clientele restrictions, I knew the two of them had it. I had been here many times over the years, and nothing was ever leaked. I hoped today was not the day that an employee went rogue and took pictures. It was a chance I took, but I also knew my team didn't play around with my protection. They, for sure, had already warned them.

"Nice to see you again, Miss Witt." The manager appeared next to me. "Thank you for choosing Prism tonight. If you need anything, please do not hesitate to ask. My name is Nick."

"Thank you," I said. "Your discretion is appreciated."

He nodded. "Certainly. We pride ourselves on it."

My phone buzzed in my hand, and I looked down at it immediately. *I'm here*, Theo's text read, and my stomach clenched again. *They put me in the private room. Can't wait to see you.*

Juan opened the door of said room and instead of answering Theo, I stepped into the doorway. My eyes immediately found him, and he stood as I entered. My knees wobbled as I took in his appearance. I knew what the man looked like—but I had never seen him like this other than photos online, and they definitely did not do him justice. He wore a dark suit, obviously made for him by the way it fit perfectly against his large, built frame. His short beard was neat and tidy on his chiseled face, and his full lips smiled at me. His blue eyes sparkled in the dim light of the room, and I felt him appraising me the same way. He stepped toward me, our gazes locked.

Juan must've said something to me, but I didn't notice until he touched my arm. I tilted my head, listening, but didn't break eye contact with Teddy. "We will be outside the room if you need us." I nodded, my gaze not wavering from Teddy's. The door closed behind me and we were alone. Finally. Not behind a screen, not thousands of miles away from each other. Together. In the same city. In the same room. Just us.

"Mallie," Teddy said, his long legs closing the distance between us in a few strides. I had never loved a variation of my name more than hearing it from his lips. He reached for me and I stepped into his arms, my eyes closing immediately at the feel and smell of him around me. I wore heels as I loved to do, and still, the top of my head fit perfectly under his chin. He wrapped his arms around me and pulled me tighter into his chest. My senses were overwhelmed by the way he smelled, the feel of him against me, and my nerves.

"You look so fucking beautiful," he murmured into my hair. I'd chosen a short black dress from my favorite designer. It showed just enough to be sexy but not too much for a first date. My hair was styled in waves down my back, and my makeup was edgy, with dark eyes and red lipstick. Playing up the blue in my eyes and my full lips was my favorite part of wearing makeup and what I was known for. I loved jewelry, and I paired my simple dress with many statement pieces. In other words, I dressed to knock him clear on his ass tonight, and it seemed to be working.

"Let me see you again." He stepped back, his gaze scanning my dress. "The most gorgeous woman on the face of the planet. How did I get so lucky to be here with you right now? I think someone may need to pinch me and make sure I'm not dreaming."

I made an exaggerated motion of checking him out as well. "Teddy, you look handsome as hell, too. You sure know how to wear a suit. Damn. I think I'm the lucky one." I reached over and pinched his arm and then pinched my own. "Seems that neither of us are dreaming."

He grinned and laced his fingers with mine. I couldn't help but notice how large his hand was compared to my own, and that made me think back to Bailey's comment. I forced a giggle back down where it came from. He pulled me into him, and I tipped my head back so I could look into his face. His dark hair was just enough to run my fingers through, and I forced myself not to do it yet. The nerves I had moments ago were replaced with butterflies, anticipation making my heart pound.

"There will never, not ever, be a time when I'm not the lucky one." Our entwined hands dropped down between us.

He rubbed my hand with his thumb and lifted his other hand to my hair. He tucked a strand behind my ear and winked at me. "I've been waiting to do that again."

I swallowed, my throat suddenly dry because I knew right where this was going based on the many conversations we'd had about this right here. "W-what else have you been waiting for?"

Theo's gaze darkened and his eyes dropped to my lips. "So many things, Mallie. So many fucking things." He let go of my hand and cupped the sides of my face. "But first, this. I've been dreaming about this moment for so long. I cannot believe you're here in front of me. Right now, I'm going to kiss you unless you tell me not to. And please don't tell me not to because I may cry like a little boy getting candy taken from him if you do."

His thumbs traced my cheeks, and I struggled to regulate my breathing. With my chest pressed against his and our gazes locked on each other, I couldn't formulate words if I wanted to. So, instead of responding, I stood on my toes and pressed my mouth to his first. Immediately he wrapped his arms around me and pulled me closer. Our mouths moved urgently on each other's, and within seconds, his tongue traced my lips. I made a sound and gripped the lapels on his jacket, wanting to be closer. When our tongues touched, I knew I whimpered. Our heads tilted and our kiss deepened. He leaned down, and I placed my hands on his cheeks as our mouths and tongues moved together like we had done this a million times before.

There was no awkwardness trying to figure each other out. Our mouths just knew what to do. The sensations of his short beard, his soft lips, and his silky tongue made me want to come undone. He tasted like something I couldn't quite place, mint mixed with something else, but I knew I could never get enough. I could feel one of his hands on my lower back, the heat of him searing me as he pulled me into him even closer. I knew without a shadow of a doubt that I had never, not ever, been kissed like this and that I never, ever wanted it to stop.

When Teddy pulled back slightly, he rested his forehead on mine and closed his eyes as we breathed together. "Wow," he said finally.

"*Wow* is right," I echoed.

"I knew it was going to be magnetic between us," he whispered, "but that exceeded all expectations. I can't wait to do that again. And again. And again."

"Agree. But right now, I'm not sure I can even walk to the table after that," I said, and he grinned.

"I guess it's a good thing I'm strong," Teddy said and winked. He held out his arm, and I took it. We walked to the table, and he pulled out my chair for me. He leaned down once I was seated and pressed another quick kiss to my lips. "I have a taste of those now. I can't make myself stop."

I grabbed his arm as he went to step away and pulled him back to me. He leaned down and our lips touched again. He gripped my chin as our tongues met. I felt his gaze on me, and I opened my eyes, staring into his. My stomach flipped and I gripped his hand that wasn't holding my chin. His thumb caressed my palm as his tongue twined with mine. I knew he held back—I could feel it in his slow movements. Lord knew he was strong enough to pick me up and hold me while we kissed. I closed my eyes again, and a groan escaped as I thought about him pushing me against the wall.

Teddy pulled back and put his lips against my ear. I shivered at the sensation of his beard on my ear and his warm breath against me. "If you make that sound again, I'm going to lose it. I'm barely hanging on to my restraint right now, and I don't want you to think this is just physical for me because it isn't. At all. But I am so turned on right now I want to carry you out of here and to your house so I can show you what I will do to make you make that sound over and over again."

He stepped back and kissed my hand before settling across from me. He immediately reached for my hand again, and our fingers twined. Identical smiles played on both of our faces as we took each other in across the table. I noticed a slight tint of my red lipstick on his mouth, and I loved it.

"We're finally here," he said, breaking the silence.

"We're finally here," I echoed.

"No one saw you come in?" he asked.

"No. This place is great. Did anyone see you?"

Teddy smiled. "No one here is looking for me. I did have a few people ask me for autographs at the airport before I left, but once I got into the city, I was just a regular guy."

I looked him up and down, my meaning clear. "Not dressed like that you aren't."

He laughed. "Well, I arrived in sweats and a ball cap, so yeah. Just a regular guy arriving on a plane to New York."

As if this hulk of man would ever fly under any radar. I could guarantee every woman within eyesight noticed him, and I'd guess most of the men, too. He was formidable at first sight and mouthwatering immediately after. I definitely broke my own self-imposed no-internet rule to look up pictures of this man in his element over the last many weeks. Before right now, my favorites were him in his football uniform, his muscles on clear display.

My eyes widened. "Sweats? Like, what kind?"

Teddy smirked and crossed his arms in front of his chest, the jacket pulling across his muscles. "What if I told you they were gray?"

I closed my eyes and put my hand over my heart. "I'd tell you that it was unfair you wore those without me."

"Oh, Mal," he said, "you can see me in whatever you want, whenever you want. This is just the beginning."

The beginning. I took a deep breath. Yes. A beginning. I

loved how up front he was with me—he'd been that way since our first conversation. Even before that, if I was honest. He was refreshing and didn't seem to hide anything. Too bad that to be part of my life, he had to be exploited just like me.

"Hey," he said. "What's that serious face for all of a sudden?" I bit my lip, and he brought his hand up to force it out of the death grip of my teeth. "Honesty, remember?"

"I'm afraid," I said. "Not of us. But of everything else." I indicated outside. "I know what you've said, and it's not that I don't believe you. But I don't think you get it. No one can really get it until they live it. The second they see us together, it's all over for you. And what I mean by that is you're going to get the scrutiny of every news outlet, social media post, and person who thinks they know me or wants to know me. It's going to be a circus. They'll look up everything about you, including things you said or people you were around years ago. They'll stalk you and take pictures of you with long lenses everywhere you go. They'll post untrue things all over social media. They'll make up lies about us. Lies so good you'll start to wonder if they're actually true. And I just wish I didn't have to expose you to this just to be around me. Right now, we are in this little bubble where no one knows about us except the people closest to us, so we don't have to deal with it."

Teddy nodded. "I know this is hard for you because it's something that you cannot control and yet is such a huge part of your life. You've explained all of it, and I'm still here right now."

"It is hard for me, and I appreciate that you are here and seem unaffected. In a way, I asked for this. I have been on display since I was a teenager. It's not that I love the attention, but I don't know any other way. I love my career and I wouldn't trade it, but this part? The part where every single person in my life is scrutinized and analyzed for their affiliation with me? I wish I could change that, but I can't."

CHAPTER 8
Theo

I HATED HOW SHE FELT, but I got it. We had talked enough over the last month that I knew it plagued her. It wasn't the first time this had come up, and I knew it wouldn't be the last.

I also knew I had no idea just what would happen *when* we went public—not *if*. I had already decided—but in my opinion, there wasn't anything that would push me away from her. I knew that before I had her in my arms and my lips on hers today, but after that? No way was I letting her go, no matter what shitstorm the media put us through.

"I know I can't convince you that I will be okay," I said, and she nodded. I caressed the palm of her hand and she looked down at our intertwined fingers, hers long and slender and mine easily double her size. "I don't know what I don't know, and I get that. I know you have had years of being exploited and talked about in the media and judged for your connection to men—and women—but I can't show you I'm okay with it if you don't give me the chance to show you that I'm okay with it. I have every confidence that you can help me through the parts of this I'm not used to, and I want you to know that I am not self-conscious or worried about what they'll say about me. That's just not who I am as a person. I'll do whatever you want in whatever timeline you want. I'll also meet with Zoey and your security team if that is what we need to do. I'll hire additional security. I'll have my PR company collaborate with yours. Whatever it takes, Mal."

She squeezed my hand and smiled. "I don't know what to do with you, Theo Nolan. You always know what to say to make me feel better about things."

I raised my eyebrows. "I could think of many things you could do with me, Mallorie Witt." Her laughter lightened the mood, and I kissed her hand again. "All jokes and innuendos aside, I think we both knew before tonight that we have something here, and I don't think I'm alone in saying that being here together feels right." I paused and she nodded. I could not put words to the feeling in my chest when she nodded in response, but I knew I liked it. Loved it. More than fucking loved it.

"You have become a vital part of my daily life, and I do not want that to stop. I want to be the first person you think of when you wake up and the last you talk to before you go to bed. Whether that means we are across the world talking to each other or we are next to each other. I have an impossible schedule, and so do you. I will never judge you for that, nor will I have a tantrum about you not spending enough time with me or having to travel or record or anything. I know who you are and what you do. That has not been a secret since I met you. It's actually one of the things I like best about you. And, total transparency here, I love knowing things about you that no one else knows and that you've felt comfortable enough to share with me. At the end of the day, I just want to be the person you turn to, and I want you to know that I will be your biggest cheerleader. I know you have a lot of them, but none that are me." I winked.

Mallie stared at me, her mouth slightly agape as she processed my words. We'd had a lot of conversations over the last month. We'd mostly skipped over the surface stuff and gone right to the heart of who we were as people. I didn't need to play the coy game. I played the field enough as a young man. At my age, I was beyond all of that. I wanted her to know who I was and that I wasn't playing with her. She matched my energy, and that was why, at this point, we knew each other on a much deeper level than most people would after knowing each other for only a short time.

"I feel the same way. I am beyond that part of it scaring me because I know how I feel, and you've been extremely honest with me the entire time. Why do I feel like I've known you for so much longer than I have?" she said finally.

I shrugged. "Probably because we have spent countless hours talking to each other in all time zones and at all times of day and night. Plus, we've both been hurt. If there's one thing we both know, it's that there's no reason to waste time on someone who isn't worth it. We are worth it. So tell me," I said.

"Tell you what?" Waiters dropped off salads and drinks, but our attention stayed on each other. "Thank you," she said without looking at them, always the picture of class.

"What do we need to do?"

Mallie lifted her drink and sipped it. "What do we need to do?"

I grinned. "Is there an echo in here?" I took a drink also and waited for her to catch up. "What are the next steps, angel?"

Mallie blew out a breath. "I really love when you call me that," she said, her voice low. I thought about the many nights she sang her songs to me. Sometimes when she was working through a new song and others when she practiced the different songs she switched out on her set list while I listened on the phone. That low, gravelly voice was my favorite. I would never forget the first night she sang for me. Life changing. I couldn't wait to be in the same room as her and witness the magic that was her voice. Hopefully tonight, if I played my cards right.

I wanted to say I couldn't wait to call her that while I worshipped every inch of her spectacular body, but I didn't. It wasn't that I couldn't be honest with her; it was that I wanted to show her respect and take her cues. I wasn't going to do anything to fuck this up and push her away.

"The ball is in your court, angel. If you want to see each other a few more times before we are seen together, I'm fine with that. If you're ready, I'm beyond ready."

"You're that sure?" She bit that damn lip again, and I swore to God I wasn't going to make it out of this restaurant.

"I didn't need to meet you tonight to know. I mean, am I stoked as hell that we got to make this work? Definitely. Do I want to see you as much as is feasible? Yes. But I don't need a certain amount of times of us 'dating' in person to be ready."

She studied me for a moment. "After dinner, can we go over our schedules and see when we can get together again?"

I guessed that was the answer, that she wanted to wait a bit, and that was fine. I wanted to make her comfortable. As long as she didn't get spooked and call it all off, I would wait as long as she needed.

"Where are we going after dinner?" I winked at her. Teasing her was my second favorite thing to do. Kissing was my first, for sure. Or maybe talking to her. Or listening to her sing. Damn, I had too many favorites when it came to her, and I knew there were other things that would be added to that list if I was lucky enough to experience them.

She blushed, and my stomach bottomed out. God, I loved how her feelings were all over her face all the time. "I-I thought maybe we'd go back to my place if you're okay with that. For obvious reasons, we can't just walk around New York or go to a bar, so . . ."

"I'm just teasing you," I interrupted her. "I'd love to go to your place. And yes, let's look at when we can get together again. How about we order some dinner so you can take me back to your place and have your way with me?" It hadn't been mentioned whether I was going back to the hotel that was booked for me or staying with her, and I figured not asking was the best way to go right now.

She blushed again and bit that fucking lip. I knew she thought about it just as much as I did. The problem was, I wasn't sure I could deny her if she gave any sign that she wanted it as much as I did, and now I knew by her reaction to my comment that she wanted it, too.

I looked at her profile in the darkness, the city blurring outside the window as we drove back to her apartment. Despite the late hour, the city bustled with activity.

She sat right next to me, no space between us, and looked out the window. I cataloged all her features, so delicate and perfect, in disbelief again that she was sitting next to me and I really was in her presence. And not because she was Allie Witt. I mean, it was there all the time. Who she was and what her life entailed. But that was not what I meant. How had I gotten this amazing woman to give me the time of day? I couldn't have predicted this if I'd tried.

My hand rested on her bare thigh, and she leaned into me. I could feel her hair tickling my face, and I loved it. There was a divider between us and Juan and Rico, and when I asked, she stated it was so people couldn't take pictures of her from the front of the car and flash into the driver's eyes. That could be the difference between life and death.

I couldn't believe just how invasive people were. I had so much to learn. Thankfully, after dinner, they took me out first and into her waiting SUV, then waited a few minutes and brought her out without any fanfare. I could tell she was relieved when we pulled away with no attention brought to us. So relieved, it seemed, that the first thing she did when she got into the SUV and the door shut was lean over and press her sexy lips against mine. It took everything in me to not slip my hand up her short dress. I settled with keeping it in a PG-13 zone until she showed me different.

Dinner was beyond my wildest dreams. Our conversation never stopped, and we vacillated between joking, discussing trivial day-to-day things, and scorching-hot sexual tension. I stole a few more kisses, and she definitely did not complain. I never wanted this night to end, and I was glad she invited me back to her apartment.

Mallie turned and smiled at me, those striking blue eyes bright even with just the city lights around her. "We're almost there," she said. I nodded and leaned over and pressed my lips just under her ear. She gasped and tilted her head, inviting me for more.

"You like that," I whispered against her ear. I'd gladly be a full-time student of learning what she liked. I kissed down her neck and back up, feeling goose bumps all over her legs. I moved my hand, stroking the inside of her thigh as I continued my slow perusal of her neck and ear. She whimpered and her legs shifted slightly, giving my hand more room. My heart thundered at the possibility of touching her, but I didn't. She said we were close to her place, and I didn't want to start something I definitely didn't want to have an audience for.

The blacked-out SUV slowed, and I put my hand back in an appropriate place and smiled at the beautiful woman next to me. She reached her hand out and stroked the side of my face, her fingers passing through my short beard. I liked it way too fucking much. A hidden garage door opened and the vehicle went in, the door immediately closing behind us, but not before I saw the crowd outside her apartment, cameras flashing. When my eyes widened, she nodded, no words necessary. This was every single day for her, no matter the time.

Within seconds, Juan opened the door and I slid out. I extended my hand to her and she smiled, taking it and stepping out into the garage. Her heels clicked on the smooth floor as we headed for the stairs into her house.

After we ate dinner, while Mallie was in the restroom, I had a quick conversation with her security, Juan and Rico. I wanted them to let me be part of her protection when I was around. Not that I didn't respect their position, but I wanted to understand every part of her life. Of course they would tell me nothing without approval from her, but I hoped to get it.

Rico handed me the small duffel I'd brought from the hotel, and I nodded my thanks.

"Thanks, guys," Mallie said. "See you in the morning." They nodded at her and glanced at me before she shut the door behind us.

I had so many questions. Where did they go? Did they have their own place? Were they outside her place all night? But before I could register to ask them, a dog ran up to us and she crouched down, short dress and all, and nuzzled his head.

"Hey, Charlie," she said to the fluffy dog. "This is Teddy. You be nice."

"Is he often not nice?"

She smiled up at me and my chest squeezed. "He's never met anyone he didn't love. Possibly too much."

Charlie eased his way over to me, and I petted his head. I loved dogs. With my schedule, I didn't have one, but I hoped to someday when my life slowed down. Then again, if Mallie had a dog, anyone could.

"Do you want a drink?" Mallie reached down and took off one hot-as-fuck heel, then the other. She held them in one hand and made her way farther into the apartment. What I wanted was to push her up against the wall and taste every part of her, but I forced myself to follow her. There was something about seeing her in her own space, her bare feet walking in front of me, that made me feral. We were truly alone, with no chance of anyone seeing us.

"I've got a full bar, so put in your request," she said. "I'm a white-wine girly myself."

"I love myself a good white," I said. Honestly, I already felt buzzed, and it had nothing to do with alcohol. I had limited myself to one whiskey neat at the restaurant. I didn't drink much during the season anyway, but I wanted to have all my faculties with her. She smiled and poured us both a glass, then filled up Charlie's food and water bowls. She indicated the other room, and I followed her. She sat on the couch and tucked her legs up under her. I sat next to her and turned my body so I faced her.

"So this is my place. Well, my New York place," she said. "I'll show you the rest later. You see my piano over there?" She gestured across the large open-concept room. The piano sat by large windows, the city lights illuminating it. "That's where the magic happens."

I tried hard not to picture a different kind of magic happening there and focused on her writing lyrics and singing.

"How many places do you have?" I knew what I'd looked up about her, but I wanted every bit of information directly from the source.

"Home base is South Florida, as you know. The beach is my favorite place, and it gives me the most inspiration. I have this place, and I do spend a good bit of time here. I love the city. I have a home in LA, too, since I am out there often for business."

"Do you have a piano at every house?"

She nodded. "It's a must. And a guitar. I have an entire studio room in my Florida house. It's soundproof and all. We've recorded there before. It's also where I house all of my awards and things. I wake up at least several times a week with a melody or lyrics in my head. Sometimes I just put them in my phone or do a voice memo, but sometimes that isn't enough and I have to actually get up and play it." She indicated the shelf next to the piano. I couldn't wait to see her work through her process. Listening to her sometimes when we talked was amazing enough. "I do keep my first Grammy here, though, because I was the underdog in the category and I won at eighteen years old. It's the one I'm the most proud of. Not to downplay the rest, because I'm thankful for every single thing I've been recognized for."

"That's fucking amazing and you should be proud as hell. Haven't you won like two-hundred-something awards?"

"Someone is looking me up on the internet," she teased.

"I can't help it. Reading about your career is so inspiring. I may have also watched every tour you've done on YouTube, your documentary you made a few years ago, as well as most of your interviews, but I want to hear about everything directly from you."

Mallie looked at me wide-eyed. "How do you have time to do all that?"

I shrugged. "I make time for what is important, and you're important to me."

"If he wanted to, he would," she whispered, looking down into her glass, obviously talking to herself.

"What's that?" I heard her, but I wanted her to tell me why she said it.

She looked up. "If he wanted to, he would," she repeated. "Something people have started saying about putting effort into relationships. If people say they are too busy, can't do this or do that, it's not that they can't. It's that they won't. You are a busy man with an important job, and yet you found the time to find out all of that information about me just so you knew more about me."

I nodded. "I did, and I will continue to, but now you can

tell me what to watch and what to stay away from. You're inspiring. It's no wonder you're as popular as you are. What you've done for the industry and women—hell, people—is just amazing, Mal."

"Thank you. To so many I'm just a pop star, you know? I'm overrated or overplayed. My music is just bubblegum crap that means nothing or whatever they come up with to try to tear me down. But I didn't start out to be any of these things. I just wanted to make music. But since then, I've found a niche in inspiring people—mainly girls and women—to never let others keep you from reaching your goals."

"Those people are just haters that don't have the talent you have in one finger. They're jealous of what you've been able to do in your life, and they're generally miserable people that make themselves feel better by tearing down someone they will never know in real life."

"Thanks, Teddy. I am over listening to them. It used to bother me a lot, but I don't let it anymore. I know who I am and I don't apologize for it. Also, you know you can ask me things. You don't have to look them up anymore, though I am impressed at your level of knowledge."

I set my glass on the coffee table, and Charlie came in and settled under my feet. "I know I can. And I want to know every single thing there is to know about you, both things that I could look up on the internet and things that no one but me will ever know."

"I looked you up, too," she admitted. "You've had an impressive career also. First draft to the Blaze and you've been there your entire career, right?" I nodded, impressed. She told me she didn't know much at all about football. "You've broken more records than anyone else in your position. You and Spencer are a dynamic duo, and all teams try to figure you out. And your charity work? Amazing. You love to cook?"

"You learned a lot! I'm impressed, too. I do love to cook.

Started when I was a kid and never stopped. I don't have much time for it during the season, but I love finding new recipes. When I started playing professional football, I wanted to use my resources to do the same with other kids. You can ask me anything, too."

Mallie smiled and sipped her wine. "This was the best night I've had in a long time. I'm so happy you're here. Thank you so much for coming. I know it isn't easy for you to travel during the season, and I'm thankful that it worked out."

There were many things that I loved about this woman, but this right here may just top the list. I loved how honest and forthcoming she was. She wasn't playing games or holding back on what she thought, and she was telling me exactly how she felt.

I reached my hand over and picked hers up, lacing our fingers together. "Mallie, I never, ever want this night to end. If I could figure out how to stop time so I didn't have to go back for practice soon, I would. It's been perfect. Even better than I thought it could be, and I built it up a lot in my head. It's like we just took our phone conversations and amplified them by a million. Plus, seeing you in person just takes my breath away. You're such a beautiful person, and while I do mean your physical self, because just look at you, I mean even more than that. I knew the day I met you that you were special, but I had no idea. The hours we've spent getting to know each other have been everything I hoped them to be and then some."

"I don't know if what I feel for you is too fast or not," she admitted. "I have always thought I was a good judge of relationships and the pacing of them, but this has me thrown off. At first, I really didn't want to get into anything with you. I told myself for quite a while that I wasn't going to contact you, that I couldn't. You know that's why it took me so long to ask for your contact information. After Josiah, I didn't believe that I knew at all what I was looking for or how to pick good people. But you took every reservation I had and made me feel so content about all of them. It scares me that it seems too perfect, but I also love how easy it is just to be with you. It's like I've known you forever."

We'd had these conversations multiple times already, but it was good to have it here, in person, and let me help her feel better. "I don't think there's a specific timeline. I think what is most important is that both people have the same feelings and there isn't one person doing all the work. That's when issues happen. Kind of like with my ex. I was the one doing all the feeling, apparently, and she was checked out. Same with you and the douchebag. I think what we have done right from the beginning is to be clear with each other and, even if it is scary, we put ourselves out there so there isn't any guessing."

Mallie nodded. "Also, one thing that will definitely come up once we are 'outed' to the public is that you're my rebound. The breakup with Josiah is still floating around, and remember that it took months for it to be public, so that's immediately where this story will go. That we are just fucking, that I'm just using you, or even that we are a publicity stunt to get the attention off yet another breakup of mine."

I whistled. "Damn, girl. I'm sorry."

She shrugged. "I'm used to it. You aren't. I'm just telling you what is going to be said so you'll know."

"Noted. It still doesn't scare me. It just pisses me off for you."

"It pisses me off for me, too, but there's nothing I can do. Let's change topics. I've been writing a song about you," she said, that damn blush creeping up her cheeks again. "Well, multiple. But there's only one that is almost done."

I couldn't help the grin that overtook my face. I knew how huge this was. Her lyrics were masterpieces. "You didn't tell me you were writing a song about me. Or multiples for that matter."

She shrugged. "I wanted it to be a surprise."

"What's it called?"

"I'm not telling you until you hear it," she said.

I stood and held out my hand for her. "Well then, let's hear it."

She stood, and I pulled her into my chest. She tipped her head back to look at me, and we both smiled. "I'm so glad to be here," I said. I leaned my head down and took her lips with mine, and she sighed into my mouth, her body melting against me. Our tongues twined, and I held her face in my hands. As much as I wanted to devour her, I didn't. I kept it soft and sensual, my emotions pouring into the kiss. She wrote me a song. Me. I wasn't sure I could take much more, and my heart may burst.

I let her go, and she took my hand and walked me over to the piano. She sat down and put her fingers on the keys. I watched as she obviously went through a process before she began. I knew nothing about playing any instruments—my talent was on a football field. I think the last time I touched an instrument was the recorder in third grade, and I was rather sure that my mother threw it out of the car window when I scared the shit out of her playing it in the back seat.

"Don't judge me," she said. "It's rough."

"Me? Judge *you*?" I laughed. "You are freaking Allie Witt. There is no judgment."

"Not right now," she said. "It's just me. Mallie."

Well hell. Way to put me back in my place and remind me that even if she was a superstar, she still just wanted to be a regular woman behind the doors of her house.

CHAPTER 9
Allie

I TOOK a deep breath and began the first notes of the song. I couldn't believe I actually told him that I wrote a song for him and that I sat here to play it for him—on our first in-person date. It should've been awkward, but it wasn't. It was anything but that. It was like I lost my damn mind when he was around. He kissed the brain cells right out of me. I could feel him behind me, but I could not see his expression, which was better.

Theo. Teddy. Holy shit, what a night it had been so far. Dinner with him at Prism was beyond any expectation I had. He made me feel like a fairy-tale princess all night. And kissing him? Never, not ever in my entire life, had someone kissed me like him. It made me wonder what else he was proficient at, but if I admitted it to myself, I already knew. The man knew his way around a woman's body. Bailey's words from earlier rang in my head, and I forced them out. I meant every word I said to Teddy. I cared about him. We fit so well together. I wanted way more than I ever had with someone this quickly. That voice in the back of my head continued to try to reason with me, to tell me that there was no way that this could happen so fast, that I needed to slow down and not play all my cards so quickly.

But I wasn't listening to that annoying little voice that made me feel like I didn't deserve happiness. I was, instead, writing songs about this man. Forgoing sleep to write lyrics or waking up after dreaming about him. I was known for leading with my emotions, but this may be a new record for me. I just wanted to be happy, damn it. I closed my eyes and let the words of the first verse fall from my lips as I rocked back and forth on the padded bench. I wasn't sure yet if these were the final lyrics or not.

In a crowded room, our eyes collided,
His gaze like the ocean, deep and undivided.
Blue eyes met mine, a connection ignited,
Little did I know, a love story was invited.

I paused, my eyes closed as I readied myself to continue to the pre-chorus. I swayed to the music, allowing it to take me with it along the journey.

Caught in the current of a fleeting glance,
A chance encounter, a serendipitous dance.
In those blue eyes, I found romance,
Love arrived unexpectedly, like fate's advance.

I felt movement, and Teddy sat next to me on the bench. I halted playing to look at him, and what I saw in his eyes stopped me in my tracks.

"I want to hear the rest of the song," he said, his voice so low a shot of lust went straight to my core. "I cannot believe you wrote those beautiful words about meeting me. I feel out of control because I can't wait for you to be done singing. I'm sorry if this is rude to interrupt when the master is at work, but I couldn't stop myself. I have to touch you. Is it okay to touch you?"

I was rather sure I knew what he meant, and my heart pounded in response. I knew if I removed my fingers from the keys, my hands would shake. "Yes," I said, my voice barely audible. Permission granted, Teddy grabbed me like I weighed nothing and set me on his lap, my dress riding up to my hips. He slid his hands up my bare thighs and I squirmed when he stopped millimeters from touching the edge of my thong underwear.

"Mallie," he said, and I wanted to shift myself against him at the tone of his voice. I never had it happen before, but it was possible his voice alone could give me an orgasm. "I want to respect you. Make sure you tell me what you're okay with. There is no pressure here. We have all the time in the world. I never want you to think I'm using you or want something from you just to satisfy my own desires. I want to give you the lyrics to write a new song."

He said the magic words. No doubt new songs would be written about this night for sure. We looked into each other's eyes, having a silent conversation. His thumbs stroked the insides of my thighs, setting me on fire. When was the last time I slept with a guy on our first date? A long, long time ago. Before I had a lot to lose and could be more careless with my choices. However, to me, this wasn't the same thing. We hadn't just met. We knew more about each other than I felt like I knew about Josiah over our five-year relationship. We'd had a lot of deep conversations and knew exactly what the other thought. We weren't young and looking to scratch an itch. We knew what we wanted and had the battle scars to show that we had put in the work to get here.

I didn't need to think it through. This was Teddy. "Do you want me to spell it out for you?"

"I kinda do, yeah. I will never forgive myself if I do something to upset you or push you away. I'm living my life on cloud nine these days, and I can't come down from that high by doing something stupid."

I put my hands on either side of his face. Over the years, I evolved from a sweet little teenager who would do whatever she had to do to get her record deal to a woman who knew who she was, what she wanted, and what she stood for. This Mallorie Witt took no shit from anyone but did it with a kind heart and a giving spirit. This Mallorie hit the top of every chart and won every award she was nominated for. This Mallorie Witt knew exactly what the hell she wanted, and she took it with no apologies. But this girl right here, on the lap of Theo Nolan? This was Mallie, a newly coined woman dating an amazing man. She could be whoever she wanted with him, and what and who she wanted to be was a woman who told her man exactly what she wanted and how he could do it.

"Teddy," I said, my voice low. "I want you to show me just what you can do with that fine-as-hell body. I want you to touch me and fuck me until I don't know who I am or where I am. I want to know what you can do with that mouth, those hands, and what I assume is that giant dick of yours. I want you. All of you. Right now." Bailey would be so proud. I couldn't even believe I'd said it, much less that I planned to do it.

Teddy blinked, registering my words. I definitely never told a man exactly what I wanted before, but maybe I should've. This was the new me. Confident in every part of my life, including in bed with a hot man. No questions on what I want—I will tell you. *This is Mallie.*

"Fuck," he said, and that was the last word spoken. He buried his face in my neck, nipping and sucking at the skin. His hands moved to my core, and he used one to shift my underwear out of the way. He groaned when one finger slid through my lips, finding me soaked for him. He pushed inside of me and I writhed on him, my head falling back as the sensations took over. I panted when he added a second finger, curling it just right. His fingers were giant and they stretched me, but it felt like they were made for me.

"So fucking sweet," he said, kissing the other side of my neck. "You have too many clothes on, angel." He moved his fingers again, using his thumb to stroke my clit.

"Teddy," I moaned, pushing myself against his hard length. The man was massive in every place, and I felt that his dick was no exception. I wanted to see him, touch him. I wanted it all.

"Pull that dress over your head and let me see those beautiful breasts." He didn't have to ask me again. I flung it off, and his eyes zeroed in on my low-cut strapless black lace bra. His one hand worked inside me while the other unhooked my bra. It fell to the floor, and Teddy immediately took a nipple in his mouth. I held his head, riding his fingers.

"I need," I said. He tilted his head up to look at me.

"You need what, my angel."

"To my room," I said. "I need to see you and touch you."

"One minute," he said and slid me off his lap. "Can I set you up here for a second?" He indicated the lid of the piano. I nodded permission, and he placed me there like I weighed nothing. His hot gaze slid down my body, from my bare breasts to the small thong. "We're going to get rid of this," he said and took the scrap of fabric off and tucked it in his pants pocket. "I've had myself a fantasy that I need to live out. Are you okay if I do?"

Whatever this man wanted to do to me, I would not tell him no. I nodded and he dropped down and opened my legs. "I need to taste you while you lie on this piano that you create masterpieces on. I need to feel you come on my tongue. From now on, whenever you sit at this piano, I want you to think about this. I want you to write songs about this and sing them in front of thousands of people that will never know you created them while I ate this beautiful pussy."

Before I could fully comprehend his words, his mouth was on me. He held me open with his large hands and closed his mouth over my clit. I screamed and lay back, holding his head with my hands as he devoured me. At one point, his fingers joined his tongue in annihilating my every sense. Never, not ever, had I had a man eat me so thoroughly or expertly. He lifted my hips to get a better angle and I groaned, my eyes rolling back. My hands gripped his hair and he looked up at me, a devilish look in his eyes I couldn't even attempt to decipher. I struggled to catch my breath as my orgasm came barreling down my spine. I cried out as his tongue brought me through the rippling orgasm. He rained kisses along both sides of my inner thighs, bringing me down slowly from the best orgasm of my life.

He crawled up my body, kissing me all the way to my mouth. I panted, the aftershocks of my orgasm still ricocheting through my body. "That is just the beginning of what I'm going to give you tonight, angel. Now that I've had a taste of you, I will never get enough." Before I could respond, he closed his mouth over mine and lifted me, carrying me easily as we continued to kiss. He stopped when he realized he had no idea where to go, and we broke apart, laughing.

"That way, second door on the right," I said. "This is super unfair, by the way." He held my naked backside against his very clothed body.

"What is?"

"That I am completely naked and you are completely clothed."

Teddy wiggled his eyebrows as he reached my door. "I don't think you should ever wear clothes again."

"That would be frowned upon in my line of work."

He stepped up to my bed and laid me down gently. "You'd be popular for a whole new reason," he joked. He ran his hands up and down my body as though he was trying to memorize me. I pulled him to me, and he caged me in, holding himself over my body. "But also, I want no one to see this. This is mine."

His possessiveness and the look in his eye as he said it made me tingle from head to toe. This man was going to show me things I knew I'd never seen before.

I reached for the buttons of his dress shirt and undid

them. When I finally got the last button undone, I shoved the shirt off him. "Undershirt, off," I demanded. He took a handful of the shirt like only guys can do, pulled it off, and tossed it behind him.

I stared. The cut muscles of his defined chest, arms, and abs were something I hadn't seen up close before. His muscles rippled as I ran my hand along his chest and down to the button of his pants, my intention clear. "You like what you see, angel?"

I ran my hands down my naked body, cupping my breasts and ending at my turned-on, ready-to-go-again pussy. I ran my hands along myself as he watched. His tongue darted out to lick his lips as he watched me. "You're fucking gorgeous, and I want you all over me."

His gaze darkened on me. "You're going to get all that you want and then some."

I reached for his pants, unbuttoned them, and attempted to push them off his backside. When they didn't fall right off, he laughed. "I have an ass."

"I'm trying to see that ass," I said. "Help me."

He shoved them to the floor and stepped out of them, leaving him in a pair of black boxer briefs. His legs were ridiculous. I'd never seen so many muscles. And then there was the star of the show, straining behind his underwear.

"You're a work of art," I said.

His gaze scanned my naked body again, and I swore I *felt* his perusal. "Says the literal masterpiece."

I sat up and he backed up to allow me to stand. I hooked my fingers into his boxer briefs and tugged them to the floor. He was so tall and large that I felt tiny next to him. My attention immediately went to his large dick, so ready for me. I reached out and wrapped my hand around him, and he groaned.

"Angel," he said.

"Teddy," I replied, pumping him slowly as I watched his

expression. "Lie back. I want to get to know this body. You had your way with me. It's my turn to explore."

He smirked and did as I asked. He put his hands behind his head and watched as I climbed over him. "I guess that's only fair, but note that I won't be able to handle it for long. I need you sooner rather than later."

I straddled his hips, and he gripped me tightly as we lined up perfectly with each other.

"Definitely not going to last long with you doing that."

I grinned and ran my hands along his sculpted shoulders, down his chest, and back up as I slid his massive erection through my folds, the friction making me roll my eyes and groan. "I'm memorizing you. God, this body is ridiculous."

His dimples appeared at my appreciation. "I'm glad you like it." He took his hands from behind his head to cup my breasts. "I've been memorizing your body for the last thirty minutes, and I plan to replay this over and over in my head for however long it takes until we see each other again."

"I want to suck you," I said, and his eyes widened. "Please."

"I want that so badly," he said, "but I also want to be inside you."

"You're going to get it all," I said, scooting down so I could put him in my mouth. The moment my tongue made contact, he groaned and gripped the blanket. I licked and sucked him into my mouth. He shifted my body so he could run his hand between my legs and touch my pussy again. I opened for him and groaned on his dick as he pushed two fingers inside me.

"God, I love this," he moaned. "I want you to ride my face, but I know I can't do that right now. I need to fuck you. Are you ready, angel?"

I licked the underside of his giant cock, then up to the head one more time. "So fucking good," I murmured.

"You got that right," he said. He sat up and rolled me so I

lay on my back, and he slid on top of me. "Protection? I have it in my bag."

"I have an IUD," I said. "And was tested after Josiah to make sure he wasn't cheating on me."

"I'm regularly tested, too," he said. "Are you sure?"

"Beyond sure," I said, squirming under him. "I need you inside me. Right now. Skin to skin." I had no idea who this person was, but I liked her. I think I may keep her.

He closed his eyes briefly as he lined himself up with me. Our gazes met as he slid inside me. I fought to keep them open when the sensation of him filling me took over.

"Mallie," he whispered. "Fuck, angel. You were made for me." He pulled out and slid back in, and I arched my back at the immediate overstimulation of my senses. Teddy caged me in as he moved inside me, filling me completely.

"Teddy," I groaned. "More. Give me more." My legs tightened on his hips and pulled him closer. He leaned on one arm and used the other to cup my breast and play with my nipple.

"I want you to ride me," he said. "I want these tits in my face while your pussy clenches me."

I groaned. "Yes. I want it all." He thrust a few more times before pulling out and rolling over, bringing me with him. God, his strength was such a turn-on. I was a slender woman, but I wasn't a small woman at almost five foot eleven. He made me feel like a peanut. I stared at his glistening cock lying against his belly and his amazing body, taut and ready for me to enjoy.

"Come here, angel."

I crawled over him, and he assisted in lining me up to take him. He slid in easily, and I gasped at the fullness of him in this position.

"Relax. I've got you." He eased in and out a few times. "That's it. You take my dick like such a good girl. You're so fucking tight."

He gripped my hips and moved me back and forth as he

stretched me, filling me to the brim. When he was in fully, I placed my hands on his chest and rocked back and forth, my hair falling around me. His hands moved from my hips to my breasts. He squeezed them together and rolled my nipples as he watched me move over him.

"Fucking heaven. I have died and am in heaven right now," he murmured. "You feel so fucking amazing, squeezing my cock like that. Mallie, shit. I'm not going to last. It's too good."

He took a breast in his mouth and sucked, then moved to the other as I rode him. The longer it went, the faster I moved on him, the sensation of him bringing me closer and closer to another orgasm.

"Teddy," I groaned. "I'm so close. It feels so good." He sat up and wrapped his arms around me, pushing himself up into me as I ground down on him. The shift in position and his meeting my movements made the sensations that much more pronounced, and I gripped his shoulders as we panted and breathed together, too into it now to do any more dirty talk.

My body shattered over him and I cried out. He held me still and pulsed into me, drawing out my orgasm and making me scream his name over and over. Just when I thought I couldn't possibly go any longer, he flipped me again and drove into me, chasing his own release. As he bottomed out over and over, I felt it coming again. I couldn't believe it. I shook my head back and forth against the bed, my body unable to process the feeling of it coming again.

"I feel you," he said. "Let go, baby. Give me that orgasm."

Teddy leaned down and kissed me. The second our tongues touched, my body let go. I gripped his back as another bone-melting orgasm ripped through me. He moved faster and finally let go, gripping my hip as he filled me. As we both came down, breathing heavily, he rolled to his side and took me with him. He tucked a piece of hair behind my ear and ran his fingertips down my face. He gripped my chin and kissed me.

"That was the most amazing experience of my life," he said and kissed me again, our tongues tangling. I ran my hands through his short hair and down to his muscular back, pulling him closer to me. I would tease him and tell him that he said that to all the girls, but I couldn't. Because he was right, and we weren't the ones that were going to give each other lines.

"I have no idea what you just did to me, but I don't think I can move ever again. You are going to be single-handedly responsible for the demise of my career because now I can never leave this room." We both laughed and Teddy cupped my breast, his gaze hungry.

"I hope you don't need sleep tonight," he said, "because there is no fucking way I can go to sleep after that. I'm going to do that over and over and over again. You know, to make sure I do it right. And give you something to remember me by."

I felt him growing between us, and I reached down and stroked him the rest of the way to life. "There is no fucking way I ever forget this. When you said it was the most amazing experience of your life? Yeah. It was that and then some for me. I don't even have words to describe it, and that's literally what I do."

"I fucked the words out of you?" Teddy grinned. "Now that's something to brag about. Give me an award for your shelf. Write me a song. Those are the only lyrics. It'll hit number one."

"By the way," I said, still stroking him. I didn't know much about male erections, but I was impressed at how fast he was ready again. "I don't want to bring her up right now, but I feel like I need to say this."

"Say what?"

"Beth was lying her fucking ass off. There is no fucking

comparing you to any man and saying you aren't good at what you do."

He grinned and laughed loudly. "Oh, angel," he said, rolling us and sliding back inside me. "Let me show you how good I can make you feel."

CHAPTER 10
Theo

I ROLLED over and opened my eyes, blinking as I tried to place where I was. A grin crossed my face as I remembered what I spent the last many hours doing. Visions of Mallie's body under mine, over mine, and the sounds she made as we made love over and over again flooded my memory.

Mallie shifted next to me, and I turned and wrapped my arm around her, pulling her back to me. I kissed her head and squeezed her to me, the sensation of her body molded to mine, giving me all the feelings. "Good morning, angel."

She gripped the back of my head, turned her face and pressed her lips to mine. Mallie turned her body and we pressed together. Our kisses quickly became frantic, our mouths and tongues displaying all the passion between us.

"Good morning," she said, those gorgeous blue eyes looking up at me. She touched my face, which she seemed to love to do.

"It is a fucking fantastic morning," I said, and she laughed. "I woke up next to you."

Her eyes went soft, and she buried her face into my chest. "I will never get tired of that."

"What's that?"

"You being so up front and honest with me," she said.

"I'm not playing games. I'm going to tell you. I am flying high on life right now. I had zero expectations of how yesterday was going to go, but waking up here with you? I was afraid to wish for that."

"Well, for the record, it *is* a fucking fantastic morning because not only did I wake up to you, but I had more orgasms in the last ten hours than I've had in my entire lifetime."

My man pride swelled so big it might burst the windows. "You know just what to say to make me want to beat my chest like a caveman."

She giggled. "Well, go right ahead." I pretended to beat my chest, but she was cuddled up to it and I wasn't moving her, making her laugh harder. "What time do you have to leave?"

I groaned. I wasn't successful at pausing time, and I had to fly home today. "I need to be at the airport by three." A quick look at the clock showed it was just after eleven.

"Shower," she whispered against my lips. "I'm going to need you to add to my record."

My eyes rolled back in my head at the thought of her body in the shower. "Fuck yes." I stood and scooped her up. She immediately wrapped her legs around me, and my immediate thought was *I could get used to this*.

"What are you going to do this afternoon after I leave?"

It was just after one, and we sat on her cozy couch, me in the famed sweatpants she wanted to see me in and her in my huge T-shirt, eating brunch from her favorite place. She said she splurged this morning because she kept herself to a very healthy diet when she was touring to keep her immune system up and her energy level stable. I respected the hell out of that because I had similar needs. However, this afternoon, we were feasting on French toast, crepes, and an amazing quiche.

"Crying that you're gone," she said immediately, then grinned. "No, I'll work out later, then do some rehearsing. I fly out on Tuesday to head to my next tour stop."

"What's your workout today?"

"Cardio first, then some weightlifting." She flexed her biceps. "Gotta keep building them up."

"I'd say you've got the cardio covered," I said, waggling my eyebrows.

She laughed. "That's true. Lots of cardio, not a lot of sleep."

"Let's talk about our schedules since we got kind of distracted last night. And this morning."

"I could get distracted again right now," she said, lifting her eyebrows up and down.

"You bet your ass I'm giving you at least another two orgasms before I leave," I said. "I have to leave my girl satisfied."

"Oh, I'm satisfied all right. I have never been more satisfied. I may not be able to walk this week, much less perform on a stage. How am I going to go weeks without it now?"

"I wonder the same thing. We may have to get creative over the phone."

She lifted that sculpted eyebrow again. "No matter how 'creative' we get, if you aren't here in the flesh, then it won't be anywhere close to the same."

She was good at inflating my ego. "You better watch it," I said. "You keep talking about me like that and I'll get a big head."

Mallie slid her gaze downward and then back to my face, her meaning clear. "Is that so?"

This girl. My chest swelled with the feelings building inside it. "Anyway," I said, forcing myself to focus on something other than the T-shirt she wore with little to nothing underneath it. "Let's talk. You're flying out to California?"

She nodded. "Yes. I'll be there for about ten days. I go a little early to acclimate to the time change and do sound checks and little rehearsals with the crew. I have five shows, three in a row and then three days off, then perform for two more. I'm going home to Florida after that because my next shows are in Atlanta."

"It's October and I just had my bye week, so I have no time off until we know if we make the playoffs or not. Plus, we've got the holidays mixed up in there. It's going to be hectic."

"So I will come to you next," she said. "I can do that. I have a small break around Thanksgiving and a bigger one around Christmas."

"Like, come to a game?" I tried to keep my voice even, but even I heard the excitement in my tone. Imagining her in the stands, wearing my jersey, made me more excited than I would admit to myself.

"I would love to come to a game. Maybe Christmas?"

"That sounds perfect. So, this would be our first public event?" *Breathe, Theo. In and out. Don't freak out and scare her.*

She nodded. "Is that okay?"

Was that *okay*? Would it be okay if I jumped up and down right now? She was ready. It may be two months from now, but she'd offered. Which also meant she thought we'd be together two months from now. "Whatever you want to do, I'm game for. I just want to make sure you're comfortable."

"The whole thing will be quite an undertaking. My security has a lot of protocols ahead of me going to something like that, so it may be good that we give them additional time. Plus, I want to protect this for a little bit longer."

"You want me to be your dirty little secret." I winked at her.

"I don't!" She giggled and put her plate to the side.

Within moments, she settled herself on my lap, her legs bracketing my hips. My hands immediately went to her hips like they belonged there. I ran my thumbs along her hip bones, desire immediately flooding my body. "I really enjoyed this weekend. I want to do it again, at least one more time, before the craziness begins and never ends. It's not very often I get to be a normal girl in a new relationship. Is that okay?"

"Of course it's okay." The words she just spoke swirled in my head. A normal girl in a new relationship. She said that. She said it with ease and not like it freaked her out. How could I deny her a chance to feel normal for a while when nothing in her life was ever normal? I couldn't, and I wouldn't.

"You don't think I'm trying to hide you?"

"You just want me as your secret sex slave," I joked, and she smacked me playfully.

"I mean, you *are* really good at sex," she said. My heart was so full. I loved everything about our time together. We played and joked so well together, but also our conversations were like nothing I ever had before.

I kissed her soft lips, sliding my hands into her hair and deepening the kiss. She moved against me, and I groaned into her mouth. I could never get enough of this woman.

"I want to continue this. I do," I said against her lips, stifling a groan as she rocked against my erection. "But if I do, we will never get to the details of when we will see each other next before the public outing, and I really need to know this so I have something to look forward to. And I also need to clarify that you just said 'a normal girl in a new relationship.'"

She leaned back and ran her hands along the sides of my face. "I really love touching your face, you know that?"

"I have noticed. I really love you touching my face, too. Now don't change the subject."

Mallie smiled. "Yes. I said that. Am I assuming wrong? It just felt like we were at the beginning of something . . ."

"Yes," I interrupted her, kissing her again. "We are. You aren't assuming wrong. I'm just on cloud nine that you said that, is all. You absolutely can enjoy being a normal girl for as long as you want. I'm enjoying our little bubble myself. Even if I cannot *wait* for the world to know that I'm lucky enough to be with you. If you decide you want to wait and not go to a game at Christmas, either, that is fine." *Please come to the game. Please. Please. Please.*

She nodded. "Thank you. But I think Christmas will be okay. Unless something comes up that they don't think I should come. I'll get the team on that now. So if I come to you the week of Thanksgiving and stay with you, is that okay, or do you want me to get a hotel? What do you normally do for the holiday?"

"We have a game that weekend," I said. "It's hard to be a pro athlete during the holidays. I usually have a big dinner after the game at my house, so you'd get to be there for that."

"It's also hard to be a pop singer on tour," she agreed. "Okay. So will we get time together if I come, or should I not bother you?"

"You will never be a bother. As long as you don't mind that I have practice, I'd love to have you in my house for as long as you can stay. It is pretty fucking awesome for you to be there for our Thanksgiving dinner too, as far as I'm concerned."

I did quick calculations. It was six weeks until Thanksgiving. I could do that. I could go without her after this weekend. Right? Right. I'd lived without her for thirty-two years.

"Okay. Done. I will have Zoey call Jamie and get everything set up. My security team will have to do their thing, too." She shrugged. "I'm a whole production. Nothing spontaneous about me. Sorry."

"Hey." I kissed her and kept her face close as I continued.

"Don't say sorry to me. Your safety is my number one priority. I will do whatever your team says is necessary to make sure you are safe."

"Speaking of, Juan told me you wanted information about security protocols."

I nodded. "Is that okay?"

She smiled. "You're going to take some getting used to."

"Is that a good thing or a bad thing?"

She ran her hands through my hair, and I barely kept myself from groaning at her touch. I could get used to this. Like, forever. "It's a good thing. I told them that you could be trusted and they could share with you whatever you wanted to know."

She trusted me. That meant more to me than just about anything. "Thank you, angel. It's just in my nature to be protective. If you're my girl, I want to be involved. It's my job to protect you, no matter how many people you have on payroll to do that. That being said, if I overstep, you let me know."

She looked at me for several moments. "Thank you, Teddy. The nice part is, at least your house is only a few hours from mine in Florida, so we can drive it. That keeps people from tracking me and knowing where I am when I use my plane."

My eyes widened. "What? That happens?"

She nodded. "Yep. Exactly why I said privacy is a challenge. It'll be okay this way. No one will know I'm there."

I was a protector by nature, and this information brought that to the forefront. "Mallie. I really don't like that."

She shrugged. "I don't like it, either, but it's public knowledge. Nothing I can do about it. My legal team has tried. If they get rid of one, another one starts up." She shifted and pushed against me, the scrap of lace she had on under that T-shirt definitely not enough to keep me from feeling her heat. "Is that enough talking for right now?" She dipped her head to my neck and began kissing and sucking my skin. "I need more cardio before you have to leave me."

I gripped her hips, tilting my head back so she could continue. I committed every movement she made and the way she felt against me to my memory so I could remember this for the next six weeks. My dick was hard as steel immediately, the sweatpants I wore not hiding how she made me feel.

"Fuck, Mal," I groaned, pushing my dick into her. She rocked against me, her eyes rolling back in her head as I hit her clit. I wanted to do fucking everything with this woman. There was not enough time left on earth for me to touch her in the ways I wanted to.

"How about you let me suck you now," she whispered in my ear. In the shower, she tried. But I couldn't let her because I needed to take her from behind, lift her up and push her into the shower wall. Her hand snaked down between us and under my loose pants. When she made contact with my dick, I hissed. "I want you to come in my mouth," she said, pumping me up and down in her silky hand. "I want to taste every drop of you."

I could not speak. No words would form. She smirked at me and slid down. When she pulled on the waistband of my pants, I lifted slightly. Mallie pushed them down just enough to free me. She licked her lips, and the feral look in her eyes made my dick jump.

"Teddy," she said, that low voice hitting me straight in the gut. Her eyes stayed on me as she closed her mouth over my head. I moaned loudly and lightly held the back of her head as she took me into her mouth. I wasn't small, and she took me like a champ. I felt my head hit the back of her throat, and I tightened my hand on her hair.

"Mallie," I said between my teeth. "You feel so fucking good sucking my cock. You're so good at that. Take it all, angel. That's right. Just like that." I ran my finger along her lips, feeling my dick inside her mouth. She licked and sucked, making my eyes roll back in my head. She was fucking incredible with that mouth. I pushed my hips up and she groaned around my cock. "You like that, baby? God, I am memorizing what you look like right now with my cock in your mouth. I bet you're wet as fuck, aren't you?" She lifted her eyes to me and moaned in answer. "Touch yourself while I fuck your mouth."

I felt her reach a hand down and when she made contact with her clit, she groaned. She sucked harder as she played with herself.

Shifting slightly, I lifted her T-shirt so I could see her delicious breasts. I tweaked a nipple and moved my leg so it was between hers. "Ride my leg and come," I said. She immediately rubbed herself on my shin. I wasn't going to last much longer. "I'm going to come down that beautiful throat of yours. Are you ready?"

She nodded and gripped my cock at the base with one hand and squeezed my balls with the other. Her movements became more frantic against my leg, and when I felt her shudder and she moaned on my cock, I erupted in her mouth. Once the stream stopped, I took myself out and lifted her up.

"Lean over the couch," I said, and she immediately obeyed. I lined myself up behind her and ran my hands along her gorgeous ass. "I will never, not ever, tire of fucking you. This body was made for me."

"Yes," she said. "Fuck me, Teddy. I need you."

I need you. I gripped her hips and thrust myself inside her. She immediately tightened on me, and I bit my lip to stave off my second impending orgasm. I needed her. Physically, yes. But it was so much more than that. I needed every single part of her, and I wasn't sure how to tell her that without scaring the shit out of her. It was so new. So early. But I couldn't help how I felt.

She pushed back against me and turned her face to look

over her shoulder. I leaned over and captured her lips with mine, our tongues immediately meeting. My hands still gripped her hips while I continued to drive into her. We moaned together into each other's mouths, and I took one hand from her hip to hold on to her chin as we fucked with our tongues and our bodies.

I felt her tighten just as I lost control, and I broke the kiss to focus on fucking another orgasm from her. She reached back and gripped my thigh with one hand as the sound of our sex filled the room.

I groaned and let go just as she spasmed. I leaned over and pressed kisses along her back, her chest heaving with the exertion of yet another round of the best sex of my life.

"Teddy," she said, her voice breathless. "I don't know how you top yourself every single time, but you do."

I pulled out gently and turned her so I could taste her lips again. "Same," I whispered against her mouth. "I don't think I can leave today. I think I'll just call Coach and quit. He will understand when I tell him why because look at you."

Mallie giggled and wrapped her arms around my chest, pulling me closer to her. I swayed her back and forth while we processed that; all jokes aside, our time together was down to mere hours.

CHAPTER 11
Allie

NOVEMBER

"We have to go over all the security protocols," Zoey said, and I nodded. I sat at the large table with everyone who was anyone in the Allie Witt world.

Bailey sat next to me, a rare break in her schedule allowing her to come with me for moral support to my first game, which meant a few members of her team were here as well. After this meeting we would head to the stadium a few hours away. I would stay with Teddy for the weekend after the game and would leave for my next tour stop from there.

My mom beamed from across the table. In the time that Teddy and I had been together, she never stopped being his biggest cheerleader. While she hadn't met him in person yet, they had FaceTimed often. They'd hit it off immediately, and she made sure to tell me daily that he was a "keeper" and "much better than any of those other puny men you dated."

She was so excited that I was about to make my first public appearance as Teddy's girlfriend. Not that we needed to have an entire discussion to be "official," but we had that conversation not long after he was in New York. And yes, it was earlier than I originally anticipated going to my first game. It seemed that his Christmas game wasn't going to be as easy for me to attend since it wasn't a home game, so we decided to make it Thanksgiving week and see how it went.

His home team was much more accommodating, it seemed. Teddy let me make the decision, and with the serious escalation in our seriousness, I decided it was time. If it went well and my security team was happy with the way things went, they may feel better about me going to an away game. As it was, it took weeks for them to make this plan and feel comfortable with it all.

However, I had a pit in my stomach the size of Texas. Not because I had any doubts about Teddy or my security while there. I didn't at all. Things with us in our bubble were amazing. I had managed to see him one other brief time in the last six weeks when we'd spent another night in each other's arms at my house in Florida. We hadn't thought it would be possible, but we made it happen. Not that we thought it was, but our second time together proved the first wasn't just a fluke. We greatly enjoyed our time together, and it felt right, which made me feel comfortable going public now.

I wished I could keep this to myself, but it wasn't feasible. If I wanted to live my life without hiding, which I did, then I had to do it. Teddy had to learn about the life I led and see if he could really handle what he thought he could before this went further. But I knew without a shadow of a doubt I would be destroyed if this ended at this point. Many of our conversations over the last several weeks had been with my team and his. Ironing out how this was all going to go and what he should and should not say on social media and to the press. And what we were comfortable "leaking" about our status as a couple after I was seen at his game.

The bags under my eyes that required extra makeup showed just how many late nights we spent talking. At this point, I could say that no one except my mom, Conor, and Bailey knew me better than Teddy did. The depths of our conversations were just so natural, and we both had the same philosophies about so many things.

"Juan." Zoey turned to him, indicating he needed to go over his part of the plan. I zoned out, not because it wasn't important, but because I knew he had it, and discussing all the things that could go wrong just gave me more anxiety. I thought through the scenarios that could happen this weekend.

First of all, and the most obvious, was the media attention that would happen the second I arrived. Selfishly, I was glad Bailey would be there too because, at least initially, the focus would be on us and why we were both there. Once they figured it out, it would shift dramatically.

Next, the suite that I would be in was his, and his parents would be there. I would meet them for the first time without him there. Cue the panic. He had me talk to them on the phone the last time we were together, but being together in person was a whole other thing. I wished my mom would be there, but she couldn't go. She promised to go with me to the Christmas game if that worked out. Thank God Bailey had a blissful opening around the holidays and she was okay spending it with me in a fishbowl of attention. She may or may not have mentioned forcing Teddy to introduce her to a single friend as her reason to come, but I knew she wanted to be there to help me with my extreme nerves.

After the game, he would come up to the suite to meet me. We would then leave the game together and go to his house, where he had planned a Thanksgiving celebration where I'd meet his closest friends.

No pressure. At all.

The stadium came into view, and my leg bounced up and down in nervous anticipation. Bailey went back and forth between watching me and watching us get closer to the most nerve-racking moment of my life. She reached over and squeezed my hand. She had never been to a football game before, either, and she was excited.

"It's okay, Allie," she said. "It's going to be fine." I took a deep breath, trying but failing to calm myself. We went through all the scenarios together. I told him what would happen. I prepared him as much as I could. And here we were, about to see what actually came of this.

My phone pinged with a text, and I looked down at the screen. Of course it was Teddy. He had a direct channel into my head at all times.

Take a deep breath. We've got this, angel. I cannot wait to see you up there today. I hope you and Bailey have so much fun. My parents are so excited you're here.

I smiled and showed the screen to Bailey. This man was preparing for a game, and he was worried about me.

Bailey shook her head. "I'm telling you, Al. This man is it for you. I called it from the beginning. You went through all the shit you went through to get to him."

I was afraid to hope for that, and she knew it. What my heart told me was one thing, but my reality was another. Plus my heart lied to me a lot in my life, so it made it hard to follow it.

We are about to pull in. I'll see you after the game. Kick ass today, Teddy.

"Are you ready for this?" I asked her. Bailey's security combined with mine today to escort us to the game, and we had a vehicle both in front and behind us with our team. Zoey was with them, too. She felt more comfortable coming with me, and I enjoyed having her around, so it worked out.

She nodded. "I'm excited. I've never been to a game before. I know hardly anything about football, but I can't wait to watch men in tight pants throw each other around."

I laughed. "Definitely a bonus, though the only one I want

to see in tight pants is Teddy. And I didn't know anything about football, either, until I googled things about him, and then Teddy taught me more. I am still a baby with my level of knowledge, but we watched some highlights of his game, and he talked me through a lot. At least I know now what his position even does."

"He's a running back, right?" Bailey asked and I nodded.

"He's one of the top in the entire league."

The SUV pulled into the stadium and I stopped talking, my hands twisted in my lap. I felt like I could vomit at any moment. My phone pinged again, and this time it was Zoey in the vehicle in front of us.

Stay in the car for a minute. Checking things out and getting transport into the stadium. Like I'd move without them telling me to. I knew who the bosses were.

Will do.

"Okay, spill it," Bailey said.

"Spill what?"

"What's the worst-case scenario going on in your head right now?"

"That I'm sick and tired of worrying about what drama me having a regular relationship with a man is going to do to my life. And his."

"I think he can handle it, Al. I really do."

"Maybe," I said. I had to stop. I was here to support Teddy and see him do what he loved, and I couldn't allow myself to get into this funk. "Anyway, ready or not, I'm doing it. I won't let them control my life, and I need to show Teddy that he's a priority for me. I am excited to see him. I just wish it didn't come with the rest of it."

The vehicles stopped almost inside a tunnel that went under the backside of the stadium. I worried my lip between my teeth and then forced myself to stop, smiling at the thought of what Teddy would say. My eyes fluttered closed at the memory of his body over mine, those blue eyes looking straight into my soul.

"Do I look okay?"

Bailey shook her head. "You never look okay. You look fucking stunning and like the sexy, confident woman you are."

She was such a great hype woman. Today, I wore my long blond hair curled down my back and pulled up halfway into a clip. I loved fashion and the color black, and thankfully, the Blaze colors were black and red, so that fit what I loved. Despite it being November, it was a warm seventy-five degrees, so I chose a black skirt, platform-heeled boots, and a red off-the-shoulder blouse. I wore stacked gold necklaces and earrings and my signature red lip.

"I'm so glad you're here," I said.

"Let's go turn a stadium full of men on their heads," she said, and we both laughed. Shortly after, the door opened and we were escorted out of the vehicle by Juan and Alex, Bailey's head of security. I looked up at the massive stadium, one that I played in many times over the span of my career, including the day that I ran straight into what may have been the best thing in my life. It looked so different today, filled with people wearing Blaze attire instead of the bright colors of my fans' outfits.

They led us into an area where workers milled around, not paying much attention to us. We could hear fans in the stadium, but we couldn't see them. Zoey stepped up next to me, and we walked with purpose through the underside of the stadium. Security flanked us on all sides. So far, so good.

When we reached a hallway and turned, I spotted people milling around in Flame gear and sucked in a breath. Bailey squeezed my hand, and Zoey gave me a small smile.

"You've got this," Zoey said, echoing Bailey from earlier. Zoey's job was to protect my image like my security was to protect me physically, and even she was a thousand percent on board with me and Teddy. I told her everything, and she had spoken to him many times both with Jamie, his publicist and without her. Zoey was hard to impress and tough to let people fully into my life, but she gave him the gold stamp of approval. Jamie would also be in the box today, according to Teddy. I liked her a lot, and she seemed to really care about him.

"I've got this," I said, forcing my shoulders back and my head up. I was Allie fucking Witt. I walked in and owned places. I didn't need nerves. I needed confidence. It didn't matter what they said about us. What mattered was what *we* said about us.

We reached an elevator, and the sheer size of our group, flanked by a lot of security, started making people stop and look at us. I watched as people scanned our group, and I willed the elevator to hurry. It was going to be seconds and they'd figure it out.

"OH MY GOD! IT'S ALLIE WITT AND BAILEY LEE!" a voice screamed from far enough away that I couldn't tell who yelled it, but they got the attention of every single person within earshot. Everyone turned and looked, and just as pandemonium started to ensue, the doors opened and we slid in. Phones pointed at us as we entered the elevator, and we both waved as the doors shut.

"Whew," I said. "That took longer than I thought, but in two seconds, it'll be all over socials."

Bailey rubbed her hands together. "Let's fucking *go!* It's football time!"

Zoey laughed at her. "Yep. It's time to have fun and not worry about the rest. You're here to see Teddy. The rest is just noise."

"And meet the parents and friends and his publicist. No pressure."

"Hey," Zoey said, "Remember who the fuck you are.

You're an amazing person, and not just because you're Allie Witt, pop superstar."

I smiled, and the elevator doors opened to the suite level of the stadium. Cheers erupted as we stepped out. Yep, it took that long for it to go viral that I was here. People shouted our names and that they loved us. We walked down the hallway toward Teddy's suite, and I imagined him there when I was here on tour, watching me. If it wasn't for him seeking me out, I wouldn't be here right now. After he helped me that day, had he not continued showing me who he was, I would've never seen him again. I made a mental note to thank him for doing what most people wouldn't.

Juan stopped at the door to what must be Teddy's suite and opened it, walking in first. I knew the routine, and I stood outside with Rico and crew until he gestured for me to follow. Most of the guys would be outside the suite, so they wouldn't take up all the space and also because now that it was out that I was here, they anticipated many people attempting to come up.

Bailey and I walked in, Zoey behind me. Several people I didn't recognize turned as we walked in, and my stomach clenched with nerves again. I was momentarily distracted by the view of the field from here. The team warmed up on the field and I searched for #23 immediately, ignoring the stares and phones I saw from the neighboring suites.

"He's over there." Jamie walked up, pointing toward the end zone. I smiled when I noticed him standing with Spencer. "It's great to meet you in person," she said, reaching out her hand to shake mine. However, instead of shaking her hand, I hugged her. I couldn't help it—I was a hugger.

"Hi, Jamie," I said. "It's so great to officially meet you. This is my best friend, Bailey Lee, and my publicist, Zoey."

Zoey shook her hand. "Definitely nice to meet you in person," she said.

Bailey shook her hand also.

"I cannot believe I'm meeting both of you at the same time," Jamie said. "Well, to be real, all three of you. Okay, that's it. That's all the fangirling I'm going to do." She squealed and jumped up and down. "Okay, seriously. That's it."

We laughed together, and I hugged her again. I liked her. Despite the years of experience with it, I still enjoyed it when people freaked out like that, especially someone like her who worked with famous people for a living. It reminded me of all the years I wanted that.

"We've done a lot to get these two here today. Nice to finally be here," Zoey said.

Jamie laughed. "For sure. Come on in. Make yourselves at home. We've got a full bar and food you can order, plus regular drinks in the fridge. Theo's parents will be here shortly. Let me introduce you to everyone here so far."

I followed her through the suite, where I met Teddy's friend Ty, his neighbor Wyatt, and two childhood friends, Marc and Devin. We finally settled ourselves in a front-row seat and got drinks. The mayhem below us and next to us was steadily increasing, but I refused to look anywhere but next to me and in front of me at the field.

"You good?" Bailey asked, sipping her beer.

"I'm good," I said. "Nervous but excited to meet his parents. Spencer's fiancée, Lacey, is here, too, but she's in the stands. She told Teddy she'd come over at halftime."

Zoey sat down next to me with a soda. She didn't drink, probably because handling my life meant she had to stay on her toes at all times. "You're creating quite a scene," she laughed. "Not that we didn't expect that, but the two of you? Yeah. Pretty sure the internet is broken trying to figure out why the two of you are in Theo Nolan's suite at the Blaze game. It was genius, though, because it will take them a bit to figure out which one of you is associated with him."

Bailey giggled. "It's me. He can pick me up and put

me in his pocket." We laughed with her, the image in my head too much. "Nah, he's all Allie's. But I am on the hunt for one of his hot single friends." She looked over at Jamie, sitting on the other side of her. "Have any candidates?"

Jamie grinned. "There are several unattached players on the Blaze. The only one I represent who is single is the safety, Briggs Callahan. He's number twenty-two."

"Hey, Teddy is twenty-three!" I exclaimed.

"Teddy?" Jamie asked.

Oops. I forgot our bubble was no longer, and I needed to remember no one called him that but me. "Sorry. Theo."

"No," Jamie said, "that is the cutest thing. You call him Teddy?"

My face flamed, but I nodded. "I'm glad I said that in front of you and not someone else. He told me his teammates called him T-Bear because a kid called him a teddy bear once, and I liked it. It fits him."

Jamie put her hand over her heart and fell back in the chair dramatically. "Swoon. I just cannot with how cute you two are."

Bailey pointed at herself. "Excuse me. Enough with those two lovebirds. Tell me about Briggs. That name is hot as hell. Is he as hot as his name is?"

Jamie pulled her phone out of her pocket and typed, then turned the phone to Bailey. Her mouth dropped open and she looked at me. "Um, *this* is the hottest man I've ever seen. No offense, Al."

I laughed. I doubted very much that he was near as hot as Teddy—Theo—but I leaned over to look at Jamie's phone. The man in the picture was hot, for sure. He had short blond hair and striking green eyes. His face looked like something chiseled out of stone, with no facial hair to speak of. Much like Theo and every other football player, his muscles had muscles.

"I'm going to need to meet this one. Will he be at Theo's later?"

Jamie grinned. "As a matter of fact, he will be. He's a rookie and Theo has taken him under his wing, so he is often at his house."

Bailey smirked. "Well, isn't this perfect. My day is made now. Does he like country music?" She sat back in her seat and crossed her arms over her chest.

"I'm not sure," Jamie said. "But I doubt there is a man on this earth that wouldn't look at you and be interested."

"Awww, thank you, Jamie."

The suite door opened again, and in stepped Theo's parents. My mouth dried as we made eye contact and they made their way directly to me.

"Allie!" His mom, Sandra Nolan, walked up to me first. She wore a jersey with Theo's number on it, her blond hair styled in a cute bob to her chin. She definitely did not look her age, which Theo said was in her late fifties. I stood and she enveloped me in her arms. Immediately, I felt safe. "So great to meet you in person. You're just gorgeous. Look at this beautiful outfit you have on. Sigh. I miss being young and able to dress in whatever I want."

Sandra pulled back and her husband, Thomas, beamed from next to us. He was tall, just as tall as Teddy, and handsome with the same dark hair as his son but with more gray than brown. He had the same smile and blue eyes.

"Allie. I can't believe we finally get to meet face to face," he said. He wrapped me in a hug, and I felt like I was in his son's arms. I saw where he got it. He exuded protectiveness. "Thank you so much for the smile I see on Theo's face again. It's been too long."

He stepped back from me and put his arm around his wife and squeezed her to him. She rested her head on his chest, causing a ball of emotion to form in my throat.

Sandra nodded, dabbing tears from the corners of her

eyes. "It's true. All a mom ever wants to see is that her baby is happy, and it is obvious to me that the two of you have something really special."

"Thank you," I said. "It's so great to meet both of you, too. Your son is amazing, which is a testament to you and your parenting. And, obviously, your love for each other."

They smiled. "Forty years together," his dad said. "The best decision I made in my entire life."

"Well, they just figured it out," Bailey said from the seat next to me, indicating all the cameras facing our way. More than likely, the professional cameras for the stadium were trained up here, too. It was Zoey's job to monitor what they said online as the game progressed. Right then, I was focused on the people in front of me. I forced myself to block out everything but the people who created Teddy.

"The game is starting!" Wyatt called, and we settled into our seats, Bailey on one side of me and Zoey on the other. His parents sat behind us. My eyes scanned for Teddy, and I couldn't help but grin when I found him. He stayed out on the field, so the offense must be starting first. Look at me; I knew things about football.

"What are they saying?" I asked Zoey without looking away from the field. She scrolled away on her phone, and I knew she was reading what was posted about us.

"Both of your names are a trending hashtag. The Allie-Cats have lost their damn minds. People are feral. A video of you and Bailey walking in was posted, and underneath it the speculation was wild on what both of you were doing here. Once you guys entered Theo's suite, the real chaos began. And then when you hugged both of his parents and Bailey stayed seated? Yeah. Losing their shit. They're wondering if this is the first time you guys are meeting each other in person."

Bailey and I exchanged a glance, and both of us started laughing. "They think this is our *first meeting*? In front of the whole world? Are they serious? Why would anyone ever do such a thing?"

Zoey laughed, too. "Right. Like I said, feral. Then the more astute Allie-Cats remembered that Theo went to your concert back in July and posted pictures from his suite and kissing the cheek of your cutout, so now the speculation is that you started talking back then, but then you were still with Josiah—as far as they knew—so they are confused. The documentary Theo was on where he mentioned you is the current fixation. They're trying to put together the puzzle pieces. They're not too far off, but they don't know all the details yet."

I blew out a breath. Well, it had begun. "Okay, so everything we anticipated so far. At least they don't know anything about our actual dates."

"Yep. The AFL has posted you all over their socials and on the live coverage of the game no less than five times already, and the game just began. They're very excited that the two of you are here and in Theo's box. At first, they were confused, too, but now they know it's you that they're focusing on."

"Hey, it could be me, too," Bailey said. "I want to find a hot man, too."

It was halftime and the Blaze were up 30–7. I stood at the back of the suite to hide a bit from the onslaught of cameras trained on me the entire game. According to Zoey, I was being shown on the television a ridiculous number of times, and that wasn't even counting the people taking videos and pictures and posting them on socials. It wasn't like I didn't expect this wherever I went, but it was a lot, no matter what.

Right now, I was waiting for Spencer's fiancée, Lacey, to make her way over. Bailey waved at fans through the glass of our suite, loving the attention. She was always giving her security a run for their money. She'd be over there taking pictures with them if Alex would let her.

The door opened and Juan walked in with Lacey. She wore an oversized jersey with the number thirteen on it and "Green" on the back, Spencer's last name and, soon to be, hers. She saw me and stopped in her tracks, a frozen smile on her face.

"Lacey?" I said. I stepped forward to greet her.

"Allie," she said, her voice barely a squeak. "I am sorry. I am a full-on, grown-ass adult, and I'm going to freak the fuck out for a moment. Am I really standing in the same room as you? Are you really dating my fiancé's best friend?"

I held out my arms and she stepped into them and we hugged. "Nice to meet you in person, Lacey. Yes is the answer to both of your questions."

She stepped back and shook her head side to side. "I just literally cannot believe you're really here. I mean, it's not that I didn't believe Theo, it's just . . . wow. I just can't seem to process this. That night he watched your concert, I was on FaceTime with them. Later, Spencer told me that Theo was beside himself over you, and I couldn't believe it. I've been a fan of yours forever."

"Thank you," I said. "To be fair, I'm still processing that I'm really here, too."

Lacey looked over at the cameras pointing at us from every angle. "Well, I guess they got the memo that you're here."

"They sure did." I laughed. "Come on. I want to introduce you to my best friend. You know Bailey Lee?"

Lacey's mouth dropped open. "You're kidding me." When she spotted Bailey in the seat, scrolling on her phone and drinking her beer, she looked back at me. "I think this is the best day of my life. Don't tell Spencer that."

I liked her already. "Girl code."

CHAPTER 12
Theo

I WRAPPED a towel around my freshly showered self and smiled at the mayhem happening in our locker room. That win was huge and one we needed badly, but even better than the final result and the two touchdowns I scored, Mallie was here. In my suite. With my parents. And my friends. She'd done it. We were not just official in our own minds, but the world now knew. Mallie may be concerned about the circus, but all I could think of was just how ecstatic I was that I could publicly declare her as mine.

I knew the media circus had started. I didn't need to look at my phone to know. The buzz was all over, so much that it even infiltrated the field. At halftime, even Coach Reynolds had asked me if it was true that Allie Witt was really in my box watching me play. I knew for a fact I hadn't hidden my elation at her being here, but I didn't really try to. Yes, Allie fucking Witt was in my box. Watching me play.

"Lacey texted me a picture of them," Spencer said, holding his phone. He was in a towel as well. He held the phone out to me, and I couldn't stop the grin from overtaking my face at the sight of them. And *holy motherfucking shit did she look hot. That was my girl.* "She said she freaked the fuck out but then realized that Allie was cool as hell and the nicest person she's ever met. They're having a great time up there. I can't believe you really did it. You got her to come to a game."

"She decided to come. I didn't make her," I said. "I just want her to be comfortable."

"NOLAN!" Briggs Callahan, one of our rookies, shouted at me. Multiple people stopped to look as he crossed the room. He looked like an excited kid on Christmas morning.

"Callahan," I responded. I liked the kid, and I'd taken him under my wing this year to help his transition to the professional leagues. He'd been a hotshot in college, but many times, that didn't always translate once they got to a professional team. He had a big personality and often commanded a lot of attention. I was working with him on tamping himself down some since he was in the public eye now, but he had a good heart.

"Dude, is it true?" His eyes were wide. "Are you really dating Allie Witt?" His voice carried, and the locker room instantly fell quiet.

"I mean, wouldn't you?" one of the other young guys, Brock Woods, shouted out. "She's hot as fuck, and I hear she's a freak in the sheets."

"Oh fuck," I heard Spencer say as I crossed the room and shoved the fucker down to the ground. The guys reacted immediately, crowding around us. They knew that if I got physical with someone, it was for a damn good reason, so they didn't intervene.

"Get your pansy ass up and say that again," I said through my teeth. I clenched my fists, ready and willing to show him just how serious I was. Woods scrambled to his feet and backed up, his hands in the air. "I will put you through the fucking wall if you *ever* talk about her like that again. Do you understand?"

Woods nodded. "I'm sorry, man. That was a stupid thing to say. I'm an idiot. If you want to punch me, I deserve it."

"You *do* deserve it," I said, "but I'm not going to punch you because I need my hand intact. However, if you ever disrespect her or any other woman like that again, I will teach you a lesson. You got it?"

"Got it."

Briggs blew out a breath next to me. "Fuck, Woods. You really have a death wish. Jesus."

"Sometimes I'm stupid as fuck still," he said. "I'm sorry, man. No disrespect."

I crossed my arms. "That was disrespectful as hell. Don't ever talk like that again."

Callahan stepped into the middle of the group. "The entire world is talking about Allie Witt and her best friend Bailey Lee in your suite, T. She was seen talking to and hugging your parents. Something you want to tell us?"

"See, how hard was that?" I asked, my eyes still trained on Woods. "But, yes, Allie Witt is here, and yes, I am dating her. She will also be at my house later for our Thanksgiving feast, as will Bailey Lee."

Briggs stared at me, processing my words. "Damn, dude. You're the luckiest bastard in the world."

I smiled this time. "I sure as shit am."

"Did you say Bailey Lee is coming too?"

"I did."

Briggs grinned. "I think I may be the second luckiest bastard in the world."

I forced myself to walk even though I wanted to sprint into the suite to get Allie. I ignored the shouts from fans. I usually would stop and talk or take pictures, but this time it was different. I knew what they wanted, and I wasn't going to give it to them.

Rico walked next to me, keeping us from being stopped.

We turned the corner, and I saw the mayhem outside the suite. People lined up, trying to see her. They held their phones, hoping to get a glimpse.

"Stadium security is taking care of it," Rico told me, reading my mind. "They'll be here in just a second and will clear it out. We will wait until they do to take her out."

I nodded. We reached the door to the suite, and I tried to block out the noise of the fans yelling about Allie. Juan opened the door and I slid inside. My parents stood close to the door, as well as Bailey and Zoey, but they were the only ones in here besides Allie. Jamie had texted me that she'd left to go deal with the caterers at my house. Allie turned to look at me, and at that moment, nothing else mattered.

She closed the space between us, and I wrapped my arms around her. She tipped her head back, and there was no damn way I wasn't going to give her what she wanted. I slid my lips over hers and breathed her in. "You're here," I said into her ear.

"I'm here," she repeated.

"You look so fucking beautiful. It's a good damn thing I didn't see this outfit from the field. I would've had my tongue hanging out of my mouth."

"Well, I did see you from here in those tight pants, and I did drool a little."

I smirked. "A little?"

She smiled. "A lot. Watching you play is hot as fuck. You know our private bubble is all over now, right?"

I smoothed her hair back. "We knew that was going to happen. You're okay, right?"

She smiled. "Guarantee this is being videoed right now as well."

"Do you care?"

She looked at me, and we had a silent conversation with each other before she said, "I don't. I really don't." I could not explain the relief that I felt at her words.

"Good. Let's get out of here." I took her hand and hugged my mom and dad with one arm. "Hey, you two. Thanks for coming."

My mom had tears in her eyes, which was typical of her when anything happened to me. "She's amazing," she whispered in my ear. "We're so happy for you."

I looked down at Allie and then back at them. "She *is* amazing. Now let's go eat some food."

———

We pulled into my driveway and the gate opened, the vehicle brigade following us in. When I bought this house, I thought having the gate was excessive. Now, I was thankful for it because it was one more way to keep her safe while she was here.

Once we left the stadium, I turned my phone off due to the sheer volume of messages and social media tags I'd gotten since the start of the game. Everyone I cared about would be here within the hour for our Blaze Thanksgiving, and the rest wasn't important.

Allie lifted her head from my shoulder and put her hands on the sides of my face. "Today was great. I know I was worried—still worry—about all of this, but I want to be clear about something. I wasn't—and am not—worried about being around your family and friends. They made me feel the most normal that I have in a long time. If I ignored the cameras pointed at me and the people screaming my name, I could almost think I was a girl watching a football game. It was a lot of fun. I have missed out all this time not watching football."

"It was great to have you there. The media frenzy will hopefully die down the more they get used to us."

She laughed and patted my arm. "You're so funny. It won't die down. Not even a little bit. Right now, they are freaking out and speculating about the details. Zoey told me about some of it during the game. The more we are out there? The more stories will surface and lies will be spread about conversations we had with people and issues our families and friends had with each other. It will never be over. Not ever. But that was a nice thought."

I kissed her lips. "I don't care."

She grinned against my mouth. "This right here is all I care about."

The door opened, and I slid out and held my hand for her. She took it and I watched as her skirt slid up her sexy legs as she got out. God, she was hot as fuck, and I really was the luckiest man in the entire universe. I reached around her to shut the door and took her hand in mine as we walked up to my front door.

"Later, I'm going to lift that skirt and feast on you," I said into her ear. "You're so goddamn sexy, and it's going to take every bit of my willpower for the next many hours to not pull you into the bathroom and fuck you on the counter."

She blushed and bit that lip. "I have a secret," she said, then stood on her tiptoes to talk into my ear. I leaned down to assist her. "I took my underwear off in the bathroom before we left the stadium. They're in my purse." She indicated the postage-stamp-sized purse she carried.

I groaned at her admission and looked down like I could see through her skirt. "You're fucking kidding me. We rode all the way here and I didn't know that? That's it. I'm checking in with Jamie and making sure everything is set, and then it's on."

Mallie's eyes widened. "You want me to sit around a table with all of your teammates, friends, and family after fucking you?"

"Even better than that," I said, "I want you to be dripping while you're sitting around the table with the people I care about the most. I'm going to find Jamie. You go to my bathroom and do not take one thing off." I eyed the boots she wore. "Especially those."

———

I held my hand over her mouth as she moaned. Her teeth grazed my skin as her eyes rolled back in her head. I pushed my cock harder into her and gritted my teeth to keep from shouting out.

This woman's body was made for me, and it had been too long. She sat on the edge of the bathroom counter. As instructed, she was still fully clothed, minus the underwear she really wasn't wearing. I still wore my suit from leaving the field, my pants undone just enough to let myself out.

"You feel so fucking good, angel," I said, using my other hand to hold her hip still to get better friction. "I want that orgasm. Give it to me. Later, I'm going to give you so many you'll beg me to stop. Right now, I need it hard and fast."

She whimpered, and I felt her contract around me. I picked up the pace and hit right where I knew she loved it the most while working her clit with my thumb, and that was all it took. Her breathing accelerated, and she scratched her nails down my back. The sounds of our sex filled the room and I let go, stifling my own moan as my orgasm took over. When she stopped making noise, I took my hand from her mouth, and she immediately put her hands on my face and kissed me.

As our tongues slid together, I felt an overwhelming urge to say words I hadn't said in a really long time. I forced them back, but just barely. The idea of the words should've scared the hell out of me.

They didn't.

———

"So, Allie, tell us about yourself," my mom started, passing rolls around the table. "I mean, everyone here knows who you are because you're the most recognizable star in the world."

I looked at Mallie's face as my mom talked, my stomach churning with nerves, but she looked calm and unaffected. I put my hand on her leg, and she wrapped her fingers with mine and squeezed.

"Tell us who you are when you're not Allie Witt, pop star."

She grinned as if this was her favorite question to answer. "I'm from Florida, a few hours from here, born and raised, though I don't get to spend as much time here as I'd like due to my schedule. Since I grew up here, the beach has always been my happy place. When I was a kid, we went on a cruise and I was enthralled with all the performers. After that, it was my plan to work on a cruise ship and travel the world until I 'hit it big.' My primary goal was to get a record deal, of course, but that happens so infrequently that I wanted to make sure to have a backup plan. I was raised by a single mom, and she's my entire world. We lived next door to my aunt and uncle my entire life, and I grew up with my cousin Conor. Our grandparents lived on the other side of me, so we were all close. He's currently my assistant, and my aunt and uncle run the Allie Witt Corporation. My grandparents both passed away in the last fifteen years. I have a dog, Charlie, and he usually goes everywhere with me. If I'm gone longer than a few days, he goes with me on my plane."

"I love dogs," my mom comments. "What kind is he?"

I stroked Allie's leg with my thumb, encouraging her. Every person at this table hung on her every word, and it was a lot of people. Bailey sat on the other side of her and caught my eye as I looked down the table. She smiled and nodded, and I felt so much from that reassurance from Allie's best friend. It wasn't too much. She was okay.

"He's a mini goldendoodle. I always wanted one. It wasn't practical for me to get a dog as much as I travel, but I did it anyway, and he is the coolest dog. He has the chillest personality and is just happy curling up next to you. He doesn't mind the planes or being in different places." She laughed. "Wow, I really just went on about my dog like he's my kid."

Everyone laughed. "What do you think you would've done if you didn't become a singer? That is, if you didn't do the cruise thing," Spencer asked. Everyone ate as Allie talked, and as much as I wanted them to leave her be, she seemed to enjoy talking to them, so I let it go for now.

"I love kids, so I thought maybe I'd be a teacher. English was always my strong suit, and playing piano and guitar. I really worked hard at my music as a young high schooler, though, thanks to the support from my family, so I put out my first album at sixteen. I have wanted to be a singer since I knew what singing was. My mom always loved music, so we didn't watch TV when I was a kid. We listened to music. I knew as many musicians' names and songs as other kids knew cartoons."

"What's it like?" Briggs asked, and I shot him yet another warning look. Briggs was a good guy, but still immature and dealing with the huge media spotlight of being a rookie on the Blaze and the attention he got from it. He'd already gotten quite a reputation for himself with the ladies, and he regretted it, hence my involvement in helping him to stop being stupid.

"What's what like?" Allie took a bite of her food and chewed, waiting for his answer.

Meanwhile, I couldn't eat, my gut in too many knots over this seemingly harmless conversation. I just wanted it to go perfectly tonight. This was the first time I got to see her with the people I loved, and I was beyond ecstatic at the way she fit right in.

"Being a globally famous pop star. Having a life no one

else can even fathom. Having fans screaming your name everywhere you go and not being able to have a regular life? Touring the world and selling out stadiums?"

"Briggs," I said, my tone expressing my warning. His attention snapped to me, but Allie shook her head at me and squeezed my fingers.

"There's nothing wrong with those questions, Te—Theo," she said, correcting my nickname. "It's perfectly normal to wonder, and I don't mind answering them."

I saw the looks on a few faces when she almost called me Teddy, but they let it go to let her continue—for now.

"To be honest, I was so young when I started that I don't know what 'normal' means. I mean, normal to me is paparazzi screaming my name outside my house at all hours of the day and night and fans wanting autographs and pictures everywhere I go. I don't know what it's like to graduate from high school with a group, go to parties that are not for awards shows or album releases, or just go to the grocery store unattended. But you know what I do know? I know that every single day when I open my eyes, I'm living my dream. It's all I've ever wanted, and I get to do it. It has its fair share of frustrations, but I genuinely love what I do and the people that have helped me get to this level of success. I have a loyal fan base that has been with me for a long time, and they keep me going when it gets hard. I've been in this long enough that some of my first fans now have kids they bring to the shows. Touring is my absolute favorite, other than being in the studio recording. It may sound cliché, but I love seeing my fans face to face and singing with them. I also love meeting them, but that has gotten harder throughout the years. Without them, I'd still just be singing to my family."

"Don't they call themselves Allie-Cats?" my adorable mother asked, and laughter broke out across the table. Someone had been searching up my girl, and it wasn't just me.

Allie laughed. "They do. They came up with that when I released my second album, and it just stuck. They are definitely loyal to me, and they keep me going on the hard days for sure."

My dad looked lovingly at my mom, and a silent conversation happened between them. If there was a reason I believed in true love, it was the two of them. Married when they were just teenagers, after a month of dating. They still looked at each other like I wanted my spouse to look at me. Mom smiled and nodded, whatever communication they had understood.

A natural silence took over the table as people ate and stopped asking Allie questions. She looked over at me and smiled, and I swore my heart skipped a beat. I leaned over and kissed her temple, unable to stop myself. She leaned into me for a moment before we focused back on our plates of food.

I heard a small sigh from down the table. Lacey, the guilty party, laughed. "Sorry. You two are just *so cute*."

"Agreed," Bailey said. "I am both so happy for you guys and so damn jealous it isn't funny."

My eyes found Briggs across the table. He stared at her, his fork midair, as he processed how to respond to that. I shook my head at him, helping him with the awareness that this wasn't the time to hit on Bailey Lee. If he wanted a shot with her, he had to do it away from the eyes of everyone here. He nodded and put his fork down but continued to watch her. I knew that look. As if she felt him looking, she met his gaze, and an interesting look passed between them before she turned away. Hmm.

Small talk continued, and with most of the table consisting of my players and their girlfriends and wives, it went naturally to our upcoming games. After a few minutes, Lacey indicated that Allie and Bailey should follow the girls to the back porch for wine and "girl talk." Allie stood, and my eyes went right to what I knew was—and wasn't—under that skirt. She leaned down and pressed her lips against my ear. I intertwined my fingers with hers, my thumb caressing her palm. I needed to touch her. All the time.

"I know what you're thinking. I'm thinking about it, too. Have fun with the boys. I'll be ready for you later." With that, she kissed my lips quickly and walked away.

Silence followed the girls, and once they were out on the back deck, Spencer, Briggs, and the rest of my closest friends all turned their attention to me.

"Dude," Marc, one of my closest childhood friends, started what I knew was about to be a serious razzing. "You're in love with her."

"It's written all over your face," Devin, my other childhood best friend, interjected. "I never saw you look at Beth the way you look at her."

"And the way you two can't stop touching each other and looking at each other?" Ty, one of my closest friends, added.

"What is this, Theo's inquisition?" I laughed, but I didn't mind. They weren't wrong, and I wouldn't discount what I felt by saying they were.

"Speaking of," Spencer said. "What was she about to call you before she said Theo?"

I grinned. I knew that hadn't slid by anyone. "Teddy." The table of my best friends all simultaneously clutched their hearts like they'd rehearsed it, then laughed once they realized they all did it.

"Teddy like T-Bear, huh?" Isaiah, one of my favorite teammates, piped up. "She likes that you're a big ol' teddy bear."

I shrugged, and I knew my face told exactly how much she liked it, but I wasn't hiding. "Guess she does."

"Notice he didn't deny being in love with her," Xavier, another of my close player friends, brought up.

I wouldn't go there before talking about it with her, so I stepped carefully into my next words. "I have never felt this way about anyone before in my life. Ever. But it's still early." I looked at my dad, still in the room. He was a quiet man most of the time but one of the most emotionally stable people I'd ever known. A small smile played on his face as he listened. "My only goal in life other than making it in the professional football world was to find a love like my parents have."

Everyone turned and looked at my dad. He dabbed his eyes with his napkin at my statement. "That makes this old man so happy to hear, Theo. Your mother is the best thing to ever happen to me. Other than you, of course." He stood as my mom entered the room, having excused herself a few minutes before. "Speaking of the love of my life, we're going to head out."

I stood from the table and hugged him and then her.

My mom had tears in her eyes when she pulled back.

"Mom?" There was nothing I hated more than seeing her cry. "What's wrong?"

My dad linked his hand with hers and smiled at her.

"She's perfect for you," she whispered, indicating the woman sitting outside with all my friend's wives and girlfriends. "There's nothing wrong at all. I just know that I spent the day with your soulmate, and that makes my mom heart so happy. I just can't help that it makes me emotional."

I opened and closed my mouth, feeling the heat in my face. My heart pounded against my sternum, and my chest heaved like I just ran sprints. "Mom," I whispered, afraid to speak any of this out loud. My mom had never, not ever, uttered those words before, not even when I talked about getting engaged to Beth.

She wrapped her arm around my dad's torso and leaned into him, nodding at me. "Ever since she walked into that suite today, I felt it. I couldn't tell you why or how, but I just know."

"I feel it, too," I whispered back to her. "Is it too soon? We've both been so burned. It's only been a few months."

She looked up at my dad, and he spoke up this time. "I think you're both ready because of what you've been through. You're not young kids like we were, and even then we knew rather soon also. Too soon for most people who doubted us. I don't think anyone can put a timeline on something like this. As the saying goes, when you know, you know."

CHAPTER 13
Allie

I SAT BACK, a wineglass between my fingers, and listened to the women around me chat. Teddy's mom had left just a few minutes ago, claiming to be too old to stay up late with us. I truly loved getting to know her.

Thankfully, due to my profession, I was rather good at remembering names, but the challenge was remembering which woman was connected to which man, which was the main reason for me to do more listening than talking. The more they talked, the more connections I put in my brain. Of course Lacey was engaged to Spencer, who was Theo's best friend and the quarterback of the team. I liked her a lot and could see us becoming good friends.

Then there was Brittanie, Isaiah's wife. She was the spunky one of the group and made everyone laugh. I could not tell you what position he played, but I knew he was one of the stars on the team and broke a lot of records. It may have been something about a tight end, but that doesn't seem like it makes sense. Who names a football position that?

Sydney was Xavier's girlfriend. He was the kicker. Then there was Lisa, Marc's wife. Marc was Theo's best friend growing up. He did not play football. Devin, his other childhood best friend, did not have a significant other, nor did Briggs, the rookie on the team.

Lacey sat on one side of me and Bailey on the other. Having Bailey here was comforting. She always fit into whatever situation she was in. Not that I didn't, because it was part of our training as professionals, but in this situation, I had a vested interest in being accepted. I worried about these people being annoyed at how much their lives were all going to blow up by being seen or associated with me, and she just got to be here as my friend.

We sat outside in the balmy Florida evening. No matter that it was November, it was almost warm enough to swim in the massive pool feet from us. A water feature made it sound like waves at the beach, and I loved it. Everything about Teddy's house felt cozy despite it being a mansion. It felt right being here, and it wasn't lost on me how quickly that happened. With always being on the road and in different locations for many reasons, home was a hard word. It was more a feeling than a place.

"You're being quiet over there," Sydney said, and the attention shifted to me. For the time we had been out here, it was nice to just blend in and soak in their conversation.

I smiled. "I'm just taking it all in. It's really nice to be here with all of you. Thank you for including me."

"I'm going to go there," Brittanie said, indicating both me and Bailey. "I've been holding it in this whole time. I cannot believe you are both here right now, sitting with us. Like, we meet a lot of famous people being around the guys, but . . ."

The girls laughed. "Go ahead," Lacey said. "Freak out. Fangirl like I did when I went into her box at halftime. Then I got over it and realized they're normal girls like the rest of us, just with a face everyone in the world knows."

Brittanie looked at Sydney and then Lisa. All at the same time, they stood up and screamed, jumping up and down like they were in the front row of my concert. Bailey and I grinned at each other.

Within seconds, the back door opened, and Theo stepped out. All noise immediately stopped. "You okay?" He looked right at me like no one else was out here. Everyone watched as he walked up to me, his brow knit with concern. I wanted to ask him what could possibly have happened to me in his heavily guarded house with my security outside, but I didn't because his immediate concern for my safety made me swoon.

"Yes," I said. "We were just having a girl moment." I looked over at them, now settled back in their seats like they were chastised by their parent. They watched our exchange in silence.

He leaned down over me in the chaise I lounged in and nuzzled my neck, his arms wrapping around my head gently. "You scared me," he said, his voice low and heard only by me.

I leaned into him and reached my hand up to the side of his face. I breathed in his scent. There was just something so —manly—about the way he smelled. I also loved touching him. I had never dated anyone with facial hair before, and I was obsessed with it. Maybe I was just obsessed with him. "Just being silly with the girls."

I felt his smile on my neck, and he stood up and ran his fingers through my hair. I fought the urge to groan. "Glad to hear it. You all take care of my girl. Have fun, but not too much fun." He pulled my hair to tip my head back and pressed a kiss to my lips before returning to the house.

When the door closed, mayhem ensued.

"Holy shit," Brittanie said. "That was so hot." She fanned herself, and the rest of the girls laughed.

"That man is so gone for you," Bailey said, and the rest of the girls nodded. Butterflies erupted in my stomach because I was just as gone for him. And with the nature of our relationship and the level of honesty we had with each other, I knew it wouldn't be long until I told him just how deep I was in.

"*My girl?* I have known Theo for many years, even when he was with the one that will not be named," Lacey said, "and that Theo is a different man."

"I have to agree. How long have you been talking?" Lisa asked.

"Since July," I said. "Well, kind of. Officially talking since September."

"Back when he went to your concert?"

I laughed. "Yes, but before the concert, my ex broke up with me while I was onstage rehearsing. I ran backstage and literally ran full steam into Theo. He helped me back to my dressing room. Later, he came for the concert and had a jersey and a note sent to my dressing room."

"Wait. That guy Josiah you were with for five years dumped you *on the opening night of your tour*? *Over the phone?*" Brittanie's mouth hung open.

I knew this was new for them because it wasn't public knowledge. It helped that every person in this house had signed an NDA before tonight, but also, I knew they wouldn't spread it. There was a girl code with the women.

"Yes. We broke up months before we actually broke the story to the public. It's just how things are done in our world." I looked over at Bailey and she nodded in agreement.

"What an asshole. Who does that?" Lisa said.

"We weren't meant to be," I said. "Was it shitty? Absolutely. We were together for a long time. But what I have come to realize since then is, the amount of time you know someone doesn't matter; it's the strength of your relationship. We were obviously not strong, but he wasn't willing to do the work to be with me. I have learned a lot over my years of dating, and now I know exactly what I want and what things I will and will not accept in my partner. Josiah did me a favor."

"I'd say," Brittanie said, indicating inside, "that you found exactly what you want."

I smiled, that feeling back in my stomach. "I will tell you all this," I said, and they leaned forward, hanging on my every word. I didn't feel like Allie Witt right now. I just felt like Mallorie—Mallie—a girl dishing about boys with her friends. "I have never felt the way I feel right now. Ever. This may sound corny—and maybe it is, but it's also true. I've spent my life writing lyrics about love. For the first time, I feel like I am living those lyrics."

The girls blinked at me for a few seconds, and I thought maybe I'd gone too far. I admitted too much. But then Brittanie sniffled, and then Sydney.

"That was the most beautiful thing I've ever heard," Lacey said, dabbing her eyes. "Shit, Allie. This is why you're so successful. You are damn good with words. Make sure you tell Theo that. For real."

I sipped my wine, momentarily embarrassed that I let that much slip, but then I stopped myself from fixating on that. I was in a safe place here. I felt it. "I plan to. Oh, and you guys can call me Mallie if you want to."

"Mallie?" Brittanie asked.

"My real name is Mallorie. That's what my family calls me. But Theo came up with Mallie, and I like it. So, since we are friends now, you can call me that, too, if you want to."

"You think of us as friends? Excuse me, I'm not done fangirling," Sydney said, and the group laughed. "No, but seriously. Thank you for letting us into your world. I know it can't be easy to trust people, and I think I speak for all of us when I say we appreciate it. If we can do anything to make any of this easier for you, please let us know." The women all nodded, and I fought the urge to shed tears at how happy I felt at that moment.

"What do you call Theo?" Lacey asked.

I thought of my favorite thing about Theo—the way he

wrapped himself around me and made me feel like not only the most important person in the world but the safest and most protected. "Teddy."

"Aw, like his T-Bear nickname," Brittanie said. "You guys are too cute. It's so nice to see him like this. That bitch did such a number on him. He loved her, but none of us were sold. Turns out, we were right."

"Yeah, we both have had some doozies," I said.

"Where are you headed next on tour?" Sydney asked. "I'd love to see a show of yours sometime."

"Atlanta," I said. "Not too bad travel-wise. I play there for two weekends and then come home around Christmas. I think I'm going to attempt to catch the game on Christmas if my security team can get it together."

"I'm sure that is a whole ordeal," Lacey said.

I laughed. "I am a whole production, but it's necessary, unfortunately. I wish I could feel safe everywhere, but there are a lot of unhinged people out there who think I'm married to them."

"Seriously?" Brittanie's eyes widened.

"Sadly, yes," I said. "Most people are just nosy or want autographs and pictures. But all it takes is one crazy, and there have been many that try to get into my house, or my car, or run at me when I'm walking somewhere. My security literally carries emergency medical equipment." I looked around at their shocked faces. "Sorry, that may be too much for our first gathering."

"No," Sydney said. "Don't be sorry." She indicated the other women. "I'm sure we're all thinking the same thing—that it is terrible that you have to deal with that." They nodded in agreement.

"Thanks. It's part of the life I have, and I wouldn't give up the rest because of that. I have a great security team, and most of the time, I feel incredibly safe. I just can't ever let my guard down because it could literally mean the difference between life and death."

"I'm sure it makes Theo furious to even think about someone trying to get to you," Lacey said.

"It does. He actually met with my security team to hear about their procedures. When he's with me, he wants to take the lead. When he heard about the incidents that have happened over the years, I thought his eyes were going to bug out of his head and he was going to run through a wall or something."

Brittanie sighed. "These men of ours are extremely protective, but I can definitely see that Theo would take that to another level with the life you have. It's just his nature to protect people."

"On a happier note, I'll share my schedule with you guys, and you let me know when you want to come to a show and I'll make it happen."

"Really?" Sydney said. "Thank you! I would love to see your show."

"When is Theo going to a show?" Lacey asked. "I'm sure whenever he can make it work is when I can go and bring Spencer. Maybe we can all go."

"Teddy says that it depends on the playoff schedule and if it looks like they'll make it to the championship. I can't even believe I know this information. A few months ago, I couldn't tell you a single thing about football." We all laughed. "But there are two weeks off in between playoff games where he—and I guess the rest of the guys—could possibly travel then. The only major downside to that is that I'm in London, so it's a lot of travel time."

"London!" Brittanie yelled. "I've always wanted to go to London! Group trip to see Mallie in London!"

"YES!" they chorused, and I couldn't help but smile. They made me feel so wanted, and despite us talking about them coming across the pond to my sold-out show, normal.

"So, do we hope for or against a championship?" I asked, and the girls gasped.

"We don't speak of that," Brittanie whispered, "it's bad luck."

"Angel," Teddy whispered in my ear. His large hand splayed on my stomach, our bodies flush with each other's.

After everyone left, we immediately went to the bedroom and took the time we didn't take in the bathroom earlier to be happy we were with each other again. We also apparently took a little snooze because he just woke me up. I wasn't sure which thing I liked better, him calling me Mallie or him calling me angel. But hearing angel in that sexy I-just-woke-up-and-have-sex-on-the-brain voice with his beard tickling my ear and his giant dick pressed into my ass? Yeah. Straight to the lady parts.

"Teddy," I said back, lacing my fingers with his. He lifted them and kissed my hand before settling our hands on my naked body. I wriggled back against him. I could not ever get enough of sex with him. I was twenty-nine years old. I'd had plenty of sex in my life, and I loved it. But it was a damn good thing I never knew it could be like this because it didn't matter how many times now I'd had sex with Teddy. Every time was better than the time before, and it was seriously like our bodies were made for each other from day one. It also helped that both of our love languages were touch, because I didn't want a single bit of space between us ever, and he agreed.

"I didn't get to tell you this before, but thank you. Thank you for coming to my game today, enduring the media spectacle and letting me claim that you're mine. I have had a lot of moments in my career when I have felt like I've made it, but seeing you up in that box tonight? Seeing you around the dinner table with my family and friends? I've never felt that feeling before."

I turned my body so I faced him, my heart pounding. I tilted my face up so I could see him, and he looked down at me. The room was dark except for a light in his bathroom shining into the room, enough that we could see each other. I kissed him softly, our tongues finding each other's. I wrapped my leg around him and pulled him close to me, channeling every feeling I had into it. It made no sense. I never thought I'd be ready this fast after someone I thought I loved crushed me into a million pieces.

But then Teddy happened, and all of a sudden, nothing—and no one—else mattered.

"Today was one of the best days of my life," I said, running my hand along his biceps to his hand. Our fingers twined together and I squeezed. "The media circus is nothing I'm not used to, so that doesn't even register on today's scale. Do you know what was the best? Seeing you do what you love. Being there with your family and friends and being accepted. Feeling like just a girl seeing her boyfriend play his game. And tonight? After the game? Around the table with them? Outside by the pool with the girls? My heart felt like it may explode with happiness. I've never felt so comfortable with people as fast as I did them. They really went out of their way to make me feel included."

Teddy smiled a slow, Cheshire cat smile that brought his dimples out. His eyes sparkled in the dim light, and the slight creases around his eyes showed me his pleasure with what I said. "Mallie. Hearing the word *boyfriend* out of your mouth does something to me."

My heart rate increased with the tone of his voice. He smoothed my hair back, his thumb caressing my cheek as he stared down at me. My breathing intensified, and I had this feeling I couldn't quite describe in my stomach.

"We have both had pasts," he continued. "Ones where we

thought the person we were with was going to be forever, only to find out in the worst possible way that they weren't the right one for us. We have had heartbreak and pain and wondered why we couldn't find what seemed so easy for others. We are both successful in our careers but have struggled with finding someone that we could connect to on all levels of our lives. I have struggled with how to voice this to you because I definitely do not have a way with words like you. I've also struggled with the timing of it. Because it has been my one goal in all of this to not scare you away or do something that will make you regret giving me a chance. I'm thankful every single day for getting the chance to know you and for you to trust me. I'm old enough to know what I want, and I don't want to waste time wondering if the time is right."

He took a deep breath, and I knew. I knew by the look in his eyes. By the way his hand shook a little as he continued to caress my cheek and by the timbre of his voice.

He pressed his lips to mine briefly, unspoken feelings passing between us like we were opening the floodgates and holding nothing back anymore.

"Mallorie, I just can't stop from telling you. I have wanted to tell you for longer than I probably should admit."

I swore my heart stopped beating and my lungs ceased to take in oxygen, waiting for what he said next, even though I felt it throughout my entire body.

"I forced myself to wait," he said, "until I knew you were ready for us to be 'out there' with the world, but I've known that I've loved you for a while. I have never been more sure about anything in my life. I don't need more time or some certain milestone to happen. There is nothing I want more than to show you and tell you that every single day. I want it all. I want the good, the bad, and the in-between. I want the successes, the challenges and the road bumps of life. I. Love. You."

Tears filled my eyes and I nodded, the lump in my throat keeping me from responding immediately. "Teddy," I said, my voice cracking. "You should really stop saying you aren't good with words," I said, "because you *are*. You're everything to me. Despite me thinking I wasn't ready and that I couldn't possibly love someone again so quickly, I do. I love you. I love you more desperately than I have ever loved anyone in my life. You have shown me what true love is. I have written about it my entire life but never really knew what any of that meant until you. I have never felt this way about anyone. Ever."

He leaned his forehead against mine, and we breathed each other in. I allowed the emotion welling in my eyes to spill over. As the tears tracked down my face, our gazes met again. "I told the girls tonight I had never felt this way about anyone before, and I mean it. I have also known that I've loved you for quite a while. I just couldn't believe it was possible."

"You told the girls that?" His voice was thick with emotion.

"I did. I told them that I've spent my life writing lyrics about love, and for the first time, I finally feel like I'm living it. They told me to make sure I told you that, and so, there you go." We looked at each other for a moment, processing all that hung around us. I felt . . . lighter. Free. And so fucking loved. He *loved* me. Me. And I knew without a shadow of a doubt that it wasn't a line. I could *feel* it. Our connection was so strong. Reinforced by hours and hours of heart-to-heart conversations and the honesty we'd promised each other from the beginning. I knew that he was for real. He rolled us so I was lying on his chest, and he stroked my hair. I wrapped my leg around his and traced his pecs with my fingers. This was literal heaven right here. I never wanted to leave.

"Did you really say it back?" he asked a few moments

later. "Am I dreaming again?" I lifted my head and rested my chin on his chest. He smiled at me.

"I love you," I said again. Tears filled my eyes without warning and slid down my cheeks, splashing on his chest. My chest heaved with the emotion swirling inside me, and I couldn't stop it if I tried.

"Hey," he said. "Why the tears?" He wiped under my eyes with his thumbs, his gentle caress making my tears flow faster. "Angel, talk to me."

I sniffled, trying but failing to control the emotion welling up in me. "I-I don't want to leave you," I cried. I felt ridiculous, but it was true. I loved him. He loved me. It felt so unfair that we had to be away from each other for so long. "I know it's ridiculous—"

"Angel," he interrupted. "It is not ridiculous." He reached down and pulled me on up so our faces were lined up. I loved how strong this man was. "I love you so fucking much, Mallie, and I wish we never had to leave each other again, but we both know we wouldn't be happy that way. We are who we are because of the passion we have for our careers. But that doesn't mean I don't wish I could keep you in this little bubble forever. Now let me show you how much I love and cherish you and turn that sadness into euphoria."

CHAPTER 14
Theo

DECEMBER

"Nolan," a reporter called out. I turned, recognizing him as Sam Wright, one of the top sports journalists who often covered our games. Spencer sat next to me, and I could feel his attention on me as he waited for the question.

We already knew that most of these questions would be directed at me, as they had been for several weeks now. The guys took it well, not giving me too much shit for my dating life taking precedence over our game. Thankfully they liked her a lot and understood that this attention came with being associated with her.

"Good to see you, Sam," I said. It was press day before our Christmas away game, and I was pumped. We were ready to clinch this game and move on to the playoffs. I had a feeling about this one. That, and Mallie was coming. One month without seeing her was torture at this point. Sure, we spent an ungodly amount of time on the phone and video chat, but I needed to touch her and love her. It was the way our lives would more than likely always go, so I had to get used to it, but that didn't mean I had to like it. Would I rather this than having never met her? Yes. One million percent. I couldn't fathom my life without her at this point.

"You've gotten a lot of press in the last month," he started, and I smiled. I had my own PR team, of course, led by Jamie, but we'd spent a lot of time with Zoey and Mallie's team in the last month, discussing what information to give out and how to talk about us without releasing a lot of information. Mallie was familiar with this, but I definitely wasn't used to the shift in attention. No one had asked me during a game press conference about my dating life after the debacle of Beth had died down. Now, though, our names were front-page news and in just about every post on social media from major news outlets.

While Mallie was quiet on her social media for obvious reasons, she was okay with me giving out tidbits about us, saying she trusted me. No pressure there. Every clip where they asked me about her had been shared and commented on all over every single social media site and news outlet. I read comments at first and laughed at the way my facial features, tone of voice, and even the "sparkle in my eye" were analyzed. But then, when people started getting sick of seeing it blasted everywhere, I stopped reading because it got ugly sometimes and I wasn't about having that negative energy around me.

"I sure have," I said, "but I'm here to win this game and not worry about the rest."

Sam nodded. I liked him and knew he wouldn't be disrespectful like some, so I was glad he was the first to talk today. Some of the questions over the last month have been interesting, to say the least. "What's it like to be thrust into a much bigger spotlight now that you are dating Allie Witt?"

Dating Allie Witt. God, I loved those words. I wasn't just dating Allie; I loved her. She loved me. But none of that needed to be shared. I grinned, unable to help my natural reaction anytime her name was brought up. The press ate that up, too, reporting on my facial expressions and slight blush anytime I was asked about her since she showed up to the Thanksgiving game. I was used to these questions now, but I still loved hearing her name with mine. And I didn't care what they said about my face. I didn't try to hide my feelings.

"It's nice to see new fans of the Blaze," I said, referring to but not naming the Allie-Cats, who had taken a vested interest in watching games since she showed up to my Thanksgiving game. In the three games we'd had since, the viewership increased significantly, even though they knew she wouldn't be there since she was back on tour. The documentary I was on with Spencer had also been number one for the last several weeks.

"Allie has a lot of people that care about her, and for good reason. She's an amazing person and performer with a sold-out international show. The additional spotlight doesn't bother me. The more fans to watch us win it all, the better." The press laughed, as did my teammates on the panel.

"Rumor has it that Allie will make an appearance this weekend at the game," Sam continued. They knew she was on a break for Christmas, so it was assumed she would come.

"I'm not sure what her plans are yet," I said, which was a lie. Of course I knew she was coming. The plans for that had been in the works since she came to the first game. But the frenzy around her and what she may wear and who she may be seen with would have to stay just that until she showed up. "She's extremely busy right now on tour, but of course I love her support."

"Will you be supporting her at a concert once your season is over?"

"Right now, all I can focus on is the game in front of me and getting to the playoffs. I would love to be able to go with her on tour, but that hasn't been determined yet." Another lie. The plans for my trip with her to London were already in progress. If we made the playoffs, we had a break that week, and if we didn't, I'd be done for the season. There wasn't much that could keep me from going with her that week, and it seemed several of the guys and their girls were going, too.

"What do you say to the people that say she's going to distract you from the game?" Another reporter piped up, and I fought to school my face. I hated this narrative going around on social media right now. This girl pumped me up. A *distraction*? It annoyed the shit out of me.

"I say that I'm not the one up here asking you questions about who you're dating instead of the football game, so I'd say the media is the one making it like this is a distraction. Allie and I both have busy lives, and we both support each other in our careers. She has done nothing but add to my life." My answer may have been a little too curt, and I knew it would be everywhere, but I kind of hoped it shut them up.

"You guys here ready to talk about the game?" Spencer interrupted, right on schedule.

The group laughed and the focus switched to him. I listened as the questions shifted to the game and the preparation for the playoffs if we won, but my mind was on Mallie. I knew she'd arrive tomorrow just a few hours before the game with Lacey, Brittanie, and Sydney in tow.

I also knew she was bringing her mom. I wouldn't be able to see her prior to the game starting, but I'd know she was there. Afterward, I could have a little bit of time with her before we had to get back on the plane to head home, but it wasn't enough. Then again, it never was. After this, I wasn't sure if I'd see her until London, and that made me sad. But this was the reality of both of our lives, and I'd take a little of her over not having her at all.

Thankfully, the press conference was over not long after that, and we filed out together to go to practice.

"Thanks for the deflection," I said to Spencer.

He shook his head. "They're ruthless, but you handle them like a pro. You think they'd be done asking you about it at this point, but Allie's name is big business. Did you see the sales of our merch since she came to the game and outed you both?"

"I did. It's pretty wild but awesome, too. I don't think they're going to stop anytime soon. As long as there's a chance she shows up, and when she does show up, it just fuels them to keep talking about it. Just imagine that what they say to me is just a fraction of what they'd ask Allie if she'd allow it. I got designated the official media person. I'm fine with it. I don't mind at all talking about us. I'm just happy there is an us."

"She's good for you, man. You two are great together. Lacey is so excited to get to spend time with her this weekend," Spencer said. "Despite how busy Allie is, she has kept in touch with Lacey quite a bit."

"Brittanie, too," Isaiah piped up, joining us. "I think she may be more in love with Allie than you are."

I laughed. "Not possible, but she is loving the friendship with the girls. She says, and I quote, that they make her 'feel normal.'"

"I don't think Sydney has shut up about her for the last month," Xavier said. "Thanks for dating a woman that the girls actually like this time."

I shoved him as we walked into the locker room, and we all laughed. To say they tolerated Beth was an understatement. "Glad I can make you all happy with my choice of a woman."

"Just don't fuck it up," Isaiah said.

"Trying really hard not to," I answered.

"Hey, good job up there," Briggs said, walking up to us. "They just love to ask you about Allie."

I shrugged. "It comes with the territory. As long as they stay respectful, I don't mind one bit talking about her. I'd shout from the rooftops how I feel about her."

Briggs studied me. I knew he showed an interest in Bailey,

and they'd spoken briefly at my house during the Thanksgiving meal, but he had been uncharacteristically quiet about it since then. For a moment, we had a silent conversation as the other guys walked away to get ready for practice.

"You good?" I didn't want to push him, but I wanted him to know I was there if he needed me. Briggs wasn't usually a quiet guy, so it was unlike him to not tell me if things were progressing with Bailey or if he had shot his shot and she denied him.

"You handle it so well," he said. "I'm not sure I could do it."

I contemplated my answer. "When it's worth it, you will handle whatever you need to handle. You've been quiet, and I haven't pushed, but you're acting kinda like you want me to push you right now, so I'm going to ask. Have you been talking to Bailey?"

He crossed his arms over his chest. "She's kind of brushing me off."

"What do you mean?"

"I thought we hit it off pretty well that night at your house. Enough that she gave me her number. We talked several other times since then, and it felt like maybe there was something there. But she's kind of ghosted me."

"Is she busy, Briggs?"

He shrugged. "I mean, probably. But seeing how much you talk to Allie, and she's coming to see your second game while she's in the middle of touring, it just showed me that maybe Bailey isn't actually into me."

"If she gave you her number, and she's talked to you, I wouldn't assume that, but you have to talk to her. The best thing I did with Allie was be honest with her from the beginning. Was it scary? Sure. But it also kept us from wasting each other's time by playing games. If you want this with her, you have to put it out there."

Briggs nodded. "I wish she was coming with Allie."

"How do you know she's not?" Allie hadn't said that she was, but that didn't mean Bailey wouldn't show up.

"I guess I don't, but I thought maybe she'd tell me if she was."

"Briggs. Text her or call her and ask if she can. Maybe she doesn't know if you want her here. You have to put yourself out there, man."

"Thanks, Theo." Briggs walked back to his locker and picked up his phone. I shook my head. I guessed this was what life experience and age did for you—I didn't want a question in my mind—or Allie's—of how we felt about each other.

―――

I'm here. Two little words in a simple text that made my heart skip a beat. I grinned at my phone screen, the chaos of the locker room around me not even registering.

It wasn't that I didn't know she was on her way—it just made me happy to confirm she'd made it safely and was inside the stadium. Today was a huge game—and I would put every bit of my focus on it—but I gave myself a few minutes to focus on the happiness that I got to see her today after a month.

I'm so glad you're here. I miss you so much. I can't wait to hold you and kiss you.

The bubble popped up, indicating her response. *Baby, you and me both. It's taking everything I have to not run through this building and find you so I can do just that.*

Baby was new. I liked it.

Don't tempt me, I wrote. *I love you, angel. I will see you right after we kick some ass and make it to the playoffs.*

I love you. Seeing those words would never get old. I still couldn't believe it, even though we said it freely and often.

"Nolan!" Coach screamed, and I shoved the phone into my bag.

"Coming!" I said, striding across the room.

"You ready?" Spencer said, slapping my back.

"Beyond ready," I answered. "It's time to put this thing away."

"Is she here?" Spencer asked.

I nodded. "Just arrived."

"Good," Spencer said. "That means all the girls are here safely. Now we can focus on getting this job done. Let's go over some plays before we head out for warm-ups."

"You're going to the playoffs!" Allie jumped into my arms the second I walked into the suite to get her after the game. I breathed her in, my face buried in her neck. I wrapped my arms around her and she held my face, pressing her lips against mine.

I thought briefly about the cameras probably directed right at us, but I didn't care. The rest of the suite was also in chaos, the other girls greeting the guys and mayhem happening.

It was a hard-fought game, and I was exhausted and sore. My elbow bled, and I tweaked my knee. But nothing felt better than having Allie in my arms. The pain from the game and the stress of it being closer than we wanted it to be melted away the moment I saw her.

"Mallie," I whispered into her ear. She tilted her head and I felt her grin. She loved when I whispered into her ear and my beard tickled her. Just like she loved when I kissed from her ear, along her neck, and down her naked body. God, I couldn't wait to do that. "I missed you, angel. You look so fucking beautiful."

She was the most beautiful woman I'd ever seen in my

life, and it didn't matter if she was wearing nothing in my bed—my preferred version—or glammed up on the stage; she made me weak in the knees. Tonight, she wore a pair of black leather pants, black boots, and an off-the-shoulder Blaze vintage T-shirt. Her hair was in a cute ponytail, and her makeup accentuated that gorgeous face. She wore a necklace with the Blaze logo I'd sent her from a local shop, then some others that were hers.

She cupped her hand over her mouth and leaned up to my ear. "I had a lot of fun watching you tonight, but you look so fine that I cannot wait to be alone. I need to fuck you like yesterday." She leaned back and looked me in the eyes, and the lust I saw there had me wishing I had a damn helicopter in the parking lot.

"You're fucking killing me," I whispered. I put my lips back on her ear. "I'm going to start the night off by fucking you so hard you see stars because I need you like I need my next breath, and these pants are fucking torturing me. But after that, I'm going to take it slow and give you so many orgasms you'll be screaming my name, angel."

I felt and heard her sharp intake of breath. She ran her hands up and down my back. "I love you, baby," she said.

My heart skipped a beat. "I love you, too, sweet girl. I am so glad you're here."

"Hey," Spencer interrupted, Lacey standing with him. "Good to see you again, Allie. Did you enjoy the game?"

"I did," she said. "They make it a lot of fun." She indicated the girls standing around the suite.

"You guys ready?" Allie asked. Was I ready? No, not really, because that meant saying goodbye to her for a few more hours. Since we weren't at home, we had to travel with the team to Florida. She was flying herself and the girls back and we planned to meet at my house. She would stay two days and then fly out to her next stop, and then I wouldn't see her again until London. Now that we made the playoffs, it would be tight, but I'd make it. If we got to the championships at the end, she could be there, but that remained to be seen if we made it that far. It would be a busy few months.

I reached out for her hand, and she indicated to her security that we were on the move. She had a team of five with her tonight, a few that were hired for the stadium only, and then Juan and Rico as usual. I nodded to them in greeting. My parents were not able to make the game tonight, which I understood since it was Christmas and an away game. I'd catch up with them after Mallie left. The next two days were solely for her. I had some gifts for her, and I wanted to be with her alone. My family and friends understood.

The second the door to the suite opened, the volume increased significantly. People shrieked Allie's name, and her grip tightened on my hand as we stepped into the hallway. I glanced at her out of the corner of my eye and saw her face frozen into what I could only describe as the celebrity face—eyes wide, smile fixed, her head held high and her shoulders back.

She knew she would be videotaped and pictures would be everywhere of the two of us. She made eye contact and smiled as we continued to walk, security indicating for people to step back or move. A few times, she waved at fans, and the volume increased significantly when they realized she had acknowledged them.

I heard my name a few times, but I followed Allie's lead and just continued to smile and walk. When we reached the elevator, a worker from the stadium held it open for our approaching group. A young girl, probably no more than ten years old, held a sign up over her head. She stood with what must be her parents. She yelled Allie's name while jumping up and down in excitement. Allie turned her head and stopped as she saw the sign, and the rest of us halted with her.

The sign read *I'm Your #1 Allie-Cat* with pictures of her at several of Allie's concerts, from the time she was a toddler until recently. When the girl noticed that Allie saw her, she stopped jumping and stared, her mouth open. Allie had a silent conversation with Juan and Rico, and she stepped closer to the little girl. I followed, and that was when I noticed she was decked out head to toe in all of Allie's *Lovestruck* merch. She even wore the Allie-Cat symbol on a necklace.

"Hi!" Allie said to her, and I couldn't help but smile at the expression on the girl's face. She looked like she might pass out at any moment. "I love your sign! What's your name?"

The little girl blinked and looked over at me and then back to Allie. A woman I assumed was her mom reached over and put her hands on the girl's shoulders, and she kind of snapped out of it. "I'm Eliza." She put her hand over her mouth, and tears filled her eyes. "I can't believe you stopped to say hi to me. I have loved you since I was so little I didn't even know what music was. I want to be a singer someday, just like you."

"It's true," the woman interjected. "I've been a fan of yours since your first album, and I played the music constantly for her when I was pregnant. Ever since Eliza was a baby, she calmed down only to your music. She was only two when I took her to her first concert. She wore headphones and soaked in every single second of it."

Allie indicated Juan, who handed her a pen without a word. This must be a normal thing. She crouched and signed her name to the sign and then stood up. "Do you want to take a picture?"

Eliza nodded, the tears still falling from her eyes. "I love you so much, Allie."

"I love you too, sweetie! I hope you always work for your dreams. If you want to be a singer like me, then do everything you can to make that happen. It's the best job ever because of fans like you." Eliza's mom took a few pictures and then got in the photo with her while her husband took another.

"Can Theo be in a picture too?" she asked. "He's my favorite player. You guys are so cute together. I can't believe you're really a couple. It's like a dream come true."

Allie turned her head and looked at me. I read slight panic in her expression, wondering whether I wanted this attention or not. But what she didn't realize was I would do anything and everything with her and for her. I nodded and stepped into the frame.

"Hey, I'm her dad! I want in on this one," Eliza's dad said, and we all laughed.

I shook his hand and noticed he wore one of my jerseys. Lacey took their phone and snapped a few pictures, and I signed his jersey.

"Nice to meet you guys," Allie said. She hugged Eliza and whispered something to her, then hugged her mom as well. She waved as we walked away, and I put my arm around her shoulders and pulled her to me. The elevator doors closed, and she leaned back against me.

"That was the best thing I've ever seen," I whispered into her hair, kissing the side of her head. "You just made that girl's entire life. You're the best human being I've ever known." She tilted her face and looked up at me and I kissed her lips. "I love you, Mallie. So damn much."

CHAPTER 15

Allie

JANUARY

I rolled over in bed and picked up my phone to see what time it was. The sun had just barely peeked in through the curtains of my hotel room, and my phone said it wasn't even six in the morning here in London, but I knew I wouldn't go back to sleep despite the long day ahead. I would have to caffeinate and hope for the best.

Teddy would be here very soon. I smiled as I unlocked my phone and went right to his message. He and the whole crew of friends were coming on my second plane and would arrive any minute. I had other messages, which I assumed were from the girls, but I needed a moment to daydream about Teddy's.

I cannot wait to kiss your face (and many other things). We will land in about an hour, I think.

He'd sent the message about an hour ago. I snuggled down into the comforter and kicked my feet. I loved this man so damn much. Did I ever feel this way with Josiah? With anyone? It was hard to remember anything before Teddy, and honestly I didn't want to. None of that mattered anymore.

I touched my fingers to my lips, in disbelief that I would

actually see him soon and get to feel his lips on mine and touch his beard with my fingertips. Since I spent two days with him at Christmas, it had felt like the longest month of my life. We hadn't left his house for those two days, spending the days in his bed, drinking coffee around the Christmas tree, talking until all hours, and exchanging gifts. He had gotten me the most beautiful diamond bracelet and matching earrings that I planned to wear at my show tonight, and I had gotten him a new set of cutlery that was apparently the best brand for chefs. He had loved them and kissed me a hundred times for them, so I guessed I got it right. He then used them to make me the best meal of my life, and I was convinced the man really was perfect.

Since we'd expressed our love for each other, our relationship was on another level. We just got each other in a way I knew I never had before. We talked about real things and consulted each other on decisions and made plans for the near and far future that involved each other. I wasn't afraid to talk about something beyond the next week or two because Teddy was unbothered by everything surrounding us.

How did he handle a guy parked outside of his house with a long lens? Waving to him. What did he do when asked incessant questions about me during his football interviews? Answered them honestly but cryptically, with an adorable smile on his face. What did he think about the press running stories of us getting engaged? He kissed me and told me he loved me. How did he feel about the press unearthing the story with his ex and using it as a reason to say we wouldn't last? He had me remind him just how hot we were together.

After seeing me at the Christmas game and realizing this wasn't a fluke that we were together, the press started to speculate about a ring for Christmas. When that didn't happen, they shifted to him getting on the stage of my concert in London during my song "Lovestruck." If not then, they said it would be after the championship on the field. It was hysterical how quickly they tried to marry me off after dragging me through the mud about Josiah just months ago. There was some conversation about it being too soon and to take the pressure off us, but the stories wouldn't stop. They were ready for him to drop to a knee and propose in a public place.

Believe it or not, we did talk about this, not because I was ready for that at all or thought he was planning it, but because people were so convinced that this would be the best fairy-tale ending to our real-life rom-com playing out for the world to see. However, this sounded like nothing but a nightmare for me, and I told him just that, not that he needed me to.

When we had the conversation, the look of horror on his face told me that he would've never done that to me anyway. I lived my whole life as a public spectacle, and it was bad enough that they watched every single part of our relationship. I definitely did not *ever* want a public proposal. I should've known that Teddy knew me better than that, even without me having to say a word. I had never been more in tune with a person in my entire life.

The story of the little girl and her family that I met after Teddy's Christmas game also ran a few-week cycle all over social media and national news. That at least was a cute story, but the main topic was not that I stopped to sign a poster for a kid or take a picture with her, but that Teddy was in the picture with me with his arm around my shoulders and my arm around his waist. There were conversations about our body language. How long we had really known each other. If I cheated on Josiah with him and whether that was what ended us. What I wore, and if Teddy had gotten me any of it. And how we would spend our first Christmas together.

Then there were photos that the mom shared of Teddy watching me talking to the little girl Eliza. I knew exactly what that look on his face was the second I saw it. The public did, too. It fueled the rumors of marriage and babies for sure.

It gave me butterflies in my stomach when I thought of it, but I also hated the instant assumption that we would get married *or* have kids. It wasn't that I didn't want all of that—I just didn't want it to be the expectation that I did it. When Teddy saw the picture, he told me it made him feel he wanted things he hadn't thought much about in years and that he loved seeing me with kids. He apologized for the drama it caused in the press, but how could I be mad about him looking at me like I was his entire future?

Eliza's mom was even invited on national morning shows to talk about meeting us. She was sweet and I loved seeing it, but it definitely kept the rumors circulating even more. I loved all my fans, but there was something about the kids that really got to me. I loved seeing them as much as I could.

Tonight was my first show out of four in a row in London. I got here a few days ago to rehearse and acclimate to the time change, though I lived in a perpetual state of, *Where in the hell am I?* Teddy and the crew would enjoy a few days in London, sightseeing and being tourists. I sadly could not do that because it would only cause a scene. Teddy mentioned staying back with me, which I felt bad about, but I wouldn't stop him only because I missed him so much. But he'd never been to London, so I wanted him to have fun while he was here and go see all the tourist things.

With his week off between playoffs, the media speculated that he would come, but of course there was no confirmation. However, the press would be extra ruthless once they saw him and the rest of the players and girls. I also knew my plane was probably tracked, so it would be amazing if they made it here without fanfare.

I texted Teddy back that I couldn't wait to see him, and he immediately responded: *Juan just picked us up a few minutes ago. We are en route to you. He says about thirty minutes. Be ready. I need you as much as I need a giant breakfast.*

I grinned at my phone screen. I would order us food once

he was here, but I knew what he wanted first because I wanted the same. I typed a message to Conor to order us food to be delivered in an hour, told Zoey that they all arrived and to arrange for transport for them later to the stadium, and then got up to make myself more presentable.

I looked at myself in the mirror and smiled. My eyes were bright despite being tired. Even with no makeup, my cheeks were flushed. I felt like I had a permanent smile on my face. I hummed one of the new songs I'd written for Teddy, one I hadn't shared with him yet. I brushed my teeth, washed my face, and brushed through my blond curls. I wore an oversized T-shirt from my first sold-out stadium show, my teenage face staring back at me in the mirror.

"If only you knew then what was coming for you," I said out loud. "Many years of the wrong ones. All to get here. You know that song you wrote, 'The Only One,' back when you were eighteen and heartbroken from who you thought was the love of your life? The one that would be one of your career-defining hits? Yeah. Now you know what those lyrics really mean."

I laughed at my naive self, the teenager who thought she knew what love was because she was thrust into the real world so young. Instead, that teenager was stupid and fell for a guy who didn't care about her at all. That stupid teenager had also given that man something she could never take back, and that had given her several years of regret.

I thought back to the songs I wrote with Josiah in mind and cringed. This was the downside to writing with your heart. You had to then reassociate them in your mind. It wasn't the first time, but hopefully it would be the last. I thought of a few of the songs on my set list that were originally meant for him. I played them for the tour, but I basically disassociated while playing them. However, Teddy would be there tonight. This would be the first time he was invited as my boyfriend to my show, and I knew that all the attention would be on us because of it. Might as well make the most of it and show him just what he meant to me. An idea came to me and I ran for my phone, pulling up my voice memo and singing lyrics, melding two songs together and changing key lyrics.

"Yes," I said to myself. "That's it." I walked around the room with my phone, singing. My brain whirled with the possibilities. I would have to talk to the band, give them the changes and updates, but they were used to me. Most of my band had been with me for the better part of my career, and my backup singers and dancers were as close as family to me. We were a well-oiled machine most of the time.

A knock sounded on my door, and I knew it was Rico based on the knock alone. It was the warning that he was about to open the door. But before he could open it, I flung it open. He stepped back quickly, surprised, but all I could see was Teddy. His giant frame filled the door. He wore a black tracksuit with the Blaze logo on it and carried a suitcase. His beard was neatly trimmed, and his eyes laser-focused on me.

He immediately stepped into the room and kicked the door shut. I squealed as he grabbed me and lifted me, crushing his body to mine as his luggage fell to the floor. I wrapped my body around his as he held me off the ground, burying his head in my neck.

"Thank you, Rico!" I called to the closed door, my giggles being silenced by the goosebumps taking over my body. Teddy walked us to the king-size bed visible in the open-concept room, his lips blazing a path from my neck to my lips and back again.

"I love you," he said into my neck. "God, I missed you so much." He lifted his head and looked at me, and I smiled, my heart skipping a beat at the look on his face. My body slid down his until my feet touched the ground, but we left no space between us.

"I love you," I said, my hands on his face, the short hairs

of his beard making me weak in the knees. "I have missed you so damn much. That was definitely too long. I need you, Teddy." Our lips met in an urgent kiss, and talking ceased as our tongues took over. My shirt rode up as he gripped my waist, his hands setting my bare skin on fire. I felt him growing against my stomach as we kissed, our kisses more frantic than I could remember them since our first time. This may even be more so because we know how we feel about each other now.

He pulled back and lifted my shirt, leaving me in only a red thong. "Goddamn," he said. "This body is fucking ridiculous. I can't be slow with you right now, even though I want to taste every part of you. I just need you too fucking bad."

"I need you just as bad," I said. I unzipped his jacket, and he helped shrug it off his shoulders. Next to go was his T-shirt and shoes. I ran my hand down his chiseled chest until I got to the waistband of his pants. His dick was at attention and straining the material of his track pants. I slid them down, taking his boxer briefs with them, until we both stood naked in front of each other. I stepped back and put my hands on my hips, looping my thumbs into the string of my underwear. I turned around so he could see the thong up my ass and looked back over my shoulder. He sat on the edge of the bed, stroking his cock as he watched. I bit my lip and moaned at the sight. Fuck, this man was gorgeous.

I played with the strings of the underwear as he watched, captivated by my movements.

"That fucking ass is mine, Mallie. God, it is so beautiful. Turn around and take those off for me, angel."

I turned and played with the straps again. His gaze went from my bare chest down to my small underwear.

"Take them off," he said again, still stroking his cock.

I could watch that forever. I slid them down and kicked them to him. He grabbed them with his other hand and then fisted them around his cock. I slid my hand down my body to my clit and rubbed it, imagining it was his hand.

"I can't," Teddy said, standing up. "I can't wait one more fucking second." He walked us to the full-length mirror against the wall and stood me in front of it. He ran his hands down my body as he watched in the mirror. "I have dreamed of this body for too long." He gripped my hips and tilted me slightly. "Put your hands on the mirror," he said, his voice so low it made me shiver.

I didn't hesitate, so turned on I could barely keep myself from trying to relieve it with my own hand. But I knew what was coming, so I forced myself to watch Teddy in the mirror. He stepped up behind me, and our eyes met in the glass.

"The most beautiful woman in the entire world," he whispered. "And she's mine. What the fuck did I do to deserve this?" He ran his hand along my ass and to my dripping-wet core.

I whimpered, pushing my ass back against him. He smiled at me with those fucking dimples and I groaned. He held my hip and slid himself inside me as we both watched in the mirror. He turned us slightly so I could see him sliding in and out. "Watch," he said, his voice tight. He didn't have to tell me to—I couldn't tear my eyes away from him. "I can't be slow," he said.

"Fuck me," I said in response. His eyes fluttered closed briefly as he gripped my hips, pushing himself harder inside me. I screamed his name and pushed back, taking him fully.

"Mallie," he said. "Fuck, you're made for me. This pussy is mine. You take my cock like such a good girl."

The sounds of our fucking made my eyes roll up in my head. I leaned back against him, and he used one hand on my stomach to push me back harder onto him. I gasped, so full that it almost hurt, but I was too turned on to feel anything other than euphoria. Teddy kept one hand on my stomach, holding me on his cock, and covered my breast with the other, pinching and tweaking my nipple.

I writhed and panted, the sensations so much and not enough all at once. He slid his hand down my body and began playing with my clit.

"FUCK!" I yelled, the orgasm hitting me out of nowhere. Teddy didn't let up, continuing his assault on my senses with his dick and his fingers. My knees buckled and he held me up.

"I'm not done with you yet, angel," he said into my ear. "Look in that mirror and watch me fuck another orgasm out of you and then come inside that pretty pussy."

Our eyes met in the mirror again and I panted as he pistoned himself inside me. My breasts bounced as he picked up the pace. This man—he knew exactly how to work my body to make me come undone over, over, and over again. The grip on my hips was so hard I may have bruises.

"That's it," he said, pulling my hips back even harder. "I feel you tightening on me. I am going to come so hard, but not until I feel you shudder on my cock again. I need your orgasm, angel. Give it to me."

The way Teddy talked dirty to me just did it for me, and I felt it. Before him, I used to think multiple orgasms weren't really a thing. Since him, there has never been a time when I didn't have at least two. If I didn't scream his name, my body going limp like a noodle, then he didn't do his job.

"TEDDY!" I yelled. I felt him pulsing inside me as I careened over the cliff again, my body giving up with the exertion. He lifted me with one arm and placed me on the bed as he finished, still sliding himself in and out slowly as we came down together.

"The best fucking thing that has ever happened to me," Teddy whispered, kissing my shoulder. "I love you, Mallie. My sweet angel."

CHAPTER 16
Theo

MALLIE SAT CROSS-LEGGED, her eyes closed and her fingers on her guitar strings as she worked through her acoustic songs for the night. I watched, transfixed, as she played a few chords, sang, and then stopped.

There were so many things that I loved about this woman, but watching her do this was at the top of the list. I loved music and always had, but as a listener and appreciator, not as someone who could sing a tune at all.

Seeing her do this was like getting national security secrets. It felt illegal and also the most amazing experience. The guys and their girls were out exploring London, and as much as it would be cool to do so, I couldn't leave her. She had her hair piled on top of her head in a bun, as she did when she was writing or practicing. I loved the little pieces of hair that refused to comply when she did that. They curled around her face and neck and were just the cutest things I'd ever seen.

She wore the outfit she'd wear to the stadium in a little bit, a pair of yoga pants and a cutoff shirt. I couldn't stop staring at her, and I wondered if it would always be this way. I was so excited to see her play again tonight. I knew she expected one of her biggest crowds ever in a sold-out stadium, and this time, I would get to watch it from the floor.

I couldn't wait to hear her fans screaming the lyrics back at her. She also told me what to expect as far as the fans with me, and I was excited about that, too. I loved interacting with the Blaze fans, and now her fans were like an extension of that. I was naturally an extrovert, so having people come up to me during the show wouldn't bother me at all.

Zoey and Mallie's mom, or *Mom* as she indicated for me to call her, walked into the room. They both smiled at me and then stood behind me, listening to Mallie sing. I recognized the song, but I definitely had homework to do to learn every single one of her songs. I was determined to do it, though.

When she finished, her angelic voice quieting, she smiled at the three of us. Her gaze locked onto mine and she bit her lip. I knew exactly what would happen right now if we didn't have an audience, but that would have to wait for later.

"You're so fucking talented," I said. "I could literally listen to you forever."

I heard her mom sigh, and I turned to smile at her. She was very vocal about her appreciation for my love of her daughter because I didn't hide it. Why would I? She was the most amazing person in the world.

"Thanks, baby," she said. "I'm playing those tonight so I wanted to just refresh myself before we go over." Mallie looked at Zoey. "Is it time to go?"

Zoey nodded. "If you're ready, yes." I loved how they respected the hell out of her artistry, and even if there was somewhere to be, they made sure she was ready to go. "We've got your stuff packed and in the vehicles. Conor is downstairs already. We're going out the back because there's quite a scene going on in the front."

Mallie smiled and stood up. My eyes immediately went to her fine ass in those yoga pants when she turned to put the guitar in its case. That made me think of taking her from behind in front of the mirror, and I had to look away before I got a hard-on in front of Zoey and Mallie's mom. I knew we didn't get to spend much time together, and that played a factor, but I swore that I would never tire of making love with this woman. She was so responsive, and generous, and also not afraid to say what she liked and how she liked it.

"You ready for this?" she asked me. I wanted to travel with her to the show and go backstage and see her entire experience.

"More than ready," I said. I grabbed Mallie's hand and the guitar case she carried.

"Thanks, baby," she said. I would never tire of that, either. It may be cliché, but I loved her calling me that. I leaned over and kissed her as we walked.

The door opened and Rico appeared. He took the guitar case from me and we headed to the elevator, where three other security guys waited.

"I love you," I whispered. I dropped her hand and put my arm around her shoulders as we entered the elevator, the entourage behind us. I pulled her to me and kissed her head, and she leaned into me.

"I love you, too, Teddy. So much."

There was something unbelievable about the energy in the stadium, waiting for Mallie to come out, but in the best way. I sported my Lovestruck concert tee that I went and got myself when we got here. I may have created a pandemonium and ended up taking pictures and signing autographs for a good hour, but it was fun and I enjoyed it. I also enjoyed seeing Spencer, Xavier, and Isaiah with fans and buying merch to support her.

Of course the girls all got things, too, but they had their

concert outfits picked out a month ago, so they didn't wear them. Each of them was dressed in a different theme, as were most of the concertgoers. Bright colors, sequins, and hearts were abundant. I recalled this from the first concert, but being in the thick of it was different.

We stood inside Mallie's VIP area, which was just off the floor section. We had an amazing view of the stage. Her opener was playing, a young all-girl band up and coming in the music industry. They were good, and I knew being here as an opener for Mallie would be life-changing for them.

Mallie's mom entered the tent, having been out in the crowd handing out hearts before Mallie came out, looking for fans to upgrade to floor seats. She did it at every show. They were little fabric hearts with the Lovestruck logo on them and *Allie Witt* on the back, and fans collected them. They often took pictures with "Mama Witt," as they called her and posted them all over social media.

"Want one?" she asked. I nodded and she put it in my hand. I looked at it and smiled at the memory of Spencer finding one of those behind her cutout at her first show. I didn't know what a treasure it was at the time, but I did now. All I knew was that it was something to remind me of her, and I kept it. It was in my underwear drawer at home. I wasn't sure that I had mentioned that to Mallie before.

I slid it into the pocket of my jeans and smiled. Now I had two. A thought came to me. I needed to collect hearts from each show I went to. Since I planned to be at all her shows this week, I would have five after this. I'd collect them and not tell her until I had a whole drawer full.

"Nice shirt," she said.

"I like it," I responded. "Definitely my color." The shirt was black, but the writing was all pink and had Mallie's face with a neon-pink heart around it and *Lovestruck* above it. I mean, I had no problems at all wearing my girl's face on my shirt. I may sleep in it every night I'm without her.

I pointed to the guys, all standing at the railing with drinks in their hands, vibing to the opener. They had different variations of the shirt on, but all of us represented.

"You guys are amazing," she said. Her phone buzzed and she pulled it out of her pocket. "Looks like I'm needed by the girl of the hour," she joked. "I'll be back."

"Tell her I love her and to kick ass," I said. I knew Mallie didn't have her phone on her before the show, and I told her I loved her an hour ago, but still. It could never be too many times.

She grinned and hugged me, her head only reaching my chest. "Thank you," she said.

"Thank you for?"

"For pursuing her. For showing her that love can be different for her. Hell, for showing all of us that. For loving her out loud and not being afraid for people to know it. For embracing who she is and loving every minute of it."

Well, hell. I didn't think I'd cry today. Tears filled my eyes as I held the older woman. "You don't have to thank me for that. She's worth all of that and more. I'm the lucky one here, and I will never stop being thankful that she gave me the chance to know her, and I will always guard her heart and keep it safe."

She pulled away and patted my chest. "You're the one she's been waiting for her whole life." With that ultimate compliment given, she turned to walk away to go backstage. I turned and Spencer stood next to me.

"Mom's stamp of approval," he said. "That's huge."

"Of course she loves me," I joked. "What's not to love?"

He slapped my back. "I'm so happy for you, man. I can't believe you made this happen." He gestured around him. "This is some wild shit. If you had told me six months ago this would be what we'd be doing, I would've laughed in your face."

"I would've laughed in my face too," I said.

"Can you manifest us winning the championship, too, since you're apparently winning at life?"

I nodded and we turned our attention back to the stage as the music changed and the countdown came on for Mallie to come out. The crowd screamed, and all of us lined the perimeter of the area, ready to watch our girl take the stage.

I held my breath as the countdown turned to zero and the lights started flashing pink. Lacey, Sydney, and Brittanie held on to each other and jumped up and down in full-on fangirl mode. The opening chords to "Lovestruck" pounded through the speakers. Mallie's beautiful voice echoed throughout the stadium, but no one could see her just yet. Deafening screams overtook her for a moment, but then her voice rang out again.

My eyes fixated on the spot where I knew she would come out. Within moments, the stage opened and she appeared in her all-pink glitter bodysuit with her matching pink boots. I held my breath at the sight of her. It wasn't that I hadn't seen it before, but being here, this close to her, seeing her in her element, was something I was not prepared for. She was so fucking beautiful I couldn't stand it.

My heart pounded as I sang along to her headlining song about falling in love quickly and deeply and being so struck by it you couldn't even breathe. *I know how that feels,* I thought, *because you did it to me.* She danced and strutted and killed the vocals in that first song, and the audience knew it. When the song ended, she stood in the middle of the stage, looking around at the audience.

"London! It's so great to be back with you again! You're looking amazing tonight!" The crowd screamed so loud that my ears rang. Mallie looked over at us and I grinned, waving at her like the fool I was. "Did you see I have some extra-special guests tonight?" She pointed at the VIP area, and my mouth dropped open in surprise.

The crowd went wild, and the guys and I held up our

arms in celebration. The girls jumped up and down and screamed again, waving at Mallie. She waved back to them before she looked right at me. I held my gaze with Mallie's and she blew me a kiss. I caught it and put it on my lips, not even caring that the whole world was watching.

"Let's make this show extra special for them tonight, okay, London?" She wiggled her fingers at me one more time, and I blew her a kiss. She held her hand over her heart before she turned to grab her guitar for the next song.

"That was the most romantic thing I've ever seen," Lacey said in my ear. "She really just called you out in front of everyone."

"She did," I said, still shocked.

Mallie sat on a stool, strumming the guitar; the lights focused directly on her. She wore a long white flowing dress, her hair slightly frizzy from hours of dancing and singing.

Sweat dotted her face and neck, and she looked like a fucking angel. The screens around the stadium showed a close-up of her face, and I stared at those big blue eyes, so expressive and full of emotion. This was the last set of her show and her favorite part. This was the part where she would sing what I watched her practice earlier.

I swayed back and forth as she played notes, watching as she looked out over the audience. "This has been such a special night for me and the band," she said, her voice thick. "I want you to know that I never take for granted being able to do this and that you care about my music. It is my lifeline to write and sing songs, and it's a bonus that you guys like it, too."

The crowd screamed and cheered, and I felt myself getting choked up. This woman.

"God, I love her," Brittanie said from beside me, wrapping her arm around mine and leaning against it. I loved the relationship I had with my best friends' women. They were like sisters to me. I nodded in agreement but didn't take my eyes off the vision on the stage.

She began singing the lyrics I heard earlier, and I mouthed the words, not wanting my off-key voice to detract from her. The audience sang along quietly, soaking in her voice as it reverberated across the stadium. Tears welled up in my eyes as I felt the emotion of the crowd. Mallie was not just a talented vocalist, guitarist, and pianist—she was a masterful lyricist and really knew how to make people feel every word of her songs. I felt Brittanie sniffling next to me and saw Sydney and Lacey holding on to each other as they sang quietly.

The song ended, and Mallie smiled out at the crowd. "The best part is hearing you sing along with me," she said. "Do you have it in you for one more song tonight?"

The crowd cheered and she got down off the stool and walked to the piano. She began playing keys, and I tried to figure out what she played. I had listened to her play so many nights over the phone, and I liked trying to guess the songs and challenging myself to see how many I could get right.

"I have a surprise for you since you've been so great." Cheers erupted. "I would like to play you something I've never played before," she said, and the crowd went wild. "But not only have I never played it before, you can't sing along this time."

Murmurs went through the crowd. I had no idea what she was doing. The girls turned to me and I shrugged.

"I have been working on a new album, and I'm not quite ready to give you the title yet. I just wrapped up recording this song. This isn't really how I usually do things, but I just can't stop myself from doing it. I told you earlier I have special guests with me tonight, and I do, but this one is for the one that is the most special, wearing my face on his chest in the VIP area and singing along to all of my songs. One who took time out of his busy schedule to fly all the way here to see me. One that showed me just how different it can be."

My mouth dropped open, and everyone in the VIP area and around it turned their attention to me. Mallie's mom nodded when our eyes met. She knew. Mallie started playing again, and I couldn't move. She just did that. She talked about me on stage. She was about to play a song just for me—about me.

"This one is called 'Out of the Blue.' For you, Theo."

"Oh my God," I whispered. I felt all the cameras on me, but I couldn't make myself care. I was frozen in love and appreciation for her. I knew the song, of course. She had played part of it for me, but she'd refused to show me the final version, wanting me to wait to hear it once it was done. I knew she went and recorded it at the studio. But to hear her singing it to a stadium full of people, full well knowing that it would be recorded and become viral, made it so real for me.

Mallorie Witt just declared her love to the world. Her love. For me. The stadium watched her silently, of course not knowing the words but also realizing what they were witnessing. The first time this song would be heard, and they were there to hear it.

She got to the chorus and looked out over the piano in my direction. I knew she couldn't really see me, as the stadium was dark and the light shone in her eyes, but I pretended our energy found each other.

Out of the blue, a love rekindled,
In the silence after heartbreak, where pain dwindled.
His gaze, a soothing balm, a healing kindled,
In the unexpected, love's flame reassembled.

"Theo," Xavier said. "Wow."

"I know," I answered. I swayed back and forth to the melody. As if it wasn't enough to know that she wrote the song and then recorded it to share with the world, this was something altogether different.

As she continued to sing about our powerful connection and love story, her mom stepped up next to me. I put my arm around her shoulders, and we swayed together as she got to the outro, a term I never would've known about a few months ago.

In the aftermath of the storm, a calm anew,
His blue eyes, my sanctuary, a love true.
Out of the blue, a rebirth, a love that grew,
In the quiet aftermath, forever with you.

The crowd literally erupted, the noise so deafening I couldn't hear myself think. Mallie stood from the piano and beamed out at the crowd. They continued to scream and started chanting her name. I saw the girls videoing, and I was glad because I couldn't tear my attention from her face. She looked from right to left, up and down, cataloging every fan in attendance and the love they poured out to her.

After so many minutes, I couldn't guess how many it actually was, she picked up the microphone. Tears tracked down her cheeks, and she left them there. "Thank you," she said. She looked over at me and smiled. "I'm guessing you love that song as much as I do?" When the screaming resumed, she laughed. "That song will be out soon, but you keep that a secret between us, okay?" She winked, knowing full well she just broke all of social media and people would be begging her for its release. "It's been amazing playing for you tonight, London!"

I watched as she walked toward the back of the stage. Just as she reached where she would disappear from sight, she turned back toward the crowd, toward me. Her face filled the huge screen above the stage. She looked directly into my soul and mouthed *I love you* before the screen went dark and she disappeared.

"Did she just—" Lacey said.

"She just mouthed *I love you*," Sydney said. "Yes. She did."

"THEO!" Brittanie shouted. "She just said she loved you in front of God and everyone! You're so going to get married!" A few laughs around us made her realize how loud she was, and she slapped her hand over her mouth.

Isaiah shook his head at her. "That's my girl," he said, pulling her to him.

"Sorry," she said. "I sometimes forget volume control when I'm excited."

"She was mouthing *I love you* to the fans," I said.

Everyone looked at me and laughed.

"Come on, lover boy," Rico joked, appearing next to us. "Let's go backstage."

I liked this dude, ex-military and ex-CIA. You didn't mess with Mallie, or he'd take your ass down. He also had a killer dry sense of humor. I followed him backstage to see my girl, people shouting my name as we walked. I waved to them but didn't stop. I had a mission to accomplish.

The moment the door opened to her dressing room, her eyes met mine. The room buzzed with people and activity, but we only saw each other. She ran for me and launched herself into my arms. I whirled her around and nuzzled my face into her neck.

"I am so fucking proud of you," I said, kissing her lips. "You killed it up there. And the song? Holy shit, Mal. You just shocked the damn world."

"I don't care about the world," she said. "I only care about what you think."

"I was shocked for sure," I said, "but in the best way. I cannot believe you did that. All of it. You calling us out at the beginning, saying my name, and then singing a song meant for me? Then, the icing on the cake was you mouthing *I love you* as you walked off."

She grinned. "You caught that, then."

"Everyone caught it," Brittanie said, and everyone

laughed. "Lover boy over there tried to say that maybe you were saying that to your fans, but we all rolled our eyes at him."

"It was for you," she confirmed.

I held her head in my hands and leaned down to her mouth. "I love you, too, angel."

CHAPTER 17
Allie

THE MUSIC PULSED AROUND US, and my body moved against Teddy's. My arm snaked behind his head, and his hand splayed on my stomach. I'd played my last show in London tonight, and while I was exhausted, I wanted to give Teddy and his friends—*our* friends—at least one fun night out together before we flew back and he got to work preparing for the playoffs.

Thankfully his final game before the championship would be in New York, so I could easily attend and then go home. We rented the top floor of a pub for the night, and my entire team was here to celebrate. I had one leg left of my tour, and that was back in the US after a much-needed two-month break. The drinks flowed, the food was good, and the music was killer. I loved all music and saw it as part of my job to know about all kinds of music.

"I'm going to run to the bathroom," he said into my ear, and I nodded. When he walked away, the girls descended on me, and we began dancing together in a circle. My security flanked the walls of the room, but it wasn't overly necessary. We were the only ones up here. There were other patrons downstairs, but they weren't allowed up. A bartender and some waiters made sure we had enough food, but that was it. I felt—free. That didn't happen often.

The music changed and I immediately knew it was a remix of a hit song, "Shooting Star," from my first album. It was played often in the club scene, not that I knew that firsthand—until now. The room realized it a moment after me, and they all turned to point at me. Lifting my drink in salute, I began to sing the words about a girl wishing for true love on a shooting star. The girls all sang around me. We used our drinks as microphones, and my team had their phones out, recording us. I knew I didn't have to worry about them posting this on social media unless I allowed them to.

The room echoed with my lyrics and the dance beat, and that was when I saw Teddy out of the corner of my eye just as we got to the lyric "guide me to a love that's here to stay." He reached out his arms and pointed at me while saying the exact lyric that played. He knew the song. The crowd split for him as he got up to me just in time for the words "her forever love, now in sight." He pointed at himself and the room awwed.

As the last chords of the song finished, I felt my face flame. He really just did that. He sang my line to me and pointed at himself. My forever love?

He gathered me in his arms and leaned down for a kiss. I closed my eyes against the noise in the room and just felt him here with me. He swayed me back and forth as we continued to kiss. Our friends, my people, cheered around us. This was really happening. All these huge moments for us. Out in public. He was fine. He handled it. He not only handled it, he loved it.

The night of my first show in London had proved that. I saw all the reaction videos people posted online. He blushed and danced and pointed to me. He blew me kisses. He sang along with my songs. And when I sang the song I wrote for him? He had tears in his eyes. He wrapped his arm around my mom. Hell, I think she would marry him at this point. We were viral for so many reasons, and this time, I had brought it on myself, but I didn't even care. I loved him, and I was done worrying about what others thought about my dating life. I was taking a page from Teddy's book and loving him out loud, too. He deserved that.

The song ended, and we continued dancing as the beat changed. When had I ever done this? I couldn't recall a time, but damn, it was fun. Brittanie handed me a drink, and we clinked before taking respective sips. Isaiah grabbed her, and they danced next to us. Before long, Spencer and Lacey were back on the dance floor with us, and Sydney and Xavier right after. We sang and danced in a circle for so long I could no longer feel my feet.

Eventually, after even more drinks and dancing, we realized it was late and we were exhausted. I indicated to Juan and Rico that we were ready to leave, and it took them a few minutes to prepare our entourage to go.

"Huge gathering outside," Rico said to Teddy, but looking at me after he said it to be sure to include me in the information. Teddy's face sobered immediately, and I kind of loved that he took my safety so seriously. It made my stomach swoop like when you dropped on a roller coaster.

"The word got out quickly. They've been out there for hours. The restaurant did a good job of not letting them in, but they're definitely waiting for you to leave. And either way we go out, we will be mobbed."

"Is there a risk to her?" Teddy asked, his arm tightening around my shoulders. I looked up at him, and his expression could only be described as lethal. The only other time I saw that from him was on the football field. I wrapped my arm around his waist and squeezed, reassuring him. Without taking his attention from the guys, he kissed the side of my head.

"No," Juan said from the other side of me. "Just typical stuff. I just wanted to let you know what we were walking out to. We will have the walkway blocked off so they can't get in your faces, but they will be flashing lights and screaming your names."

"Okay," he said. "We can deal with that. You ready, angel?" He looked down at me, and despite the fuzziness of my brain after the last four days of performances and the many drinks I'd had tonight, I felt everything when our eyes met.

"Ready," I said. I turned back to our friends. "You ready for this mayhem?"

"Born ready!" Brittanie yelled, and the group laughed. Forever the party, Brittanie was always ready.

"Remember," Teddy said to the group. "Do not engage with them, no matter what they say." He looked pointedly at Brittanie, and the group laughed again. My head spun with happiness and love for this man. I didn't need anything or anyone else ever again. At this moment, I had everything I'd ever wanted in life.

"Yes, boss," Brittanie responded.

Juan and Rico led the group as we descended the stairs into the main part of the restaurant. People stopped to watch us as we weaved through the room and to the door. Teddy held my hand, walking next to me and looking around the room like someone might jump out at us. People recorded us and clapped, but no one tried to approach.

We made it to the door, and Juan and Rico stood on either side of the walkway. My eyes widened at the sheer number of people standing out there at this time of night. Flashes immediately started, and Teddy used his other hand to take over holding my hand so he could put his arm around my waist. His large hand gripped my body like he was afraid I would disappear. It was hot as hell, and I was here for it.

"Stay close," he said, his voice so low it made me shiver. He definitely didn't have to tell me twice to stay close to him.

The shouts began the second we came into view, and the flashes were blinding. He walked with me slowly, his attention moving from the crowd to my face. He winked at me and his dimple showed me, as serious as he was, that he was playing around with the bystanders. I squeezed his hand and smiled up at him. We reached the waiting SUVs, and he opened the door for me, turning back toward the screaming crowd. He still held on to my hand, and he did not let it go as I slid into the seat. He followed me in, and Rico slammed the door shut.

Teddy pulled me to him as soon as the door shut. "That was so hot," I said.

His eyes darkened and his hand went right to my thigh. "What was?"

"You, being all protective and unbothered by all of that."

He smiled. "Mallie, I am protective and unbothered. Nothing will ever happen when I'm around, that's for damn sure. You're my girl, and they'd have to kill me to get to you. Also, it doesn't bother me. I am proud as fuck that you're mine. I welcome them to take pictures of us."

Well, hell. I was over here making this about lust, and he turned it into one of the sweetest things he could say.

"I love you," I said in response. "You continue to show me just how much." His dimples appeared, and I leaned over to kiss them. "I also love these fucking dimples. You make me weak in the knees every damn time I see them."

"How about wet in the panties?" he asked, waggling his eyebrows.

"Oh, definitely. The way you were dancing with me in there? Rather sure I had several small orgasms. I've been horny for hours."

Teddy groaned and scrubbed his hand over his face. "It's a damn good thing you're wearing pants right now because I want to know just how wet you are."

"We will be there soon," I said and kissed my way up his neck and to his lips.

"This night was so fucking fun," he said against my lips. "Thank you, Mallie."

"Thank you," I said, "for being here with me. I love spending time with you and your friends."

"They're our friends now," he said. "And I love spending time with your people, too."

"What's going on with you and Briggs?" I asked, sipping my drink. Bailey and I looked out over the field, watching for the guys to come out to warm up. I was exhausted, but I wouldn't miss this playoff game for the world. This was it for the Blaze. They'd either win this game and go on to the championships, or their season was over. I loved when Bailey was able to come, and it just happened to work out this time. I knew she'd talked to Briggs some after that first game months ago, but she hadn't mentioned much about him.

Bailey shrugged. "I don't know. I mean, he's hot as fuck. Seems to be a fun guy."

"But," I said.

"He's younger than me," she started. "And in girl years, that's a million. He's a playboy. I've seen his social media and the press coverage of him. He always has girls hanging off him at every event, and never the same one twice."

"Recently?" I asked.

Bailey looked over at me. "No. I have seen nothing since we started talking a few months ago. He swears he is done with all of that."

"But you don't believe him," I said. Bailey had a hard time trusting for many reasons, all of which I understood.

She shrugged again. "I want to, but I'm not convinced. So I'm holding him at arm's length, and he's getting tired of it."

"How do you know he's getting tired of it?"

"He basically told me. He asked me a few weeks ago if I was interested in him or not, and I appreciated that direct question, but when I told him I just wasn't sure yet about pursuing something, he kind of said he wasn't going to wait around forever."

"You have to understand that. You have to either give him a chance to prove it to you or let him go find someone else. He's young and hot, and as much of a catch as you are, he won't want to wait around forever. If it helps at all, Teddy likes him a lot," I said, "but he still has a lot to learn. He basically just got out of college and was drafted first round to the Blaze with one of the highest-paid salaries for his position. This is his first year with them, and he has made it to the playoffs. He is a little cocky and loves the attention, and now he has set his sights on a superstar, so he's feeling himself." I shrugged. "I mean, you can't blame him."

Bailey looked down at her phone and smiled. "Speaking of." She turned the phone so I could see it.

I can't wait to see you today.

I wouldn't tell her that the smile I just saw on her face was way more than "holding him at arm's length." Okay, she was scared. I could help her work through that. From all the times I had spoken to Briggs, he seemed like he had a heart of gold.

"Give him a chance. A real one. Not a half one," I suggested. "And see what happens. I know all about being scared. You know this."

Bailey sighed. "Honestly, the only reason I am even thinking about it is because of you and Theo."

I smiled. "That's a good reason. You know how I felt months ago."

"I am so happy for both of you," she said.

"You know the little hearts Mom passes out at the shows?"

Bailey nodded. "Yeah. They are so cute. People lose their shit trying to collect them. I've seen so many social media videos of people freaking out over your mom giving them one."

"So we were packing up to leave London and I found one on the floor in our room. I was so confused about how it got there because Mom was in her own suite when Teddy walked in from the bathroom. He walked right up to me and said, 'Oh, thanks! That's mine,' and tucked it in his pocket like it was totally normal for him to have a heart from my show. When I asked him about it, he told me he found the first one at my first show back in July and kept it ever since. At the time, he didn't know what the significance was, but he kept it in his underwear drawer at home to remember being at the show that night. Now he collects one every night when he goes to my shows. So he had four of them with him for the four nights of London."

"Is this man for real?" Bailey said. "Jesus, Al. How the fuck did you get so lucky to get this guy to pursue you? He's literally perfect."

I shook my head. "Honest to God, I have no idea. I was so dumbfounded by him caring about these little felt hearts, and he was like, 'What? They make me think of you when I'm not with you.'"

"Tell me you dropped to your knees and sucked that man's cock after that because I totally would've."

I laughed loudly, glad Teddy's parents weren't there yet. "I definitely showed him my love and appreciation for his sentimentality."

"You two are totally getting married," Bailey said. My heart fluttered at her words. It wasn't that I hadn't thought of it, but I tried not to. It was so early and I didn't want to jinx myself after years and years of disappointment.

The door opened and Teddy's parents walked in, so I got up to greet them. Lacey, Sydney, and Brittanie would be here soon, according to their texts, so fun was about to happen. It was cold, it being February in New York, so I was bundled up in a vintage jacket I'd gotten custom altered to have Teddy's name and number put on the back. I wore a red scarf under it, and then the rest of my outfit was black, as I preferred. I had my hair curled and down under my black beanie.

"Hi, sweet girl." Teddy's mom enveloped me in a hug. "You look gorgeous, as usual. It looked like you guys had fun in London. Your show was amazing. Theo sent me some videos. I'd love to come see you sometime."

"Anytime and anywhere you want to come, I'll make sure you're taken care of," I said. "We sure did have fun."

Of course every angle of our walk from the pub to the car had been posted all over, as well as tons of footage of us from the shows. However, on top of that, someone from the pub had leaked videos of us dancing, singing, and kissing. To say that our relationship was viral would be an understatement. I knew for a fact it wasn't anyone in our group, so it had to be one of the workers.

As much as I wanted to be upset about it, I actually wasn't. The videos were fun and showed us having a good time together, and I just couldn't stress over it. I had to have fun in my life, and Teddy helped me do that. They were going to talk about me anyway, so they may as well talk about me being in love with an amazing man who truly loved me for who I was.

"Have we told you how much we love you?" Teddy's dad said, hugging me also. "It's my new part-time job to watch pictures and videos of him with you. I have never seen my boy love someone as hard as he loves you."

"It's beautiful," Sandra said, dabbing her eyes. "All we

want is for him to be happy and loved. He's had the career he wanted, he just needed someone to love. He has always done everything with his entire heart, and it is so great to see him channel that love into you."

I sniffled. I didn't expect to cry today. "I feel the same way," I reassured them.

"Oh, we know," his dad said. "Neither of you have to say a word. We know."

CHAPTER 18
Theo

"LET'S FUCKING GO!" I shouted to the locker room full of guys. My guys. Today was it. The final game to decide whether we made it to the championships or not.

The cheers were deafening. We all held up our helmets in solidarity. Spencer had just finished his motivational speech for the day, and now it was my turn. "But in all seriousness, let's finish this, boys. We have gotten this far with hard work and dedication. We need to rely on each other and know we are ready. We've practiced our asses off. We've worked through injuries and other issues. We are here. Let's leave it all out on the field today."

After our huddle and our Blaze cheer we headed for the tunnel that would take us to the field. I had never been more excited in my life for a game. I knew we could do this.

"Nolan, hold up," Briggs called as we walked out. I waited for him and he fell into place next to me as the guys filed out. "Guess who is here?"

"Did she really come?" I figured if he was asking me to guess, it was Bailey.

He nodded, the youth in his face showing as he beamed. "She's up there with Allie." He pointed above us, where we knew the suites were. I wasn't sure exactly where she was, but knowing she was in the building was enough for me.

"Did you guys finally talk?" This kid was trying; I'd give him that.

"We are going to talk tonight, get things out in the open. I think she's just scared."

I nodded. "I would guess that is true. Just be honest, but really listen. You can't get it from her perspective if you don't. We are football popular, but we have no idea what it's like to be them. While it's amazing to be so well known and successful, it comes with its own share of insecurities and trust problems."

We stepped into the main walkway, where fans lined both sides, and the conversation was over due to the sheer volume of their voices. Cheers, screaming, and people yelling our names took over any chance of talking. We waved to both sides of awaiting fans, always happy to increase their love of our team. If it wasn't for their support, we wouldn't be the team we are.

I moved over closer to the right edge, where I could high-five kids and read signs. This was my favorite part, which was why I understood Mallie's need to see her young fans. I high-fived some kids in the front and some on the shoulders of their parents, and even stopped for a few selfies. We couldn't dally, but I always made time to do a few.

"THEO!" a loud voice rang out over the crowd. I didn't think much of it, as it was typical. When the same voice shouted it again and added "Nolan" to it, I looked over, as did Briggs.

"That dude is really trying to get your attention," Briggs shouted over the noise, pointing to a guy right behind the rope.

I looked at him, and he immediately made me stop in my tracks. Briggs almost ran into me. The guy wore the other team's jersey, which made me wonder why he cared so much about shouting out my name, but there was something about him that was so—familiar. Did I know this guy?

Once he saw that he had my attention, he gestured for me to come closer. I wasn't afraid of him, as he looked about a buck fifty at the most and came up to my shoulder, but I stopped a few feet from him just in case. The guys slapped my back as they passed me, but I didn't have long. We had to get out and warm up.

"She used to write songs about me, too," the guy said.

I furrowed my brow, wondering what the hell he was talking about. Was this some sort of deranged fan of Allie's? I looked at him closer, hoping he didn't have something he could hurt me with.

"What?" Briggs looked back and forth between us. I was just as confused.

"You're not special. Right now, she's telling you she loves you and writing songs about you. But she will always pick her career over you. She needs the attention. She has to have it. She will never be the wife or mother to your children that you want, so don't waste your time."

It was then that I realized who this was. I recalled the pictures of them I saw online when I first started looking up information about Allie and who the putz was that broke her heart. I looked over at Briggs and then back to Josiah. My heart pounded in my ears. Oh, he *was not* here at this game, trying to start shit about her.

Before I could say a word in response, his face contorted and he spewed more filth. "I mean, I get it. She's hot as fuck, and being with her is good for your career, right? You're even more popular now than you were before. It's the Allie Effect. And she's a good fuck, right? Does she still do that thing with her—"

I reached over and gripped his shirt before he could finish. "You better shut the fuck up right now," I said between gritted teeth. "I don't know what your reason is for being here, or if you just want your five seconds of fame, but if anything else about her crosses your lips, I will end you right here and now. You gave up the right to speak about her ever again when you broke up with her over the phone like the pansy you are."

Josiah must have a death wish because he wasn't fazed by my threat or my hand gripping his shirt. I could literally throw him with the grip on his shirt alone. I shit bigger than this prick. The people around us were all quiet, watching this. I knew it was being recorded, but there was no way this weasel was getting away with this.

"She will ruin you. Once you realize she's not all you want her to be, she will tell everyone it's your fault. She will write songs about you, and her fans will attack you. Believe me, the pussy isn't worth it. End it now while you still have some dignity—and your career—left."

That was it. I saw red and I had cocked my hand back to hit him when Briggs grabbed me. I fought him as he dragged me away. Once a few of the other players realized what he was trying to do, they assisted in pushing me down the corridor toward the field.

"Briggs, let me fucking go," I said, my chest heaving with anger. I needed to put him in the ground. How dare he talk about her like that—and in front of others. He didn't want her anymore. He threw her away, so what purpose did he have to stir up shit with me?

"Do not, under any circumstances, let go of him," Briggs said to the other two guys holding me. My feet moved away from the scene by sheer force, but if they gave me one second of reprieve, I would run back and finish him. "Nolan, I'm saving you from yourself right now. Think about what you would tell me if this was me. I know that was shitty. But you will get suspended from the game if you don't stop. Take a deep breath."

We reached the field, and Briggs walked me right to

Spencer. "Spence!" Briggs got his attention. When Spencer saw my face, he dropped the ball and ran to me.

"What the fuck happened?"

"Allie's ex was in the tunnel. He said some awful things, and Nolan almost lost it. Thank God I was there, or we'd have a murder scene on our hands. You need to talk to him and get his head straight."

Spencer put his arm around my shoulders and walked us away from the rest of the guys. "Talk, Theo. Get it out."

I breathed in and out, but my hands shook and my heart raced. Spencer walked us up to Coach Reynolds, and all it took was him looking at my face for him to walk away with us.

"What happened?" Coach was like another dad to me, and I respected the hell out of him.

"Allie's ex was waiting for me in the tunnel. He called out my name. He said some horrible things about her, and people videoed. It's going to be all over." I closed my eyes, the urge to sprint back to the tunnel so huge I had to breathe in and out several times. "I wanted to kill him, Coach. I may have done it if it wasn't for Briggs. He-he disrespected her—" My voice broke, and I threw my helmet down. "FUCK!" I yelled.

"Hey," Coach said, his hand on my back. "I get it. There is nothing that makes us more angry as men than for someone to do something to someone we love, and when it's on the scale of Allie, it makes it even worse. There is nothing you can do about the fact that he decided to make a scene today, but you can decide right now that you won't let it affect your game, too. It's what he wanted, obviously. He wanted to get into your head. About her, of course, but also before the game to make sure you were off. He's jealous as fuck. He let her go, and now he sees that she is happy and he can't handle it. He probably has a small dick."

Spencer laughed out loud, and I couldn't help it—I laughed, too. God, I loved this man. "He for sure has a small dick because I could've flicked him across the stadium with one finger."

Coach nodded. "See? Think about what Allie would tell you right now." He pointed in the vicinity of the suites. "Would she want you to worry about this, or would she want you to channel that anger into getting us into the championship?"

I paced back and forth, yanking at my hair. Spencer stood to the side, letting me figure out my shit. "I am going to murder these players today," I said. "You need to keep me in the whole time. I'm going to single-handedly win this game for us."

"Hey," Spencer said, pointing to himself. "You gonna QB, too?"

"I just might," I said. My hands still shook with anger, and I felt like I could run through a brick wall, but they were right. I needed to use it to fuel the game. I wished I could talk to Mallie right now and tell her what happened before she saw it on social media, but I couldn't. She may already know.

"You can't talk to her," Spencer said, reading my mind. "You have to focus. Remember, she's used to the media talking about her. I bet she doesn't even give it a second thought."

I closed my eyes, the things he said echoing in my head. The cameras pointed at us once they figured out what was going on. *I'm sorry, angel,* I tried to telepathically tell her. *I just couldn't walk by and let him disrespect you.* Why didn't I just keep walking? I could've avoided this entire thing.

"Come on," Coach said. "Get out there and warm up and run some plays."

I ran off the field after yet another set of four downs that we couldn't move the ball on and threw my helmet down, with it bouncing away from me before I collapsed on the bench. I put my head between my knees and screamed every expletive I could think of. I was so goddamn frustrated. It was the third quarter, and I had touched the ball three times so far. We were losing the game by two touchdowns. Our team was not working together, and I didn't know why.

I was off. Very much so. Spencer started averting plays that involved me having the ball after the second quarter. When we talked at halftime, I promised to get my shit together. I tried, but I couldn't. The anger I felt was not being relieved by running down guys or scoring because we couldn't seem to do either. I had, however, gotten two penalties for unnecessary roughness.

"Nolan!" I heard Spencer's voice, and I lifted my head. I respected the hell out of his position, and despite that, we were best friends and basically brothers. When we were on the field, this guy was my chief. He lifted me up by my pads so we looked eye to eye.

"You need to get your fucking shit together, or I'm telling Coach to take you out of this game," he said. It wasn't often that Spencer got mad, but he was furious. "You have no business getting penalties for that shit. This is rookie shit you're doing." He pointed upward. "This is what you want to show her, that this is how you handle someone saying something about her? Do you know how many people talk shit about her on the internet?"

"That's not to my face, and it's not her fucking ex that she was with for five years."

"Take a walk and get it together. When we go back in on offense, if you have one more penalty, I'm telling Coach to bench you."

He walked away and I did what he said. We may be equals in a lot of ways, but on this field, he was my boss.

I walked up and down the sideline, my teammates watching me warily. I got it. They weren't used to seeing this

Theo. I could see the headlines already running all over social media, and my thoughts immediately went to Mallie, wondering what she knew. I also knew she could see me playing like absolute garbage, and I was sure the cameras were on Spencer in my face a few minutes ago.

I sighed. I had to stop. I was making it worse. There was nothing I could do right now but not give the media something else to say about me until I could talk to her. I looked up into the stands behind our sideline, seeking out the signs for our team. I smiled at the sheer number of them that were focused on Allie's attendance here. *We're Lovestruck for the Blaze* caught my eye, with her heart logo and our flame together.

I walked back to the bench just as the other team got a field goal, putting them up by seventeen. "Fuck," I muttered. I picked up my helmet and walked over to the offense, huddled up around Spencer. His gaze asked the question he didn't voice, and I nodded. I was here. I had to be. This was my team. They deserved the best of me.

"Let's fucking get this done," I said. "We have to work together."

Spencer looked relieved as he called out plays. We had a little more than one quarter to get this shit done.

I let the water run down my face, hiding the tears as they continued to fall. We fucking lost. Our season was over. And while it was not my fault, I didn't help matters much, either. While I did get my shit together in the fourth quarter and scored one touchdown and got over a hundred yards, it just wasn't enough. We lost by one field goal, which almost hurt worse than being blown out because it was *that fucking close*.

Now I had to apologize to Mallie for what happened before the game and see what mayhem I had caused online. I was afraid to pick up my phone. I guaranteed both Jamie and Zoey had contacted me to talk about damage control. With the two of us, they often worked together now on what was going on. I sighed and ran the soap over my sore body. Most of the guys were done showering, but I was stalling. I had to deal with shit I didn't want to deal with. Shit I created with my own mouth and hands.

What would she think? Was she mad at me? Did this put her right back into her insecurities with us? I dropped my head and let the water go down my back. God, London had been so amazing. The press ate up our time there together, and everything was good. Seeing her in her element so many nights made me love and appreciate her even more. Then, the night we were at the pub, even after it got leaked, made her so happy. She didn't even care that the whole world had watched us dance, sing, and make out.

Now this. Fucking Josiah. What was his endgame here? Did he want her back? Or was he just so angry that she was happy in the media, something he hated, that he had to try to mess it up for us? And why did I fall right into his trap?

I shut the shower off, refusing to allow myself to wallow another minute. Mallie waited for me, and I needed to get to her and hopefully salvage this situation. Despite my foul mood, I had to make it right.

I dried off and walked to my borrowed locker and grabbed my outfit. The locker room was quiet, most of the guys wearing headphones and zoning out to deal with the loss. We'd already had our postgame meeting, and now we were just waiting for our bus ride to the airport. However, I had plenty of time to go up and see Mallie before she left. I knew she was staying in New York for a few days to record before we would meet in LA for our first awards show together. She was up for multiple awards for both *Lovestruck* the album and Lovestruck the tour, and if she won Entertainer of the Year for the third time in her career, she would set a record. That is if she still wanted me to go. I grabbed my phone and bypassed all notifications to text her.

I will be up in a few minutes.

Her response was instant. *OK.*

OK. That was all. How did two letters seem so ominous?

Spencer walked over. "You okay?"

I blew out a breath. "Yeah, I think so. It fucking sucks, man. We worked so goddamn hard."

He nodded. "We did."

"I'm sorry I wasn't the best version of myself today," I said.

"You got it together in the end. None of us played our best. It just wasn't meant to be." He indicated my phone. "Did you talk to her?"

"I just told her I'd be up in a few minutes and she said okay."

He nodded. "Briggs and I are waiting for you to go up. Spencer, Isaiah, and Xavier already went up. We have less than an hour until boarding."

I wanted to be excited that Briggs was going up to see Bailey, but I was too worried about Mallie to respond. I nodded and tucked my phone in my pocket. They would load our bags, so I set mine in front of my locker and made my way out of the locker room.

Juan was waiting for me, and I nodded at him. He led the way to the elevator that would take me to her. Fans still milled around and shouted once they saw us. I waved, even though it was the last thing I wanted to do. I looked straight ahead, hoping Josiah was not there again because there was no way I had enough resolve not to kill him now.

"She is a distraction for you!" a voice shouted, clear as day. "It's your fault we aren't going to the championships!" Other people shouted in response, seeming to agree. I bit my cheek to keep from responding. Juan glanced at me but said nothing.

"Go up and get your girlfriend and tell her to get out of here! We need you back as a player, not as a pussy!"

"Yeah! Maybe if your head wasn't buried in her pussy, you'd have your head in the game!"

"Fuck you, Nolan! They should've benched your ass!"

"Guess you should've stayed here and practiced instead of vacationing in London!"

The elevator doors closed behind us, and I leaned against the wall and closed my eyes. I fought the urge to turn around and punch the wall.

"Shit, man," Briggs said. "You okay?"

"Leave him be," Spencer warned.

I had less than a minute to get my shit together. It wasn't that I didn't think she'd care that I was upset or that I lost, but I had to do damage control first and make sure she was okay after Josiah showed up here and made a spectacle of us. My feelings could come after that.

The door opened, and thank the Lord, the hallway was clear. No more screaming people to deal with. Juan walked ahead of us, and Spencer put his hand on my arm before we went into the suite.

"Hey," he said. "Focus on her. Let it go. This is the kind of shit she deals with on a daily basis, times one million. You know people are always talking shit about her online, and there's nothing she can do but just keep living her life."

"I know," I said, "but this time, I contributed to it."

CHAPTER 19

Allie

I PACED THE SUITE, Zoey on the phone for the millionth time in the last four hours. She, of course, had been discussing with Jamie what to do, if anything, with the debacle that had been Teddy and Josiah and then Teddy's behavior on the field.

My stomach was in knots, as it had been for hours. I barely watched the game, instead dealing with all of this. I knew, of course, that Teddy had a horrible game and they lost, but the moment I saw Josiah on the phone screen and heard the things he said, my day was shot.

Lacey, Brittanie, and Sydney were rock stars, trying to do anything to help me. Teddy's mom paced like a worried mom does, both for her kid and for me. There wasn't much of the game that was watched from this suite. Fucking Josiah. Why? Why did he do that? He had been silent since our breakup. What in God's name possessed him to do this now, on the most important day of Teddy's season?

The door to the suite opened and Teddy walked in with Spencer and Briggs, looking destroyed. Everyone quieted, and Lacey went right to Spencer, hugging him tight. He buried his face in her neck, and they swayed back and forth, no words said. Bailey stood next to me, eyeing Briggs. He looked right at her and smiled, it not quite reaching his eyes. I hadn't been around yet when Teddy lost a game, even though he had when I wasn't in attendance. But none of them were the magnitude of this one, and for the assumed reasons it was lost.

"I gotta go," I said to Zoey. "Teddy is here. Whatever you and Jamie decide is fine. Just let me know. I'm fine with doing nothing and just letting it play out. I'll be in the car on the way home in the next hour, so call me if you need me."

Zoey hung up, and I slid the phone into my pocket. He hugged his mom briefly before releasing her and coming to me. He took my hand and pulled me to the corner of the suite, out of most of the vantage points of any lingering cameras. He wrapped his arms around me, and I melted into him, tears pricking the back of my eyes at the relief of being in his arms and the stress of the last four hours.

"Angel," he said, his voice cracking. "How much of a mess did I create?"

I sighed. "It's a mess," I said, "but you didn't create it. Well, not entirely anyway."

Teddy pulled back and looked into my eyes, his jaw working as he processed the mess I admitted to. "I couldn't let him talk about you like that."

I thought about the video I had watched so many times I had it memorized. The vile words Josiah tossed at Teddy and the immediate physical response Teddy had to defend me. The people, recording from every angle, catching every word between them. Briggs and two of the other guys had carried Teddy away to keep him from attacking Josiah. And Josiah had continued his vitriol after they'd walked away, getting his full five minutes of fame with those warriors with cell phones.

So much for our London trip being all over the internet. This was front and center, that and Teddy's many outbursts on the sidelines, from throwing his helmet to cussing and then getting two unnecessary roughness penalties. Now, of course, the narrative was that he had no business being with me in London when he had a game to prepare for.

"I appreciate that," I said, "and he was completely out of line. I'm sorry you had to deal with that before your huge game. I feel terrible."

Teddy shook his head and cradled my face in his hands. "I made it harder for you. The one thing you didn't want was me making things harder for you," Teddy said. He stepped back and pulled his hands through his hair. "All I wanted to do was be the best person for you, and the first chance I have to prove to you that I can handle it, this is what I do."

"Hey," I said, trying to stop his tirade, but he was pacing the room now.

"All I had to do was win this fucking game," he said. Everyone in the room watched as his emotions caught up to him. "I let my team down. I let *you* down," he said to the room, waving his arm around. He turned back to me. "If only I hadn't had to deal with your ex showing up like some sort of fanboy talking about your pussy, wanting some sort of pissing contest with me. Maybe then none of us would be in this place right now."

The gasps that rang out around the room made tears fill my eyes and my mouth dropped open in shock.

"Theo," Bailey said, her voice low and deadly.

"Theo," Sandra interjected softly, and Theo's gaze went immediately to his mother. His face crumpled as he saw the disappointment there.

Briggs stepped forward and got in Teddy's face. "You better fucking watch yourself, Nolan. You're upset, and we all understand." He turned Teddy to face me. "Look at her face. What the fuck are you doing right now?"

Teddy looked at me, and tears filled his eyes as he took in my crushed expression and the tears tracking down my face. I didn't need a camera to know what I looked like right now because my exterior look was nothing compared to the shredding of my soul.

Teddy sat and put his head in his hands. His back shook as he worked through the emotions that overtook him, but I was frozen. I wanted to go to him, but every single one of my insecurities stopped me from moving. I stood stock-still, wondering if I was dreaming or if this entire thing was really happening right now. Did the man who loves me really just talk about my pussy in front of an entire room of his family and friends? Did he just inadvertently say that it was my fault that his team lost the game? I felt my face flame at the realization of exactly what he said.

Bailey held on to my arm as tears dripped down my face. Teddy's mom walked over and put her arm around my shoulders. She whispered something in my ear, but I had no idea what she said because my ears roared with the embarrassment of Teddy's words. The girls assembled next to me as we watched this man crumble in front of us. After what seemed like forever, Teddy stood up. Everyone in the suite watched as he strode to me. His eyes were red, and his hands shook as he took mine. I couldn't move as his gaze searched my face, looking for reassurance I didn't have.

"I'm sorry," he said, his voice cracking. "That was totally uncalled for. I should not have said that. It isn't anyone's fault but my own that this happened."

My heart squeezed, seeing him this upset. All I wanted to do was make him feel better. But then I caught Bailey's look over his shoulder, and I remembered what he said in front of this entire room of people. I wasn't accepting this kind of treatment from anyone anymore, no matter how much I loved them. What he said was out of line, no matter how upset he was. We both needed some space to think things through. I needed to get out of this room, away from the possibility of being recorded with this debacle happening in front of anyone left in the stadium, and for the first time ever—away from Teddy.

I removed my hands from his, and he glanced down at them before looking back at me. I saw the panic in his eyes, but I couldn't deal with it right now. I had to deal with the fact that my own was bubbling up my chest, threatening to take me down. "I'm going to go. Lord knows how much has been recorded in this suite in the last few minutes to make things even worse, and I need some space." I looked over his head to Juan. "Juan, tell Rico I'm ready to go."

Juan immediately opened the door and had a quick conversation with Rico.

"No," Teddy said. He grabbed my hands and I pulled back. Bailey crossed her arms next to me, understanding my vibe. I stepped back, putting space between us, and his eyes widened with realization. He shook his head, and we had a silent conversation. He pleaded for me to forgive him, and I put up my wall. A wall I'd never had to have with him.

"I'm going home, Teddy," I said out loud. "I'll talk to you later." The door opened and Rico gestured to us, and I turned to walk away.

"Please, angel," he said, tears in his eyes again. "Talk to me now. I'm so sorry. I love you so much, and I lost it. Please forgive me."

"I will talk to you," I said, stepping around him, "when I'm done being mad and you are done being an asshole. Right now, I'm going home, and so are you."

I hugged his mom and the girls. I nodded at Bailey, and we crossed the room to utter silence. Just as we reached the door, Teddy called my name again and tried to move. Spencer held him and said, "Let her go, man."

Bailey turned back to Teddy. "Fucking dumbass," she muttered.

I closed my eyes, the video with Josiah and Teddy replaying again and the horrible words echoing around me. I didn't know why I was still watching, but I couldn't stop.

The reports were just as bad as I anticipated—Theo had a temper. Theo almost punched a guy half his size for talking crap about me. Never mind that Josiah, my known ex, had instigated it and said awful things that would incite anyone. The only thing that mattered was Teddy's reaction. Then the clips of him throwing his helmet, yelling on the sidelines, and the two penalties he had gotten added fuel to the fire. Let's also not forget that his going to London was a distraction when he should've been focusing on the game, so the loss was his fault and his dating me was bad for his career.

Then there was the suite. Yeah, someone had video of him coming into the suite looking distraught. They were far away and there was no sound, but the "expert" lip readers supposedly cracked what he said. The only part that mattered, of course, was the part that seemed like he said to me, "I don't want to deal with some fanboy that just wants your pussy. I don't want this." Of course, shortly after that, I left the suite without him and left the stadium before he got on the bus to fly home. I had unknowingly fed into the rumors by leaving, but I had figured no one was left to record us. Lesson learned.

The news coverage was, of course, that I should leave him, that I did leave him, that I realized what a red flag he was and walked out on him. Video footage of Theo arriving back in Florida, looking forlorn, only made that seem true. Somehow Josiah still smelled like a fucking rose in all of this.

On top of it all, some of the Blaze fans were first in line with the firing squad, calling for him to be fined or benched or, in extreme cases, fired from the team. Coach Reynolds, whom I'd met several times, even did a press conference to address the issues. He reiterated that Theo didn't do anything wrong, that what had been said about me was terrible and that Theo's reaction was normal for anyone. It didn't matter.

They were judge, jury, and executioner right now, and the criminals were us.

I wiped my eyes, unable to cope with any of this. Teddy had hurt my feelings, for sure, with what he had said. Did I see him as a red flag? Not at all. He had texted me a million times since I left, and I did respond. I was a fucking adult and wasn't going to ignore him, but I also didn't want to talk to him or see him yet. I had to dig through my hurt and this shitstorm before I could decide how we'd move on from this. I knew he didn't mean what he said and instantly regretted the bad choice of words, but he had been taunted all the way up there from what other videos I saw. It didn't excuse him lashing out at me in front of everyone, but his emotions had been in hyperdrive for almost six hours at that point.

Now that what he said had been misconstrued and put out there to make it sound even worse, he was even more of a disaster. I was not breaking up with him. I loved him. I expected something like this once we were out in public, but I now had to deal with it and figure out a way we could come out on the other side and be out of the drama news cycle. Zoey and Jamie were currently in constant communication, trying to get ahead of this and figure out damage control. I never said anything publicly. It had been years since I did an interview due to the invasive nature of these vulture reporters. But it just may be time to set the record straight.

Bailey and my mom were just as incessant with their texts. I responded, but I wanted to be alone. They both offered to come home with me, but I couldn't deal with talking right now. It was just me and Charlie, curled up on the couch, obsessing over my phone. Okay, he was obsessing over the new toy Conor got him, but whatever.

The phone rang and I sighed. It was Zoey, which meant I had to answer it. "Hey, Zo," I said, sounding as exhausted as I was. I could sleep for a week. Too bad that wasn't possible in my life, and definitely not with this amount of drama.

"Hey, Al," she said back, just as tired. It was hard work to run my life. "Jamie and I have a plan; I just need your approval. Well, both of you, but she can't get ahold of Theo right now. Do you have any idea where he is?"

"No," I said. "The last time he texted me was several hours ago. I told him I needed some time and that I'd talk to him tomorrow. What's the plan?"

"You're scheduled to go to the PMA Awards next week," Zoey said.

"Yes, I know. I'm leaving on Wednesday to go to LA."

"Theo is attending with you," Zoey said. "He will wrap up his responsibilities with his team on Wednesday and fly out with you."

I sighed. Teddy already planned to accompany me there, so I knew there was another reason for her to bring this up now and more than likely, I wasn't going to enjoy what she said next. "And then what?"

"We will arrange for you and Theo to sit down with a reporter on Thursday before the awards on Sunday."

"No," I said immediately.

"I know," she said, "but we have one that promises to let you guys lead the questions and answers. I've worked with him in the past. He has actually flown around the world covering your shows. The company he works for has him as a full-time Allie Witt reporter."

"Jesus," I said. "There is such a thing?"

Zoey laughed. "You're big business, Al. You know this. Sometimes I think you forget just how much power you wield. Anyway, he knows how huge this is. You haven't done a sit-down interview in over five years. He has been told that if you agree to this, you will get final say on whatever he publishes."

"You think we need to do this?" I asked. Zoey didn't tell me something unless she tried all the alternatives.

"I think you do. With the shit going on right now, we need

something positive from both of you. He will sit down with you, have some pictures done of both of you, do your interview, and write the article that night. Once you approve, he will put it out no later than Friday. That'll give it almost two days in the news cycle before the awards. Then you and Theo will be seen on the red carpet together, a first for you, and hopefully it will turn the news cycle back around and calm things down."

"I definitely want that," I said, "and I believe you that this guy wants this exclusive, so he will do what we want, but I still hate that we have to go through this dog and pony show just to live our lives."

"I know," she said, "but you are both well-known people with high-profile jobs. This is just part of it. You plan to stay with him, right?"

I knew she had to ask, but it annoyed me at the same time. "I love him, Zoey."

"I know you do. I'm just making sure I'm not doing something you don't want."

"Jamie is on board with this, too?"

"Yes. As soon as we get Theo to approve, we will confirm with Scott—that's the reporter."

"And you will be there?"

"Jamie and I will both be there, yes. We will not throw you to the wolves or leave you alone. He is aware that this is an exclusive of a lifetime and that how he does this will determine whether he's given exclusives from you guys in the future. He has promised that you can veto any and everything you don't want. This is all about you guys."

"This is video, or just print?"

"Both," she said. "They'll also take some pictures of the two of you prior. You will be able to decide if those are used as well."

A text popped up on my screen, and it was Rico. *I need to talk to you for a minute in person.* Rico and Juan shared the downstairs apartment when we were here in New York, so all he had to do was come up through the garage. I sighed again. What could he possibly have to talk to me about at this time of night? Hopefully there wasn't a security issue outside. I knew people were all outside, even more so after the shitstorm of press.

"I have to go," I said to Zoey. "Rico needs me for something." I texted him back: *Okay, come on in. I'm still up.*

"Is everything okay?" she said, concern in her voice.

"He didn't say it wasn't, so I'm guessing so," I said. "I'll talk to Teddy tomorrow and let you know the final answer, but I'd say he will be fine with whatever I want to do."

I knew he would do whatever I wanted based on the disaster that just happened, but that was not why I wanted him to agree to it. I wanted him to be okay with the spectacle we had to make of ourselves. He was used to doing interviews, but this would be like nothing he'd ever done before. I sighed. Welcome to my life.

We disconnected, and I stood up just as my door opened and Rico stepped inside, but that's not what I noticed the most. I noticed the giant man standing behind him, holding the most beautiful flowers I'd seen since the last bouquet he sent me.

"Rico," I said, my eyes on Teddy's.

"Listen," Rico said. "He made such a good case for me letting him in to see you. I like this guy, okay?"

"And what is that case?" I said, my eyes still on Teddy's. He looked so handsome in a pair of fitted jeans and a long sleeve button-down shirt, but his eyes were red-rimmed and tired. He had marks on his head from the game, and scrapes lined his forearms where his shirt was pushed up. God, I loved his arms. He stood next to Rico, holding the flowers, not moving until I gave the go-ahead, apparently.

"That I love you," Teddy said. "And that I'm the biggest moron in the history of morons, but I could not let you go to bed tonight without knowing just how in love I am with you. I know you wanted space, and I'm sorry. I will go if you want me to, but I just couldn't stand not seeing your face and telling you how goddamn sorry I am that all of this happened." His voice cracked and he cleared his throat, making tears fill my eyes. "I will never, not ever, intentionally hurt you. I said something really shitty that I didn't mean, and even worse, it's now misunderstood all over social media. I did that. I took what Josiah did and played right into his hands. He won that round, even if he was an awful human being for doing that."

He stepped forward and I nodded at Rico, who immediately disappeared out the front door and back to his apartment.

"You've got him wrapped right around your huge finger," I said, pointing at the closed door.

Teddy laughed. "Rico is a great dude. I got Juan, too, but they decided that only one of them should come up here just in case you fired them, so one of the two would be left. I've been down there for an hour trying to work out how to get you to let me in."

I laughed despite the heaviness in my gut. I stepped up to him and took the flowers, motioning for him to follow me into the kitchen to put them in a vase. "They've been with me for over ten years, and you come in here and win them over in just a few months."

"They apparently hated Josiah," he said, "because they took me to his apartment first."

My mouth dropped open and I stopped, the flowers in my hand. "What? Oh God, please. Don't tell me there's more for the press to find out."

"Oh no," he said. "There was no one there; we made sure of that. And Josiah is going to keep his fucking mouth shut about you from here on out and stay the hell away from any football games. We have an understanding now."

"Is he—dead?" I whispered.

Teddy laughed and slapped the counter. As much as this day had been emotionally wrecking, his laugh was infectious, and I joined in. "Mallie," he said. "No. I didn't touch the guy, but he sure thought I might. We had a conversation man to man. That's all you need to know."

"Are you sure?" I asked.

"Do you trust me? Even after I acted like an idiot today?"

I nodded. That was not even a question in my mind. "Of course."

"Thank you. He is taken care of and will not be showing up at any games or saying anything to anyone." He walked around the counter and stood in front of me. "Angel," he said. "I need to hold you. Can I please?"

My hands shook like it was the first time he was about to touch me all over again. Despite the amount of times that this man had touched me, this was the first time after any sort of fight. I bit my lip and nodded, giving him the go-ahead.

"You know what this does to me," he said, pulling my lip from my teeth and leaning over to kiss my lips. I gasped into his mouth and wrapped my arms around him. Our tongues met, and his hands gripped my rib cage like he was keeping me from floating away. My knees buckled, and he lifted me so I sat on the counter, never breaking the kiss. He nipped at my lips and tongue, shifting so we could kiss deeper. I held his face, his beard tickling my palms like I loved. I ran my thumbs along his cheeks as we kissed. I pulled him closer with my legs around his hips as we both turned this shitty day into the love we had for each other.

He slowed and rained kisses along my face, nose, and forehead. He rested his head against mine, and we breathed each other in, our eyes closed and no words being said. I ran my hands down his chest and around his torso, then rested my head on his chest.

"Mallie," he said, kissing the top of my head. "I have

never been more scared in my life than I was when I saw you walk out of the suite today. It took everything in me not to drop to my knees and beg you to stop. I never want that feeling again, angel. You are everything to me. Flying home with the team, I was the most insufferable man you'll ever meet. Once we landed, I told Coach Reynolds I had to go to you, and he chartered me a plane himself. That's how I got here so fast. I am so sorry. Please forgive me for being a complete asshole and embarrassing you in front of our family and friends. Trust me, they've all told me what an idiot I am, too."

He rubbed his hands up and down my back as I listened, feeling the reverberation of his voice through his chest. I closed my eyes and drank it in. The words he said, the way he made me feel. We'd had our first real test as a couple today. While things were thrown at both of us that we couldn't have predicted, and the shitstorm wouldn't stop for a while, right here and now, we were together. He came to me even though I pushed him away. He wouldn't let me doubt us.

"I accept your apology," I started, tilting my head back to look at him. Teddy's dimples popped as he smiled in relief. "I know you were upset and your emotions got the best of you, but that is your one free pass. Unfortunately, in our lives, we do not have the luxury of allowing emotions to overtake reason when every move we make is recorded and posted all over social media."

"I know," Teddy said, clasping my hands in his. "I knew better, even before being with you. I know now we are on a scale I've never witnessed before, and that was a complete rookie move. I promise you that will never, ever happen again."

I nodded. "I believe you, and I'm sorry you have to be held to the unattainable standards I'm held to now, too."

He shook his head. "No. Don't apologize. I am in the fishbowl with you, angel. I don't want it any other way. I made a really stupid mistake in a very public way, and I promise this is the only time you will ever have to deal with press because of me."

I buried my head in his chest, the relief I felt at his words overwhelming my emotions. Tears pricked at my eyes again. Despite how shitty this day was, what he said just now was what I needed to hear. No matter what unattainable standard the media held me to, Teddy was still okay with being part of it with me. My thoughts spiraled over the last few hours, wondering once again if love would ever be enough for me to have true and utter happiness.

I squeezed him tightly, my hands gripping his T-shirt. Despite fighting them, tears began sliding down my face and onto his shirt. Ever in tune with me, he knew immediately and shifted back so he could see my face.

"Mallie," he whispered, using his thumbs to wipe my tears away. "Baby, don't cry. I hate seeing you upset, and especially when I know it's because of me. I love you so much. I am so sorry."

I shook my head, trying to stop the stream. He held my face in his hands and studied my face. "I was so scared," I whispered.

"Scared?" His voice was little more than a breath.

"That love wouldn't be enough for you to endure this with me," I admitted. "That this whole thing messed up your game and you'd decide I wasn't worth it."

Teddy's eyes widened. "Baby, that makes me literally sick to my stomach that I made you feel that way. There is nothing —literally nothing—that you could do to not make me want to do this life with you. You're it for me. I'm all in, in every single way. I love you more than anything else in this world, Mallorie Rose Witt. Are you hearing me? You're worth every single thing. There is no question in my mind, and there never will be."

I sniffled, the tears from happiness this time. I felt every word he said deep in my soul. They filled in the cracks from earlier and reassured me that this was, in fact, my person.

"I have never been more relieved in my life," I said, smiling through my tears. "I'm all in, too, Teddy. Just so you know. I wasn't going to end things; I just needed to get away from the situation and think."

He blew out a breath and kissed my lips softly. "I was so scared, too, baby. Scared that you'd think I wasn't worth the drama, either."

I shook my head and put my hands on his face. We looked into each other's eyes, a silent conversation reassuring both of us that this was just our first bump and it was going to be nothing more than a blip on our relationship road.

"Thank you for coming," I said. "I'm glad you didn't listen to me. I needed you."

"I needed you, too," he said. "So fucking much. Hey, you know what?"

"What?"

His tired eyes sparkled, and a smirk played on his face. "We had our first fight."

I laughed. "I guess we kind of did."

"You know what that means?" He ran his hands up under my T-shirt, and I shivered.

"What does that mean?" I asked, his touch sending a signal that my body definitely heard.

"Our first session of makeup sex."

CHAPTER 20
Theo

"HOW DO I LOOK?" I asked, walking into the living room of Mallie's LA house. It was a massive mansion that made my house look like an apartment. Some things I would definitely need to get used to. The interview would be done here, so there were people milling around and professional lighting being set up.

Mallie turned at the sound of my voice, and my mouth dropped open. I wore a custom suit given to me by a top designer who wanted their name on our article, and I knew one of the designers Mallie often worked with had created something for her for this that matched her aesthetic for the awards show on Sunday, but knowing about it and seeing it were two totally different things.

Her long hair was put in some elaborate updo with curls framing her face and neck, and her makeup was flawless, as always. Her eyes were done heavier than she wore for daily use, and her classic red lip was on display. She wore a pair of skintight black leather pants that left literally nothing to the imagination. Her shapely legs taunted me. My eyes lifted to the red-sequined tank top she wore that showed just enough cleavage and her hard-earned abs to make me salivate. She held a black cropped jacket with one finger, ready to put it on. Her sculpted shoulders and sleek, bare neck made me want to put my face there and devour her.

"Fucking hell, Mal," I said. "How the hell am I supposed to sit through an interview with you like that?"

She grinned and stepped closer, and that was when I saw it, the #23 on the diamond necklace that hung between her breasts. It took everything I had in me to not drag her from the room right this minute. I reached my hand out and touched it, and she shivered.

"The same way I'm going to look at you in this custom suit and make it through the interview." She looked me up and down and I felt the heat in her gaze like a touch. I was already hard, and her look wasn't helping. "You are hot as fuck, Teddy. I'm going to need to study how closely this was made for you later."

She licked her lips and I swore to God I wasn't going to survive this.

I blew out a breath and whistled. "Goddamn, you look fucking amazing." I took her hand and twirled her around so I could see the back of her outfit. The top crisscrossed and tied behind her, showing her back muscles and also that she wore no bra. The pants were a fucking miracle of God. I couldn't stop myself from touching her round, taut ass. She smirked over her shoulder.

"You aren't wearing a fucking bra," I said, my erection becoming a problem in these custom pants.

"I'm also not wearing underwear," she whispered.

I closed my eyes and adjusted myself. "What the hell am I going to do with this massive problem?"

Her eyes dropped to my *problem* and she giggled. "I can verify that it is indeed massive," she teased. When I groaned, she giggled again. "Baby, I promise I will take care of that later after you're a good boy and survive this interview with me."

"I'm not going to survive shit. You need to go change. Into something that doesn't remind me how fucking perfect your body is."

She put her hand on the side of my face and winked at me. "Just think, after they leave, I can suck you right here in my living room to thank you for being a good boy."

My dick jumped. "Mallie," I said. "You're not helping."

She cupped me through my pants, and a wicked look came over her face. "I'm not trying to help. I love keeping you on your toes and seeing you unhinged for me." She leaned up for me to kiss her cheek so I didn't get lipstick on me, and I grabbed her and hauled her body to mine.

"This fucking body is mine," I growled in her ear.

"All yours," she promised.

"Scott is here," Zoey said, entering the living room.

I turned from her to try to get my situation under control. She didn't need to see that. Bad enough she had been around for many of our make-out sessions.

"All okay?" asked Zoey.

Mallie giggled. "Teddy likes my outfit."

Zoey looked at her, then at me, before she realized. She shook her head and turned away. "Get yourself together and behave. Remember what we discussed."

Oh yes. The many-hour discussion flying from New York to Los Angeles yesterday, during which Zoey and Jamie gave us all the things to say and not say during this interview. They'd be sitting off to the side and would help if needed. We even had to have a discussion about body language, as if Mallie and I had any issues with that. If anything, we couldn't keep our hands off each other. But I knew not to fuck this up and to defer to her if I wasn't sure how to answer. While I had a good amount of media training, she was the pro here.

Scott Lively, the reporter, walked in and shook both of our hands. He was a handsome man in his late twenties and had an aura about him that put both of us at ease immediately. I wasn't nervous at all about this, especially since the press was part of my weekly routine with the team, but Mallie hated it. She had been cornered too many times in interviews.

"Thank you so much for this opportunity," he said. "I promise that everything I told Zoey and Jamie I will hold up. I do not want to do anything to jeopardize our working relationship. I am honored that I get this chance to sit down with the two of you."

Mallie smiled. "We greatly appreciate that. Is it true that you are really assigned to cover just me?"

Scott blushed and nodded. "It's true. After the success you've had on this album, then the tour and your overwhelming worldwide popularity right now, they wanted a dedicated Allie Witt reporter. I get to travel the world to all of your shows, interview your fans, and keep up on all of the happenings. Like you and Theo," he said. "People have been dying ever since you showed up at that game, me included. They will be foaming at the mouth for this story. Well, whatever part of it you want to share, of course."

Mallie laughed. "That's crazy. How did you get that job?"

Scott smiled. "I have been a huge fan of yours since your first album. About five years ago, I got pretty popular online posting content about what was going on with you. I got the attention of some higher-ups in the media world, and here I am. I'm proud to say I'm one of the OG Allie-Cats. Have the necklace to prove it," he said, lifting said necklace from under his collar. Mallie's eyes widened and she laughed. She really had no idea how much people loved her.

"Wow. That's great," she said. "It makes me feel better that you were a fan first. And not just a fan, but an Allie-Cat, too. With official club merch."

"Damn right. Allie-Cats forever," he joked and tucked the necklace back under his shirt. Scott gestured to the camera setup. "Do you mind if we do pictures first? I will just take a few shots 'behind the scenes' with my phone and then we will start the interview. Remember, anything and everything I do can be approved or denied by you, no questions asked."

I took Mallie's hand, and we walked over to the neutral backdrop. A white fabric bench sat in front of the backdrop, and the photographer indicated for me to sit. He positioned her behind me with her hands on my shoulders. She rubbed my shoulders with her thumbs, and I tilted my head back to look at her. She smiled at me, and my heart turned to goo. God, I loved this woman. I couldn't believe I almost fucked up the best thing that ever happened to me. I'd do a million interviews if I had to, to make this go away.

I could hear the camera clicking, but they hadn't even told us what to do yet. Mallie looked over at them as she heard the same.

"Just getting some candids," the photographer said. I glanced at Zoey and Jamie. They stood together off to the side, small smiles on both of their faces. "Those were so good," he said to them, and they stepped up to look at the small screen.

"Adorable," Jamie said. I knew how stressed she was the last few days because of me, so I was glad to make her happy. The photographer continued, alternating between posing us and just taking pictures as we enjoyed the shoot. After about thirty minutes, they called it a wrap, and Scott motioned to the interview area. I could've done that all day. Taking pictures with the woman I loved, looking into her gorgeous eyes, and touching her body was not a hardship, to say the least. I even controlled the beast in my lower region—the one with a mind of its own—during the shoot.

The interview area was also set up with lights and cameras, but had a white couch that was brought in from somewhere for us to sit on instead. Mallie sat close, no real space to speak of between us. I put one arm around the back of the couch and rested it on her shoulder, then rested my other one on her thigh—in a respectable place. She placed her hand on top of mine. I leaned over and kissed the side of her head, and Scott sighed happily from the chair next to us.

"Off the record, you two are just the cutest thing I've ever seen," he said. He looked at Mallie. "It's so great to see you happy."

She blushed and bit that lip that drove me wild. "Thanks. We kinda like us, too." Everyone laughed and Scott cleared his throat.

"You ready?" he asked.

Mallie looked up at me and I nodded, forcing myself not to kiss her. We had to focus. This was the key to getting people to stop talking about our debacle last weekend. "We got this, angel. Just be yourself." Scott smiled at my whispers and indicated to start recording.

"I'm here with Allie Witt, the woman who needs no introduction. Allie is a global phenomenon and has been since she first came on the scene as a teenager. Currently on the most successful tour of her career and breaking records left and right, Allie seems unstoppable. But like the rest of us, she's still human, with the same desires we all have. To love and to be loved. Be seen as the person she is. And to do what she dreamed of her entire life. She was gracious enough to let us in her beautiful home for this interview today."

Scott paused, and Allie's hand tightened slightly on mine. I ran my thumb along her shoulder, calming her, and I felt her take a deep breath. She hated every minute of this, and she was doing this for me. To fix the mess I made of things last weekend.

"Also with her is Theo Nolan, star running back for the Florida Blaze and, just recently, Allie Witt's boyfriend. This is the first time anyone has had the privilege of talking to either of them about how they got where they are today and what is going on in their lives. We've seen Allie at several of Theo's games and Theo at a few of her concerts. Now, we get a little insight into what it's like to be them."

The camera panned to the two of us, and it was showtime.

"Thanks for taking the time out of your busy schedules to sit down with me," Scott said. "Theo, can you tell me about you sending Allie a jersey the night she played in your stadium? You were the one that reached out first, right?"

Allie looked at me, our answer to the question we knew would come first already practiced. She was ready. "Actually," Allie said, diverting Scott's attention to her, "I met Teddy earlier that day."

"Teddy," Scott said.

Allie blushed but nodded. "Teddy. That's what I call him."

I squeezed her shoulder. "She's Mallie to me."

Scott pretended to swoon. "Stop. You two are so cute. Okay, go on," he said, gesturing to Mallie.

"I was practicing on the stage and Josiah called and broke up with me over the phone after five years together and said he met someone else." She looked pointedly at the camera, ready to set him straight. "I ran off the stage and directly into Teddy. He helped me that day but never said anything to anyone about it. When he sent me the jersey and a note, I was thankful, but my whole world had just imploded. It wasn't until a few months later that we started talking."

Scott turned to me. "You shot your shot with Allie Witt, and it worked."

"To be fair, I wanted to just make sure she was okay. I sent her flowers not long after the breakup with Josiah became public, but I didn't expect anything from her. I just wanted her to know that someone cared."

"He was very sweet," Mallie interjected. "He didn't ask for my number or try to hit on me."

"So how did we get here?" Scott asked, indicating the two of us on the couch.

"I reached out to him," Mallie said. "We just started talking. I wasn't in a place where I wanted to jump into something else, but there was something about him immediately.

He gets me like no one I've ever known in my life. So it wasn't long before we both had feelings." She smiled up at me and I looked down at her, the love I had for her pouring out of me.

"We decided to meet for a date," I said. "I flew to New York and met her. We were able to see each other without anyone knowing, and that really kept the pressure off us for quite a while."

"People speculated that the game you went to was your first date." Scott laughed, and we laughed with him.

"I saw that," Mallie said, a laugh still in her voice. "That is ridiculous. We knew exactly what would happen once I showed up there, and there was no way that would've been us 'seeing where things went' in the public eye. No, we were solidly a couple before that game."

"You and Bailey Lee really caused a ruckus that day," Scott said.

"We did. It was nice for her to be there to keep all the attention off me for a few minutes."

"What kind of pressure was that for you?" Scott asked me.

"I loved that she came. She warned me what kind of attention it was going to garner, but honestly, none of that bothers me."

Scott nodded. "You sure seem to be able to handle the chaos that comes with her fame without being ruffled at all."

I looked down at Mallie. "It doesn't bother me. She's worth it."

Scott cleared his throat, and I knew he was about to go there. "Let's talk about what happened last weekend," he said. "Of course everyone saw her ex yelling some terrible things at you before the game, and like any man in love with a woman, you reacted in her defense. Did things get blown out of proportion?"

I took a deep breath. This was me. I could see Jamie nodding at me from off camera, encouraging me. "It was uncalled for, and I will never be okay with anyone talking about a woman that way, especially mine. However, I should've just walked away. He got me in a moment of weakness, and I let him affect me, my team, and Mallie."

"The media has been ruthless," Scott said, and I stopped myself from laughing. That was the understatement of the evening. "They're saying you have anger issues and Allie should run far away from you. What do you have to say about that?"

I was ready for this question, so I chose my words carefully. "They have. The media will run with any story they can, especially if it involves Allie. Funny that none of them are saying anything about a guy who decided to be horrible to a person he used to love just for media attention, though. I didn't handle myself the way I should've. I have apologized to her"—I squeezed her close to me as I spoke—"and, honestly, she's the only one that matters. Just because the cameras were pointed at me in a moment where someone said something so awful about the woman I love that I reacted doesn't mean the same wouldn't happen if any other person was in my position. It made it much worse that he said those things knowing all of the cameras would be on us and it would be viral. I was, and am, upset for her, not for me. This woman is a bright light in this world and does nothing but try to lift others up and make them better. For her to be disrespected like that was unacceptable. I will defend her with my life if I have to, so if that's a red flag, then, well, I will accept that."

I looked down at her to gauge how I did, and that was when I saw the tears shimmering in her eyes. She also hated to cry in front of people, so it alarmed me, but the little shake of her head told me it was okay.

"Allie, what do you have to say about what happened? And the video afterward in the suite?"

"This man right here is the love of my life," she said, squeezing my hand.

Scott's eyes widened, and my heart pounded so hard I heard it in my ears. She just told everyone that. I saw Zoey and Jamie whispering to each other.

"Everything he says and does is to make sure I am okay," she continued. "The media took a private moment after the game where he was upset and misconstrued what was said to fit their narrative of him and tried to paint him as the bad guy. He is not the bad guy here. We all know who that is. I do not want to speak his name again or hear anything else about him."

I wanted to pick up this amazing woman of mine and haul her out of here and propose marriage right there and then. She was such a fucking badass. But since I couldn't, I leaned over and kissed her temple and whispered, "I love you" in her ear. I couldn't let that comment pass without acknowledging what it meant to me.

CHAPTER 21
Allie

I SHOCKED every person in this room, including myself, but I had to say it. Teddy *was* the love of my life. I couldn't listen to this shit about him anymore. I wanted Scott to publish his story and set the record straight. I knew it wouldn't stop the gossip rags, but hopefully most people would put this nonsense to rest and let me never hear Josiah's name again.

I hated reporters. My entire career, they always had an angle they worked when they talked to me. It was to belittle me as a woman, make fun of me for my dating life, or downplay my talent as a singer-songwriter. But Scott just reminded me that there are still good ones out there. It must be because he's an Allie-Cat. So funny.

"What is next for you two?" Scott asked.

"Well, my season is over, so I'll definitely spend some time with my kids' cooking club. I love cooking, and it means a lot to me to share my passion with our younger generation," Teddy said.

"I will go back on tour in a few weeks. I have several months left of the Lovestruck tour," I answered.

"And will you be joining her on the rest of her tour?" Scott asked Teddy.

"As much as I possibly can," he answered. "There's nothing I love more than watching her do what she loves."

"And as far as your relationship?"

I looked up at Teddy. Our gazes locked and I felt the answer, knew it in my bones, just like the night we told each other we loved each other for the first time. But this was not the time, and I was not the person who was going to give that kind of information to the public. Some parts of my life had to be kept for just me.

"That's between us, but when we're ready to share what is next in our life, you'll be the first to know," Teddy said, turning his attention to Scott and winking at him.

"Fair enough. People are obviously clamoring for information about you, and you've been called the next royal couple. What do you make of that?"

Teddy laughed. "Did you hear that, Mal? We're royal now."

I shook my head. "We are not royal."

"Well, you're a romance novel in real life," Scott said. "People of all ages are tuned in to what happens when you show up at a game or he goes to your concert. Social media posts every single angle of every interaction you have and anything you wear." Scott indicated my necklace, and I put my fingers on it. "Rumor has it you will walk the red carpet together on Sunday also."

It was a big deal for me to have someone walk with me on the red carpet. In my entire career, the only person who ever walked with me was my mom. It was the biggest statement I could make that Teddy was it for me.

"You'll have to tune in," I said. "Better yet, why don't you come? You can be my guest." I wasn't sure what the hell had gotten into me, but I liked him.

Scott's eyes widened. "Seriously? I planned to be there, but of course just as a reporter."

"You've been great with all of this." I motioned between Teddy and me. "I appreciate you letting us control what we feel comfortable with. And plus, as the official Allie Witt reporter, you should report me breaking a record from the front lines."

"I cannot tell you how much that means to me," he said. "I will take you up on that for sure. I will freak out once I leave, so you don't see me as unprofessional." We all laughed, and he stood. "Thanks so much for your time today. I appreciate you giving me the chance to tell your story. I will get everything together and send it to you for approval before it is posted anywhere." He nodded at Zoey and Jamie. "And I guess I will see you Sunday!"

The SUV rolled to a stop, and I looked over at Teddy's handsome face. He had cut his beard short and gotten his hair cut today, and between that and yet another custom suit, this time pinstriped, I could definitely get used to these fancy events with him. He people-watched out the window, seeing all the celebrities getting out of their vehicles and heading for the main area.

As far as I was concerned, Scott was the new Allie Witt and Theo Nolan reporter. I would never work with anyone again if I had a choice. He did amazing and exactly what he said he was going to do. Integrity in a reporter—imagine that.

The pictures of us were stunning, the piece he wrote perfectly said and not sensationalized. The videos clearly showed two people madly in love, and it brought tears to my eyes to see it. We didn't have him change anything. He published them on Friday, and our story was now everywhere.

News stations across the world played our video, and every social media page shared and reshared our pictures with our story attached. People were feral for the story of us, and Josiah was long gone from the attention of the media. With Scott meeting us tonight, the positive press would only continue. Obviously people had nonsense to say no matter what I did, but at least I could get on the right side of it, for the most part.

People were everywhere, and it was almost our turn to get out. I wasn't nervous at all—I was ready. I was up for five awards tonight, and it was anticipated I would win most, if not all, of the categories. I loved these events because I got to catch up with a lot of people I normally didn't have time to see. Sadly, Bailey would not be here tonight, as she had prior commitments, but I had many other friends who would be. I would get to introduce Teddy to most of my colleagues and show him off to the world on the red carpet. Plus, I loved the songs. It was like getting to go to a concert of all the people I admired. At heart, I was just a music girl.

Juan opened the door and Teddy stepped out. Teddy always sat by the door now so he could help me out of the car. In his mind, that was his job and his job only. He turned and held out his hand, and I took it, sliding out carefully.

He held me until I smoothed my dress and made sure I was stable. I wore a floor-length strapless red evening gown slit up the right leg. Diamonds lined the slit. My hair was down around my shoulders and curled. A diamond clip held up one side. The back of my dress dipped low, just above my ass. The front dipped low enough to show some cleavage but not low enough to have a wardrobe malfunction. It fit me like a glove, and I knew I looked like a goddess. Of course I wore red stilettos in my signature brand.

Teddy then reached behind me and helped Zoey out. Juan and Rico led the way as the SUV drove off. We walked in silence toward the red carpet, where we would make our debut. The second bystanders noticed us, the volume increased significantly.

"Stay close," Juan said. Rico dropped back behind us as the crowd got louder. We made our way through the countless people screaming our names. The red carpet area wasn't quieter, but I at least recognized a lot of faces. I introduced Teddy to many people as we walked by, but we didn't stop.

"You ready for this?" I said, referring to the spectacle we were about to enter.

"Ready to be on the red carpet with the hottest woman here? Bring it fucking on."

This man, always good for my self-esteem. I linked my fingers with his as the cameras started flashing. We walked up to the step and repeat area and Zoey fixed my dress. We posed in every way they wanted, and I would've thought we were at my sold-out concert rather than an awards show if I didn't know better. We waved at the people yelling for us as we turned to walk inside.

"Geesh," I said. "I need a drink now for sure. That was chaotic."

"They all want to see Allie Witt," Teddy teased. He looked me up and down. "I don't blame them, you're hot as fuck. But only I get to see what is under that sexy dress."

"That's right," I said. "And you will definitely get to take this off me later. Now let's go have some fun."

Teddy held my hand as the announcer talked about the most prestigious award of the night, Entertainer of the Year. If I won, I would break the record for the number of times it was won by the same artist. I was favored, but you just never knew what would happen. Scott sat on the other side of Zoey. He hadn't stopped smiling the entire night.

I had some stiff competition, so I would be okay if I didn't win. I took home three out of the other four I was nominated for tonight, so it was a great night already. Plus, Teddy being here with me made it perfect, even if I won nothing at all. He made everything better. The buzz throughout the room was palpable.

The announcer read the list of names, the pictures of the nominees flashing on the screen behind him. When my picture appeared, it was me on the cover of *Lovestruck*, lying on a bed with hearts spilling out all around me. When I wrote this album, I had no idea I would really live it. I thought I loved Josiah. Ha. What a joke. There was nothing in comparison to this love.

"That picture is fucking hot," Teddy whispered in my ear. "Remind me I need that album autographed on my shelf."

Scott snapped a picture of us with his phone, and I smiled.

"Just for you," I teased, my leg bouncing in nervous anticipation. He rested his hand on my leg and I stilled.

"You got this, angel. There's no one else it can be."

His confidence made me smile.

"And the winner of Entertainer of the Year is . . ."

God, I hated this part. The pause for dramatic effect. Teddy squeezed my hand.

"The unstoppable…Allie Witt."

Thunderous applause and screaming made me jump to my feet, my hand over my mouth. No way. I really got it.

"This is Allie's third Entertainer of the Year award, breaking the tie she held with two. She is now the record holder."

Theo stood next to me and wrapped me in his arms, lifting my feet off the ground temporarily. "That's my fucking girl," he said in my ear. "You're such a queen. Get up there and accept your award."

I pulled away and put my hand on the side of his face, my eyes brimming with tears. I hugged Zoey and then made my way to the stage, the room standing for me and the applause still echoing throughout the room. I saw Scott taking pictures, but for once, the intrusion was welcome.

I stepped up to the microphone, my smile so big it could crack my face. The award was thrust into my hand and I hugged the announcer, an up-and-coming country star who knew Bailey well.

"Thank you," I said, my voice echoing throughout the room. "I am thankful every single day that I get to live my dream of writing and singing songs and people liking that I do so. I will never stop because it is who I am. My fans, my Allie-Cats, continue to be there for me and allow me to live this life. I love you guys so much. This tour and the *Lovestruck* album changed my life, but even more than that, I am in love with the best man I've ever known, and he changed me forever. Teddy, thank you for helping me live out the lyrics I write about. Here's to the next year."

I lifted the award up and smiled down at Teddy. He stood during my entire speech, as he did for every award I got tonight.

I love you, he mouthed and blew me a kiss.

"I am so glad we're home," I said as the SUV pulled into Teddy's driveway.

He grinned at me.

"What?" I asked.

"You just called this home," he said.

"*You* are my home," I said, "and this place allows us to be alone, so yes. Home."

He kissed me softly and slid his hand up my bare leg. "How did I get so fucking lucky for you to be mine, Mallorie Witt?"

"The same way I got lucky that you're mine," I said against his lips. "What do you say to starting our first night home with a shower? I feel disgusting." I wanted a shower, to love my man, and to curl up in his amazing bed.

"You don't feel disgusting," he said, his fingertips touching the edge of my underwear. "But yes, we can take a shower after I show you a surprise."

"A surprise?" I sat up. "You got something for me?"

Teddy stepped out of the vehicle, extending his hand to me as usual. The warm Florida sunshine made me smile.

"I did," he said. "I hope you like it."

"How could I not?" I said as he opened the front door. "You know me better than anyone."

He closed and locked the door. What I noticed first was— silence. No one was in the house with us, in our world, that didn't happen often.

"We're alone?" I asked.

"Alone. Security will be outside. But just us inside."

I wrapped my arms around him and melded my body to his. He tilted my head back and kissed me softly. "I love you, angel. Come on. I want to show you. I've been waiting a long time for this."

He took my hand and led me through the front of the house to the back. He had a large sitting room off his formal dining room. It had large windows to the expansive backyard and was one of my favorite places in his house.

"Close your eyes," Teddy said as we approached the entrance to the room.

I obliged, my stomach fluttering in anticipation of what it could be.

"No peeking." He held my hips as we moved into the room.

"I'm not peeking," I said. "But you're killing me."

"Open your eyes, angel."

His gruffness made me shiver. I loved the timbre of his voice. It usually meant amazing things for me.

I opened my eyes, and it took me a second to realize what

I was seeing. An identical piano to the one in my Florida house sat in the middle of Teddy's sitting room. I knew this wasn't the same one because it had my Lovestruck logo on the lid. I attempted to say something, but no words would come. Next to it was a custom guitar in my favorite brand with the same logo. And covering the piano and the floor? Hearts. But not just any hearts. The hearts from my show.

"Teddy," I said. "What is all this? Where did you get all of these?"

I stepped farther into the room and saw there were hundreds of them all over.

"Seems I have a connection with the supplier," Teddy joked.

My mom. Of course. I couldn't stop staring. He did this—for me. He remembered what I said about loving my room in my Florida house, so he re-created it in his. He even had shelves put along one wall, and I watched as he took the awards I just won from a bag by the door and put them on one of the shelves.

"This is amazing. I love it so much. Thank you, baby." Tears stung behind my eyes. He was the most thoughtful person I had ever known.

"Go sit at the piano. It's the same one you have at your house, just done with your logo."

I sat on the bench and lifted the fallboard. Four hearts lined the keys, and I looked down at them. I furrowed my brow as I read them, one word on each in his signature block letters, and then read them again. I put my hand over my mouth and turned, and that's when I saw him behind me on one knee.

"Mallorie Rose Witt," he began, and I gasped. "I love you so much. I never saw you coming, not in a million years, but now I can't imagine one second without you. I have no idea how I lived before you, but I don't want to ever live without you again. Every single thing we've gone through has gotten us here. I want you to be mine forever. I want to wake up next to you when we are both in the same zip code and look forward to it when we aren't. I want to be the one you come to for everything. I want to be your husband and the father to your children. I want every up and down of life with you. Forever. Will you marry me?"

Tears fell steadily as I looked into the eyes of my soulmate. The love of my life, on his knee in front of me with a giant diamond sparkling in front of him. The man I never knew I needed and now could not live without. The one who showed me what true love really was. Who showed up for me at every turn and amazed me more every day with who he was at heart.

"Yes," I said. "A fucking thousand times yes."

Teddy grinned and slid the ring on my finger. I threw myself on him, and he fell backward, me on top of him. We laughed together, and he grabbed my face and kissed me, the tears from both of us mixing as we registered that this was for real. Teddy just asked me to marry him. I was going to be his wife. After almost thirty years, I had someone who saw me for who I was and loved every part of me. I could love him out loud and not worry about what he thought. He was mine. I was his.

"I love you," I said against his lips. "You're the best thing that has ever happened to me."

"I love you," he echoed. "We're going to be so happy together. I promise."

"Are we really engaged?"

Teddy sat up and I bracketed his hips with my legs. He lifted my left hand, the large diamond glittering in the soft light of the room. "We really are."

"This was so perfect," I said. "Thank you for this." I loved that he knew I needed this to be private. It wasn't that I didn't love our unpredictable life together, but I wanted this for us.

"There was no other way. I have had this planned for a long time."

"A long time?"

"I knew I was going to marry you a long time ago," he said. "I just had to wait for the right time to not scare you off."

"You're perfect," I said.

He laughed. "I'm not anywhere close to perfect, but we're perfect for each other."

"We should send Scott a pic of us with the ring and see if he notices," I said. We'd decided we liked Scott and had exchanged numbers. He was a good one.

"We will," Teddy said.

He stood while holding me. I would never stop being amazed at how strong he was.

"But first, I promised you a shower," he continued. "And the only thing I want you wearing is that engagement ring."

Epilogue

Scott Lively, official reporter for Allie Witt-Nolan and Theo Nolan

THIS IS SCOTT LIVELY, the official Witt-Nolan reporter, with an exclusive report on the wedding of the century.

I met this amazing couple last year in the midst of a whirlwind romance, a successful international tour, and a hectic football season. I was blessed enough to be named as an exclusive Allie Witt reporter months before this from Star-Stream Media, but that didn't mean I would ever get the chance to meet her in person. Imagine my surprise when I got a call that Allie Witt herself agreed to a sit-down interview with her boyfriend, Blaze star running back Theo Nolan.

Not only did I have the distinct pleasure of meeting these two in person for an exclusive interview back in February, but Allie herself invited me to the PMA Awards, where I got to witness her making history from the front row with her third Entertainer of the Year award.

Since then, Allie has been gracious enough to share with me many of her exclusives. Her engagement to Teddy, as she calls him, a selfie of the two of them sent to me via a sweet text message that said, *Can you see me over the bling of my ring?*

A backstage look at her international tour and even a sit-down at the recording studio as she worked on her new album, *Soulmate*, which is being released today. But all of that pales in comparison to the exclusive she gave me this time, and I've never been more excited to report a news story involving our favorite pop princess.

Today is her wedding day. A day that Allie and Theo have purposely kept media-free, the location even top secret to the guests they invited to keep it from being leaked. Their guests, including me, were instructed to report to an airport to be flown to an undisclosed location. As much as they both love and adore their fans, this couple wanted this day to be about them, and I don't think anyone can blame them. Except they allowed me to record video, take pictures, and write about the most beautiful day I've ever seen. The marriage of America's sweethearts was something out of a fairy tale—the end of this rom-com that we've been jonesing for since the first day Allie showed up at a Blaze game and turned the world on its ear.

Allie stunned guests—and her groom—in a custom-made strapless bridal gown from Ellie Blake. The fitted dress showed off her flawless figure and the long train added to the dramatic effect. She wore her hair curled around her face and a long veil that matched the length of her train. Teddy wore a custom gray pinstripe suit made by Eryc Johnson. It was a star-studded event. Most of Teddy's teammates and his coach were in attendance. Bailey Lee, Allie's best friend, was the maid of honor, and many other artists and teammates' wives and girlfriends that Allie is close to were there as well.

When the ceremony started, the instrumentals were written and recorded by Allie. When Theo spotted Allie, he immediately sobbed. There wasn't a dry eye in the place. The vows were extremely personal and will not be repeated—but let me just say that the trend of crying at this wedding continued. I have never witnessed with my own two eyes such palpable love between two people. When they were pronounced husband and wife, Teddy held Allie's arm up and cheered, and the crowd reciprocated.

Then, the party began. These two love to enjoy life, and enjoy it they did. The drinks flowed, the music slayed, and the party was lit. Theo and Allie, the newly married couple, did all the traditional things, but in true Allie and Theo fashion, they put their own spin on a lot of it. Theo danced with his mom and Allie's, and Allie did the same with his dad. Allie sang a new song to Theo, one she produced for the new album she never told him about. It was the title track of the album, also titled *Soulmate*, and once again, there wasn't a dry eye in the place. Allie barely made it through the song. Emotions were high, and for good reason. Everyone at that wedding knew what they saw in these two, and it was summed up in the title of Allie's album—*Soulmate*.

By the time the party ended, it was in the wee hours of the morning. Partygoers stumbled to their rooms at the resort, but not Theo and Allie. They took off down the beach to enjoy the last moments of this day together. I didn't follow but instead sat by the fire and waited for them to return. When they did, the flush of love was evident on both of their faces. When they saw me, they sat next to me to recap what will no doubt be considered the best day in their lives—so far.

I asked them what was next, and a secret look passed between them. I had seen this look once before when I asked them this same question the first time I interviewed them. The answer they didn't give me then was the inevitable engagement and marriage. Now, I could only imagine what these two superstars had up their sleeve. Whatever they do and wherever they go from here, Allie Witt-Nolan and Theo Nolan will take it on together.

Theo put his arm around his wife, pulled her closer, and said to me, "You'll just have to wait and see, man. Our story is just beginning."

About the Author

Liane Mae has loved words since she knew what they were. As a kid, she carried a notebook everywhere she went and has a collection of stories over the course of her lifetime to prove it. She also is, and has always has been, an avid reader. One thing that has always stayed the same was her love of love. From the butterflies of new love to the idea that soulmates really do exist, her writing has always followed the same track– stories that make people believe in romance and happily-ever-after. While this is her first book under this name, Liane has been publishing in the romance world for over ten years.

Acknowledgments

To all of my readers, the ones that have been with me when I wrote under my other name and are here now to support me on my new venture, and the ones that will pick this book up as the first one you will read by me. Your support means everything and I couldn't do this without your support.

To Joanne/Carina, this book would not exist out in the world without your encouragement, insistence, and constant support. Thank you for spending many hours answering my messages, reading snippets, and giving advice. Love you.

To my editor, James Gallagher at Castle Walls Editing. I'm thrilled to be working with you again. I appreciate you and your attention to detail! You're the best.

To my proofreader, Rosa at Fairy Proofmother Proofreading. Thank you for taking me as a client and doing an amazing job.

Kari March at Kari March Designs. I'm so glad I was recommended to you for my custom illustrated cover. I gasped when I saw it. You took my vision and made it come to life. I cannot wait to continue working together. Thank you so much for bringing Lovestruck to life!

To all the influencers, thank you for the time you spend supporting authors and reading our stories. You take time out of your personal lives, and I am very thankful.

Lovestruck Playlist

www.ingramcontent.com/pod-product-compliance
Lightning Source LLC
LaVergne TN
LVHW011947060526
838201LV00061B/4240